Cat Got
Your Cash

Also by Julie Chase

Cat Got Your Diamonds

Cat Got Your Cash

A Kitty Couture Mystery

Julie Chase

CROOKED
LANE

NEW YORK

Published in the United States by Crooked Lane Books, an imprint of The Quick Brown Fox & Company LLC.

Crooked Lane Books and its logo are trademarks of The Quick Brown Fox & Company LLC.

Library of Congress Catalog-in-Publication data available upon request.

ISBN (paperback): 978-1-68331-267-3
ISBN (hardcover): 978-1-68331-108-9
ISBN (ePub): 978-1-68331-109-6
ISBN (Kindle): 978-1-68331-110-2
ISBN (ePDF): 978-1-68331-111-9

Cover illustration by Anne Wertheim
Book design by Jennifer Canzone

Printed in the United States.

www.crookedlanebooks.com

Crooked Lane Books
34 West 27th St., 10th Floor
New York, NY 10001

Hardcover Edition: April 2017
Paperback Edition: August 2017

Chapter One

Furry Godmother's advice for the budding designer:
Never meet your hero.

I hefted an armload of miniature couture onto the counter at Furry Godmother, my pet boutique and organic treat bakery nestled in the famed New Orleans Garden District. A rainbow of crinoline and sequins splayed over the freshly cleaned space near a box of matching accessories. My heart fluttered. "I have thirty-eight minutes before I meet with Annie Lane. That gives me thirty minutes to make the final selections, pack up, and get to her house. And then eight minutes to freak out."

Imogene, my old nanny and new shopkeep, watched silently as I turned in a small circle, looking for a place to put the keepers. Every clean, flat space in sight was already covered in adorable creations.

I turned back to the counter and flipped through a flood of tiny formal wear. I hung my favorites over one arm with newfound discernment. "You know what? I'm starting to sweat. I should use the extra eight minutes to freshen up. I'll freak out on the drive over instead."

Imogene clucked her tongue. "Annie Lane is going to love you and your designs. Whatever you decide to take will be perfect."

I gave her an incredulous look.

Imogene had been with my family for decades. First as my grandmother's caregiver, then as my mother's estate keeper, and eventually as my nanny. She was heavily biased in my favor. At the moment, she was also wrong.

Annie Lane was a world-famous fashion designer. I was a budding pet couture creator. The pieces I chose to take with me to represent my brand mattered. A lot. This appointment could change everything. My career. My entire future. Together, Annie and I could be an unstoppable force in fashion. I just needed to convince her of that. When I'd heard she was returning to New Orleans for Faux Real, the annual arts festival, I pitched a meeting to her people, suggesting a companion line for Annie's Mardi Gras designs. I sent snapshots of my feline and canine king capes and nearly fainted when she wanted to see more.

Being crowned king or queen during Mardi Gras was one of the highest civic honors in New Orleans, so the pair dressed to impress. The royal garb was so significant that some of the most epic gear from over the years was enshrined in a French Quarter Mardi Gras museum. I'd loved going there as a child, imagining the designers' workspaces piled high with sequins and gold lamé. Royal apparel could weigh as much as forty to sixty pounds, not including the headpiece. In fact, one of the queen's gowns had had more than one hundred fifty yards of tulle over satin. Wheels had to be sewn along the hem to help her get around. Those costumes made the most elaborate Vegas show girl ensemble look like amateur hour. With a little luck, one of my designs could be tucked safely behind museum glass one day too, if I made good choices. A partnership with Annie Lane was a very good choice.

Imogene eyeballed me from a closing distance. The tails of her red silk headscarf fluttered behind her, secured tightly around a puff of salt-and-pepper hair. "You're flushed. You should sit down before you fall over. Have a glass of water. I'll cleanse the air in here and try to clean up the bad juju."

My arm drooped under the weight of too many favorites. The logoed garment box I'd intended to pack my items into wouldn't hold half of what I wanted to show Annie. "I'm going to need a bigger box."

"I thought this was a Mardi Gras proposal? Why are you packing an Easter Bunny costume?" She handed me an ugly brown box from behind the counter.

"I want to show range." I offloaded the garments from my arm with a sigh of relief. It passed quickly as her words slipped through the clutter in my mind. "Did you say bad juju?"

Imogene was known to dabble in things I didn't understand, and she claimed she'd come from a long line of shamans and other mystics. I didn't believe in any of it, but the last time she'd said anything about my juju, my life had gone completely bananas.

"I can help." She fixed me with a pointed stare.

A bead of sweat formed on my upper lip. "I think I just need a moment to channel my inner debutante." I'd hated the years of grace and etiquette training forced upon me as a youth, but lately, I was thankful for the takeaways. For example, if I stood straight enough, strangers seemed to assume I knew what I was doing—and also that I wasn't having an internal meltdown.

"If you say so." She stuffed a roll of bundled sage back into her apron pocket and scanned the ceiling. She said burning sage cleansed the air, but as far as I could tell, it only made smoke and caused me to sneeze.

I thumbed a pile of headbands, hoping to accessorize the selected outfits. "Did you know Annie is half the reason I went to design school?" The other half had been to peeve off my mother. "A companion line to Annie's Mardi Gras pieces would put me on the map as a legit designer." Pet couture doesn't get the respect it deserves, but she could change that. Furry Godmother could be a pioneer brand in my field. A maverick.

Imogene delivered a bottle of water to the counter.

I dropped two headbands into the box, then sorted a stack of rhinestone-studded collars and optional charms. "Annie was born and raised in New Orleans like me." Unlike me, she'd chased her dreams around the globe, found stardom, and graced magazine covers. I'd made it as far as Arlington before a chance mugging and a cheating ex-fiancé had sent me packing back to the Garden District where my mother and her friends ran the world.

Determined to succeed in spite of my perceived failure, I opened Furry Godmother and put my fashion degree to work making designs for fur babies. As fate would have it, this was an opportunity I'd never have gotten in Virginia. I pulled my shoulders back and lifted my chin. Honey-blonde curls dropped over my shoulders. "I think I'm ready."

Imogene chuckled. "Be careful, Lacy Marie Crocker. You look like your mother when you get in that disposition."

I shot her a droll face. The similarities between my mother and I ended at the molecular level. I looked like my mother, right down to our narrow frames, blue eyes, and ski-slope noses, but I didn't care about keeping up appearances or embracing a legacy of social power like she did. I wasn't interested in marrying into the right family or accepting my family's bottomless coffers of cash. I wanted to make my own path in this life, and honestly, I could've also done without the pointy nose, but I had no control in that matter. "If only I could turn on Mom's Conti-Crocker charm and insist Annie love me."

"Why not? Works on everyone else. Annie Lane is no different. She's just people."

I could think of a certain homicide detective who'd disagree about my charm. Detective Jack Oliver had sauntered into my life four months ago, accused me of murder, pushed all my buttons, saved my life, then walked away. Was he also "just people"? Because so far, my Crocker charm hadn't done much for him. It seemed as if every time I thought our friendship was solidifying, he'd disappear for a few days and return emotionally distant. I squeezed my eyes shut and counted to three before reopening them. Part of me was determined to find out what was going on with him. The rest of me refused to spend another minute down that rabbit hole.

Imogene smiled. "Him, too."

I turned my face away and folded a sequined flapper dress onto the top of my pile. "What?"

"You forget I've known you a long time, Miss Lacy." She passed me a matching headpiece with scarlet plumes. "These look nice with the flapper dresses."

Imogene dropped a handful of business cards and store literature into the box.

"Oh!" I snapped upright. "I should take a few treats for Annie's kittens. They're nearly as famous as she is."

"I'll get those." Imogene hustled to the bakery display and slipped a pair of plastic gloves over plump, wrinkled hands. "I'll make them a sampler box."

"Thanks. That's perfect." My pet treats were one hundred percent organic and baked fresh daily. Baking added balance to my life. Some days it was the only thing that soothed my busy mind. As an added bonus, I could cater a pet's big party *and* dress him or her for the occasion. My life was kind of fantastic.

A line of bagpipers marched past the shop window. I pulled in a cleansing breath and smiled. "I love this town."

Banners for the Faux Real Festival hung from streetlamps up and down Magazine Street. The sidewalks teemed with locals and thespians in all manner of stage attire, enjoying the annual art fest. Tourists snapped photos with men painted silver and posed as statues with the Magazine Street sign. A cluster of mimes begged passersby to free them from invisible boxes.

My tabby, Penelope, leapt onto the counter and rolled in a shaft of sunlight. Happy vibrations rumbled through her lean body.

"Hello, gorgeous." I scooped her into my arms and nuzzled my cheek to her head. Penelope had been held captive, briefly, by my cheating ex-fiancé, but cheaters never win.

Imogene tied a ribbon around the little bakery box and set it inside my open purse. "Two tuna tarts, two kitty cakes, and two pawlines." Pawlines were pet-friendly versions of New Orleans's famous pralines and by far my best-selling treat.

"Thanks. I don't know how long I'll be with Annie. If I run late, don't wait for me. Go ahead and close up."

"Should I set Spot loose before I go?"

Spot was my vacuuming robot. I'd added large googly eyes, felt ears, and some yarn hair to help him fit in at Furry Godmother, but he mostly worked nights. "Yes, please. Do you have any plans after work? Visiting your granddaughter?"

Her smile faltered. "Not tonight."

"No? Is everything okay?"

Imogene clutched the pendant hanging from her necklace. "A friend in the Quarter needs help. She's got a ghost problem, but I'm sure things will be fine in the morning."

I blinked, lost for a response. "Should I tell you to have fun or be careful?"

She pulled Penelope from my arms. Her wide brown eyes twinkled. "Don't worry about me. You'd better get going before you're late. Those dopey mimes are slowing down traffic."

Right. I grabbed my leather hobo and big box of kitty couture. "You can leave Penelope here when you lock up. I'll be back for her as soon as I finish."

"What about Spot?"

"Spot's fine. She likes to ride him."

Imogene gave Penelope a funny look and set her on the counter.

I hustled to my car, dropped my bag on the floorboards, and buckled the box onto my passenger seat. I slid behind the wheel and attempted to settle my racing pulse. Air conditioning blasted my face as I gunned the little VW engine to life. November in New Orleans was beautiful, but it wasn't always cool. I plucked white angora away from my chest and directed the vents at my neck, uninterested in accessorizing my favorite short-sleeved sweater with perspiration or three layers of deodorant.

The drive from my shop was short once I'd escaped the beautiful chaos of Magazine Street. Six miles of artsy shops, good food, and good times. Magazine was to the Garden District what Bourbon Street was to the French Quarter. A tourist magnet. A melting pot. But unlike the French Quarter, the Garden District was home to the elite, the megawealthy, and several eccentric aristocrats.

Annie owned a home on First Street, where sprawling mansions protruded from the ground in every form imaginable. Century-old Victorians with scrolling gingerbread designs stood beside mock chalets and austere Gothic architecture. Garden District homes were historic and sold more often by word of mouth than realtor involvement, moving from one socially acceptable owner to the next. Residents were choosy about their neighbors. After all, without proper vetting, who knew what sort of riffraff might buy the multimillion-dollar mansion next door?

According to my mother, I misinterpreted the intents of local customs.

I puttered along side streets toward First. Sunlight streamed through the canopy of reaching oak limbs above, filtered significantly by their mossy beards. I powered down my windows to enjoy the beautiful day. Hard to believe that only a few months ago, a dead body had turned up outside my shop and I'd found myself at the center of a murder investigation. Eventually, the killer had come for me too, but things didn't work out for him. I was recovering slowly from the trauma, but at least I'd met Jack and reunited with Chase Hawthorne in the process. Chase was a childhood acquaintance who'd helped me rescue Penelope from my scheming ex-fiancé. Chase was great. Twenty-eight, a professional volleyball player, and a refugee from the Garden District, much as I'd been a short while ago. Unfortunately, he'd returned to his life-in-progress, probably on a sunny beach somewhere far from New Orleans. I missed Chase, but I had a complicated friendship going with Jack, and I'd grown closer to my mother, so there was that.

I stretched one palm against the rushing air outside my window. Knots of tourists jaunted after tour guides, snapping pictures of the historic homes and learning the most commercial facts about our area.

My phone buzzed to life inside my purse as I slid my car against the curb outside Annie's home and settled the engine. I found my phone and frowned at the little screen. "Hi, Mom."

"Lacy, it's your mother."

I pressed a palm to my forehead in exasperation. "Hi, Mom," I repeated more slowly. *At least it isn't Annie calling to cancel on me.*

"I'm having a gathering tonight to welcome a new neighbor. Cocktails and hors d'oeuvres. Nothing fancy. The caterers will set up around seven. My hairdresser and stylist will be here at six. I gave the stylist your dress size in case you're interested."

I rolled my eyes. "So nothing fancy then?"

"That's what I said. Nothing fancy."

"You know, in some parts of the country, delivering the new neighbor a plate of cookies works, too."

"Don't be so pedestrian."

I bit my tongue. If I wasted any more time, I'd be late for my meeting. "Mom I'm meeting with Annie Lane in a few minutes. I need to get off the phone. I don't know how long I'll be, but I'll keep your party in mind."

"It's just cocktails."

"And hors d'oeuvres," I said.

"Exactly. Invite Annie along. She'd love it."

"Okay. I've got to go. Have fun tonight if I don't see you. Welcome the new neighbor for me." I disconnected without waiting for her good-bye.

Mom's parties were out of control. She was a party addict. It was in her genes. The Contis had been throwing elaborate soirees in the city for the better part of a century. Contis were "old money," a group endlessly concerned with appearances and local influence. Mom was the last of her family line, so she hyphenated. Conti-Crocker. Dad's family was what the Contis called "nouveau riche," a.k.a. the *wrong* kind of rich. While Conti money had been handed down through the generations, Crockers had established personal wealth through a tedious combination of labor and penny-pinching. Both families thought the other was doing it wrong, and I'd been trapped in the Conti-Crocker cold war for thirty years.

Regardless of my feelings on the matter, I was Mom's only offspring, and I had a duty to support her. Unfortunately I'd already skipped two events last week. Tonight made three rejections in ten days. There was no getting out of whatever she came up with next.

I checked my face in the visor mirror and reminded myself to breathe. "Here we go," I whispered. I hung my purse over one shoulder and hustled to the passenger side. I hefted the giant box into my arms and hip checked the door shut. This was it. I was thirty feet away from meeting my hero. I marched forward, head high, and slipped through the front gate, moving confidently up the brick walkway as if I wasn't sweating bullets beneath my angora.

Annie's home was a stately Gothic number with black plantation shutters and galleries lined in stout iron railing. A famous author had once owned the home, and like everything in town, the place was believed to be haunted.

I'd toured the property with my parents years ago, but it had changed hands many times since then. I couldn't help but wonder what it might look like inside these days. The interior was beautiful in my memories. More than seven thousand square feet of ambience and history. Six bedrooms, six baths, stained glass dating back to the 1800s. The structure was such an astounding piece of architecture. I wanted to weep or pet it. Neither reaction was remotely acceptable or sane, so I rang the bell with my elbow.

A row of gas lanterns dangled above me. Gold-and-blue flames flickered behind ancient glass panels. I crossed the broad wooden porch for a look at Annie's rose garden in the side yard. The rear gate rattled. I leaned over the railing for a better look. Her gate bounced and banged against the supporting wrought-iron fence. Was I supposed to meet her outside? "Hello? Ms. Lane?"

I went back to the front door and tried the bell again. Nothing.

I checked my watch. Maybe she was in the bathroom. If so, where was her assistant? If no one answered the door soon, Annie could think I was late. Not to mention my box was getting heavier by the second.

I peered through the leaded glass transoms around her door. Had she forgotten our appointment? I rapped the door with my elbow three times. The giant wooden barrier swung open under the assault. "Oh, my goodness. I'm sorry." I leaned in to continue the apology, but no one was there to listen.

My stomach knotted. Silent homes with unlocked doors screamed horror movie. "Hello?" Was it trespassing if I let myself inside? Even if I had an appointment? "Ms. Lane?" I took a timid step over the threshold and wedged the box between my hip and the wall. I liberated my phone and dialed the number Annie had given me.

"Wow." I absorbed the incredible beauty of intricately carved mahogany woodwork, baseboards, and crown molding. A massive cantilevered staircase stretched up one wall, lined in ebony-stained wainscoting. Thick wooden spindles carried a curved handrail into a loft overhead. An enormous chandelier scattered light fragments over the polished wood floor. I imagined nineteenth-century couples striding arm in arm through the space, dressed in their best and preparing to dance or flirt coyly in the parlor.

The muffled sounds of a ringing cell phone sprang to life somewhere in the house.

"Ms. Lane?" The call went to voice mail on my end.

One of Annie's Siamese sauntered into sight, rubbing its ribs on an interior doorframe.

"Oh, hello." I shoved the phone into my pocket and regained control of the box. "Is your mama home?" I gazed expectantly into the room behind the kitty.

"Meow." She inched closer, tail erect, and stopped several feet away.

I'd read a detailed article about Annie and her kittens, Cotton and Cashmere, in *Feline Frenzy* magazine last spring. She'd rescued them several months ago, and they meant everything to her. I related deeply. "Are you Cotton or Cashmere?"

She turned away with a flick of her tail and trotted back in the direction from which she'd come. A series of dark paw prints remained in her wake.

A bout of panic seized my chest. "Ms. Lane?" I checked behind me before following the crimson paw prints into the next room.

I followed the kitten through a stately doorway, careful not to trip over the jamb, drop my box, or ram it into anything. A series of stunning granite countertops lined the backsplash between a massive refrigerator and a stove that cost more than my house. One kitten perched on the center island, licking its paws and mewling.

A second Siamese stood in a puddle of scarlet goo.

I stubbed my toe on something and toppled my box of couture. "Oh!" I dropped on instinct, stuffing items blindly into the box until a handful of cloth came up heavy. I unraveled the gowns, now smeared at the hems with what looked too much like blood for my liking. Beneath the stack of my fallen designs was a Crystal Saxophone award. The base was covered in blood.

I held my breath and scrambled back against the counter. I dropped the award and grabbed my cell phone, dialed 9-1-1, and hovered my thumb over the green call button. For the sake of due diligence, I forced myself to peek around the kitchen island before sending the call. I prayed Annie had simply cut herself chopping vegetables and run to a nearby bathroom to bandage her hand. Anything other than what I knew in my terrified heart had happened here.

I sobbed on an intake of ragged breath. Inches from where I sat, on the other side of the gorgeous gourmet island, Annie lay in a growing circle of blood. Arms splayed, legs askew. Her skin was pale. Her chest no longer rose or fell. Unseeing eyes pointed at my shoes. Shoes now sticky with her blood. "Oh, no." The crystal award lying beside me, the one I'd handled, accidentally covered, and lifted with layers of my designs, was her murder weapon.

The glass-shattering scream filling her kitchen was definitely mine.

Chapter Two

Furry Godmother's pro tip: Details are everything.

Thirty minutes later, a somber parade of uniformed officers, medical personnel, and crime scene investigators treaded the gruesome path between Annie's kitchen and front door. Tiny numbered teepees stood sentinel at each set of bloody paw prints. Her kittens were locked in metal crates, and everything was being tested for fingerprints. I pressed myself into the corner at the base of Annie's staircase and did my best to stay out of the way.

Curious eyes coursed over me as they crossed the threshold in either direction, collecting evidence and taking calls. One set of eyes in particular made my skin crawl with each hard glance. Those eyes belonged to the man I'd ultimately called instead of 9-1-1. Detective Jack Oliver, New Orleans homicide division. Having him here seemed like the smarter move than rolling the dice with 9-1-1. With any luck, Jack would accept my honest explanation of how I'd wound up at another murder scene and why my fingerprints were on the probable murder weapon. He'd heard me out on the phone, then told me not to leave. I wasn't sure if he'd meant town or the premises, so I'd positioned myself near the closest exit until further notice.

Emotion tightened my chest. How could this have happened? Annie was one of the most talented women in fashion, a beloved philanthropist, and a mentor. The art world would be devastated, and our city had lost a hero.

Images of Annie's lifeless stare clawed ice fingers down my spine. I caught a renegade tear on the pad of one thumb and did my best to woman up. I had to keep it together for now. Freaking out would only draw more attention to me. There would be plenty of time for a proper breakdown later.

"Okay, Crocker." The familiar tenor jerked me back to the moment. Detective Oliver motioned me from my post. "Let's go."

I followed him into the dining room.

He pulled a chair away from the table. "Why don't you take a seat and start from the beginning."

I forced my wooden legs to bend, and I collapsed onto the antique cushion. All things considered, I didn't like the hard edge to his voice.

He widened his stance and leaned over me, palms pressing the table. "You want to start with what you're doing here?"

"I told you."

"Tell me again."

I bit my tongue. Forcing me to repeat the story was probably protocol, a way of catching liars in their lies, but Jack and I were friends. Weren't we? I did my best to relax and cooperate. "I had an appointment with Annie." I cleared my throat, willing it not to crack again. "Why are you glaring at me like that? This has been an awful day. You've been dodgy for months," I complained, "and now you're angry when I'm in a crisis?"

His eye twitched. "Have you considered that maybe I'm not too keen on finding you at the scene of another murder? This makes two in five months."

"I'm well aware of that, Jack. How is it relevant? What are you trying to say? That I had something to do with this because of what happened to me in July?" I was still seeing a therapist to deal with that one, when I could afford her.

He stepped back, his ice-blue eyes trawling over me. "Your prints are on the murder weapon."

"I know." Emotion choked my words. I rested my elbows on the table. I covered my mouth to hide a tremor in my bottom lip. "Annie was my idol."

A woman in a navy shirt and khaki pants headed our way. "Detective?" She gripped an evidence bag in her blue-gloved fingers. "We confirmed the murder weapon."

Jack took the bag from her and grimaced. "Thanks. Anything else?"

"Some footprints out back by the trash cans and the rear gate. The ground's too hard and dry for a good imprint."

I dropped my head into waiting palms.

Jack set the bag on the table near my elbows. "Any idea what this is for?"

I peeked one eye in his direction. "It's the Crystal Saxophone. A humanitarian award. Annie won three years in a row for her efforts in the Ninth Ward following Katrina."

He grunted and stretched his back, jostling the shiny detective badge he wore on a beaded chain around his neck. Eventually, the badge settled against his chest.

I pried my gaze off his shirt and mentally kicked myself. "What's that supposed to mean?"

"What?"

"You grunted. Does that mean you don't think she deserved the award?"

He tented his brows. "I don't know what she deserved. Probably not this." He waved toward the gurney being rolled into her kitchen. "But typically, murder victims have ticked someone off. Offenses vary."

"You didn't know her."

"Did you?" he asked.

I crossed my arms over my chest. "Why have you been avoiding me?"

He made a sour face. "I've been busy."

The woman still standing at Jack's side turned on her heels and walked away.

"No," I said, suddenly obstinate. "You're around. We run in the same circles, remember? You're friendly at one event. Evasive at the next. What's going on with you?"

Jack was more than an annoying detective. He was sole heir to the Grandpa Smacker empire and a regular at every hoity engagement Mom dragged me to. When his grandpa passed unexpectedly last year, Jack inherited the kingdom. "I don't know what you're talking about."

"Are you kidding me?" I forced my gaping mouth closed.

He shrugged. He didn't like to talk about his social status.

I didn't care. "You're never the one to say hello, and when I attempt to make real conversation, you vanish."

He averted his gaze, trailing a pair of uniforms through the front door. "Don't take this the wrong way, Crocker, but you're nosy, and I'm in the middle of something."

"So you admit to dodging me?" *Interesting.* "Why?" I focused on the pale blue of his eyes, willing the truth from him. The last time he'd seemed truly present was at the Animal Elegance Gala last summer. That exchange was our first of many to end abruptly. He'd kissed my cheek and told his grandpa's girlfriend I was his date, which I wasn't. I was still waiting for an explanation on that one. "Is this about Tabatha?"

He winced. "You see? Nosy."

"Curious," I corrected. "Besides I thought we were friends. Friends talk, and they don't call each other names."

"I need your official statement." He dropped a notebook and pen on the table. "Wait here." He gave me a pointed look and carried the bagged murder weapon outside.

He was actively avoiding me because I was curious? That was ridiculous. What didn't he want me to know?

I considered drawing angry faces in his notebook, but poor Annie came rushing back to mind, and my stomach knotted. What a horrible time to have such a petty argument. I rubbed the creases off my forehead.

I peered through her open front door at the men and women exchanging information on the porch. A small crowd had gathered on the sidewalk, snapping photos and otherwise rubbernecking a tragedy. I was no better, ensnared by a million selfish thoughts. *Why does this keep happening? Why do I find dead bodies? What about my companion line with Annie? What will locals think when they learn I was here? What will my mother say when she hears? How will I get my designs into the Mardi Gras museum now?*

I pushed Jack's notebook away with no idea what to write. I wasn't ready to relive the last hour.

I needed to move. Clear my head. Breathe. I slipped away from the table and tiptoe jogged into the next cavernous room, careful not to touch anything. They'd taken my bloody shoes and handed me blue stretchy booties, all the better for silent wandering. The downstairs was immaculate, dust-free, and excruciatingly perfect. Either housekeeping had come this morning, or Annie didn't spend any time at this house. I wrapped weary arms around my center and squeezed. Annie's chance to enjoy her beautiful home was gone. All her plans were irrelevant. She was barely forty and dead. It didn't seem real.

Framed photos of Annie and her kitties lined the mantle over her living room fireplace. Matching satin pillows anchored the hearth. Her kittens' names were embroidered on the little beds. A bubble of grief welled in my throat. She'd loved them so much, and they'd seen her on the floor. What had they thought? Did they understand? Had they watched her die?

I inched through the rooms, circling each perimeter, absorbing the moment, enveloped by sadness. Upstairs, light crawled under one closed door, drawing me closer. I pressed my back to the wall and waited for a break in uniformed traffic, then hurried up the steps. I pushed the door open with my bootie-covered toes to avoid leaving prints. The room was covered in books, magazines, and manila folders. Bolts and swatches of fabric in every texture and hue covered the window seat and two wingback chairs. *So this is where Annie spent her time.*

I crept inside and tapped the door closed. Floor-to-ceiling shelves were packed with books of every size. A rolling ladder attached to a metal guide over the tallest row.

A mess of papers littered her workspace. An open binder marked "Shannon Martin" centered the pile. I recognized some of the work inside as Annie's Mardi Gras line. So who was Shannon Martin? Was Annie working under another name? Why would she do that?

A sticky note fluttered to the floor. *Coffee @ 11 Thursday, Café du Monde.*

Today was Thursday.

The library door creaked open, and I went rigid.

A twenty-something in pigtails and horn-rimmed glasses sneaked inside. She closed the door in slow motion. Her shoulders hiked up to her ears.

I admired her willowy figure and fitted blue dress, clearly one of Annie's designs.

"Hello," I said.

She screamed.

We stared, wide-eyed, at one another as heavy footfalls pounded the staircase beyond the door.

Jack busted inside, tossing the door wide and nearly whacking the young woman in the process. He gave us a long look, holstered his sidearm, and frowned. "Why are you up here?"

I had no idea.

He turned his eyes on the girl. "Who are you?"

"I'm Josie Fresca. I'm Annie's PA." She squinted at Jack. "A PA is a personal assistant."

"I know what a PA is. How'd you get in here, and where were you for the last two hours?"

"I used my key in the side door. I was running errands all morning. Annie had an appointment with someone about cat costumes. I went to fetch beignets and coffee."

"Where are they now?"

"In my car." Her cheeks turned scarlet, and her voice cracked. "What happened?"

"That's what we're trying to find out." Jack edged deeper into the room. "Did you speak with one of the officers downstairs?"

The girl tugged the ends of her ponytails. "No. There're so many people. No one spoke to me, so I came up here."

"Why?"

"To keep working, I guess." Emotion had nearly extinguished her voice. She pointed to a stack of boxes with red *X*s on the sides. "I promised Annie I'd get her satin pillow collection in the mail today."

Jack beat her to the boxes. "Nothing leaves the house until I say so. This is a crime scene until further notice."

The girl looked confused. "I thought the crime scene was downstairs."

"We'll let you know when the house is open for business. Until then, you'll need to answer a few questions and return your house key." He appraised the box of tiny pillows. "You worked closely with Ms. Lane?"

"Yes."

"Who'd want to kill her?"

Josie barked a laugh. "Figuratively? Everyone." She shook her head as if Jack was a clueless child instead of a hard-nosed detective. "No one gets to be as big as Annie without acquiring her fair share of haters."

Jack stared at her, blank-faced. "I'm going to need a list of anyone who might've done this to her. Stalkers. Crazy ex-boyfriends. Bookies. Dealers. Anyone potentially capable of murder."

Josie stretched her eyes wide. "I said *figuratively*. Her haters were jealous, not homicidal."

"I've got a body that suggests otherwise. Murder weapon indicates a crime of passion." He glanced my way. "Anyone upset about her humanitarian efforts or the fact she won the Crystal Saxophone three years in a row?"

I stifled an eye roll.

"I don't know." Josie released a long breath. "I didn't keep up with that stuff."

I moved away from Annie's desk. "Do you know who Annie had plans with this morning?"

"No. She kept her private life private. I was looped in on business-related appointments only." She dragged her gaze to Jack, digging through the box of pillows. "We weren't friends, and she wasn't needy. She was busy. I helped cull her load, and she taught me about fashion on the side."

So the eleven o'clock appointment was personal? I joined Jack at the box and scooped a pillow out, trying to look casual. "Josie, do you know Shannon Martin?"

"No."

Jack frowned. "Who?"

"I'm not sure. Her name's on a binder full of Annie's designs. I know because my companion line was meant to pair with them." I pointed to the desk. "Whoever Shannon is, I think she might've met Annie for coffee today. I accidentally knocked a sticky note onto the floor when I came in here."

Jack marched around the desk and examined the open binder. He lifted his gaze to mine.

I pointed at the sticky note.

He pulled an evidence baggie from his pocket and stuffed the note inside. "This room is officially off-limits."

He opened his arms and moved toward the door, herding us forward with undeniable authority.

I clutched the little pillow to my chest as we fumbled down the steps ahead of him.

Halfway to the foyer, Jack snapped his fingers, and a group of people looked up. "We need to get a statement over here. This is the victim's PA, Josie Fresca."

An officer extended his hand toward the stairs and ushered Josie away.

I hurried onto the marble floor and scooted out of the way.

Jack fixed his attention on me. "I asked for a written statement, but my notebook is blank, and you let yourself into Annie's personal library. Why would you do that?"

"I don't know."

He harrumphed. "Are you difficult on purpose, or does it come naturally?"

"You first."

"Funny," he deadpanned.

A greasy-looking man stepped into the foyer. "Someone call animal control?" He hooked meaty thumbs under his belt and yanked his pants up to cover his boxers. His face looked like he'd gone ten rounds with a baseball bat, and his breath smelled like whiskey.

"No," I said, a little louder than intended.

"Come on in." Jack waved him through the tightly knitted crowd. "Cats are in the kitchen. Wait here."

I chased after Jack. "No," I whispered. "Stop." I grabbed his hand and dropped it when he turned on me.

"What?"

"You can't let that guy take Annie's kittens. She loved those babies, and he's . . . well, he's gross, and he smells like alcohol. You can't put her kitties in a car with an inebriated driver."

He didn't look convinced.

"Someone beat him up, so he's probably not a nice guy. You said that about Annie. Innocent people aren't usually attacked. He stinks, and he's wearing his pants under his butt cheeks. I hate that. Aren't there some kind of standards for animal control officers?"

Jack's cheek twitched.

"This is serious."

He sighed.

"Please?"

He pressed tanned fingertips against his forehead. "What am I supposed to do with two kittens? Someone has to care for them until they're claimed by Annie's people or adopted by a new family. I don't have time for that. I'm a homicide detective, not a rescue operation."

"But," I stumbled.

"I'm sorry." Jack lifted the crates and turned for the next room.

"Stop!" I scurried in front of him and opened my arms to block his path. "They're potential witnesses."

"Are you planning to question them?"

I gave each carrier a careful look. "No, but please don't send them to the pound. They've had a terrible day, and they were rescue kittens. What if they have flashbacks or think they've been abandoned again? It would break Annie's heart. I'm sure someone from her family will want them once they've heard the news."

Jack set the crates on the floor, defeated. "What do you want me to do?"

I bounced onto my toes, sensing imminent victory. "I'll take them." I squeezed the little satin pillow in my sweaty hand. "I'll keep them until they can be collected by whoever Annie preselected. I'm sure she has a will to clarify all that."

Jack's expression softened. His resolve washed away. Jack was an animal lover and a cat owner. No matter how infuriating he was from time to time, he'd always have that going for him, and I respected it deeply. He slid his eyes closed for one long beat. "Fine, but no funny business."

I drew an *X* over my heart. "Promise. I'll be a model caretaker."

He dipped his head in one sharp bob of approval. "And you can't leave until you write up your statement like I asked."

"I'm on it." I tucked the pillow under one arm and grabbed the crates from the floor near his feet. I hustled past the greasy guy in the foyer—"You can go. They're coming with me. Buy some coffee. Call a cab. Move along"—and motored through Annie's house in search of Jack's notepad.

I might not have arrived soon enough to save Annie from her fate, but I could protect Cotton and Cashmere until their new family arrived. I had enough love and cat treats to last forever.

Chapter Three

Furry Godmother's warning for the hostess:
What's yours is theirs.

I set the metal crates with Annie's kittens in my living room and hurried back to my car for Penelope, who'd ridden shotgun in her travel pack. She wasn't thrilled that I'd rushed her off of Spot the vacuum and into the car with two strangers who meowed all the way home.

Annie's kitties growled and complained as I locked my front door and opened their crates.

"Welcome to my home." I hurried to the kitchen and wiped out two cereal bowls for food. The ordeal with the police had taken hours, and based on the empty food bowls at Annie's place, these girls had to be starving. I set two fresh places beside Penelope's dish and freshened the communal water. "Dinner." I plopped a generous selection of my baked goods into the trio of bowls. "I know it's not technically a meal, but you little sweethearts have been through so much. You deserve a special dinner."

The twins slunk into the kitchen like runway models, winding their bodies around every chair leg and corner they came to. "Mew. Meow. Mew."

I crouched by the bowls. "Here you are."

They sat across from me with judgmental blue eyes.

"Don't be shy." I pinched a piece of tuna tart between my fingers and offered it to them, hoping not to instigate a catfight.

They took turns sniffing and rejecting my offering. "Mew."

"Okay, well, I have pawlines and peanut butter kitty cakes." I lifted the next selection from their bowls. No response. They jumped onto my counter and stared.

"No, no." I scooped them up and set them on the floor. "Here you are." I lifted the bowls to them. "You'll love these. I made them myself this morning."

"Mew." They turned their heads away in unison, one looking east, the other looking west.

Penelope watched from the back of my couch.

I put a treat into her bowl. "Are you hungry, sweetie? Come on. Meet our houseguests."

She leapt silently onto the floor and strode toward me, head high.

The Siamese hissed and pawed as she drew near.

Penelope backpedaled. She looked at me with an expression of betrayal.

"I didn't know they'd do that," I explained. "No." I nudged their paws to the floor. "Be nice kitties." I retrieved Penelope and set her beside her bowl. "Eat."

The Siamese charged her, wailing and growling.

"Shoot! No. No. No. Hey!" Someone bit my ankle. "Naughty! I know you've had a bad day, but let's all try to get along." Good grief. I carried Penelope and her bowl to my bedroom and shut the door.

I returned to find the Siamese on my counter. "Hey. No." I set them on the floor by the food bowls, and they walked away.

My blue betta fish jumped and splashed in her tank on the counter, as excited to see me as any puppy. "Hello Buttercup. You'll eat your dinner, won't you?" I twisted the lid on her food and dropped a few brine shrimp pellets onto the water's surface. She pounced on them with vigor. "Good girl." I ran a fingertip across the glass, and she followed it with enthusiasm.

The Siamese watched with rapt attention, gently swaying their tails.

Yikes. I gave poor Buttercup another look. "Good thing your tank has a lid."

"Fish are friends, not food," I quoted *Finding Nemo* to Annie's kittens. "Your dinner is in your bowls."

Something caught my eye outside my front window. My silly heart hoped it was Jack following up on the day's events, but whatever it was had vanished. Probably a neighbor or a jogger. I opened my sheer curtains for a better look.

My phone rang. I swiped it from my purse and sandwiched the little phone between my ear and shoulder. "Hi, Mom. Sorry I didn't make it tonight." I did my best to sound more upset than I felt. I washed my hands and ripped a wad of bleach wipes from the container by my sink. "I'm getting ready to bake tomorrow's treats."

"Baking treats? That's why you aren't here?"

"I was at Annie's longer than expected," I hedged. Music from her party poured through the phone. "I should let you get back to welcoming the new neighbor." She and I could talk tomorrow when I felt more emotionally stable and less like arguing. Mom was guaranteed to flip out when she learned I had been at another crime scene. She'd been doing her dandiest to make me a proper District bachelorette, and finding dead bodies didn't mesh with her vision.

"Are you aware," she asked, "that I am not an idiot?"

"What?" I rubbed a handful of disinfecting wipes over the space where I planned to organize my pupcake ingredients. "Of course I don't think that. I don't think anything like that."

"I have my finger on the pulse of this district, Lacy Marie. Or lack thereof," she muttered the afterthought.

I dropped the fistful of wipes on the counter and pulled a wineglass from my rack, then filled it to the top. "You've heard."

"Yes I've heard!" she snapped. "Of course I've heard. My only daughter was at the scene of another murder today. Do you know how that looks? Never mind. I'll tell you. Sketchy."

"You sound like Jack."

"You should've called me. I shouldn't have to keep hearing about these things through the grapevine. Our attorney is threatening to raise his retainer."

I swigged the wine. "I don't want to talk about it yet." I resumed scrubbing the counter with enough elbow grease to rub grooves in the cheap Formica top. "I just got home. I'm still processing."

"That's what I'm for," she said. "I'm your mother."

"You're having a party."

"You were invited!"

I had another gulp of wine. "I wasn't going to interrupt the party to give bad news. I planned to call and fill you in when I got to work tomorrow."

Two Siamese landed on the counter, attacking my hands and the cluster of wipes. "Mew. Mew. Mew."

I jerked the wipes away before they poisoned themselves.

"Well," Mom huffed, "at least tell me you're okay."

"I'm fine. Shaken, but alive and unharmed. Jack didn't even accuse me of murder this time, so that's an improvement."

"Very funny."

I turned my back to the kittens and slid onto a barstool at the island. "How do perfect days go completely awry?"

"It happens." Spoken as if she had a few of her own in mind. "Can we bring you anything? I can send your father out for whatever you need if we don't have it here."

"No. I'm fine."

The kittens stretched off my counter. One landed in my lap and rolled around until she nearly fell off. The other gripped my head in her paws and sniffed my face. "Mew. Mew. Meow. Mew." I batted her paws away from my nose.

"Do I hear a Siamese?"

I pulled the phone back and made an obnoxious face at the screen. "How on earth can you tell a Siamese by their meow?"

She hacked a throaty noise into the phone. "Your father loves the incessant little devils. We had a pair when we were first married. The blessed things never shut up, and

31

forget about relaxing. They won't be ignored. Why are they there?"

I smiled at the idea of kittens making Mom crazy. She loved cats. Though, these particular two were a bit needy. I craned my head away from their reaching paws. "They belonged to Annie. I volunteered to keep them until they can be united with their new family. I'm sure Annie made provisions. She loved them dearly."

"Good luck. You'll owe Penelope big time after this."

A paw slapped my cheek. The other kitty worked the material of my skirt under her feet until my skin was fully exposed.

I covered my legs and struggled to hold the soft wool in place.

My phone buzzed against my cheek. I checked the display. "Mom, that's Scarlet. Go back to your party, and we'll talk tomorrow when I'm less crabby."

"Very well. Remember to set your alarm system, and you might want to invest in some earplugs."

"Thanks." I switched lines and sighed into the receiver. "I'm having an awful day. How about you?"

"Aw," Scarlet said. "So it's true? You found another body? You're going to need a nickname if this keeps up." Scarlet had been my best friend since we were in diapers. Our moms put us together for playdates so they could drink coffee and have a break, but it backfired. We weren't the kinds of friends who complemented one another. One shy, one outgoing. One timid, one brave. No, we were the kinds of friends that necessitated phrases like "double trouble." We were cut from the same cosmically ornery cloth and loved it.

Our paths diverged when I left town following high school graduation, but the minute I moved home last spring, Scarlet was on my doorstep with a DVD collection from the 1990s and a box of cheap wine. We were caught up by dawn, as if we'd never parted. Scarlet was the kind of friend everyone needed and I aspired to become.

I swirled red wine around my glass. "I found Annie Lane on her kitchen floor. It was awful. Nothing wrong with the local grapevine, though."

She laughed. "The rumor mill is a well-oiled machine. We take gossip seriously around here."

I offloaded the kittens and went in search of my lap-top. "Yet I'm always the last to know anything that doesn't directly involve me."

"That's true," she agreed. "Uh oh." She lowered her voice to a whisper. "I think the children are headed my way. I told Carter I went to take a bath. He was supposed to keep them busy until I came out."

"Are you hiding in the bathroom again?"

She scoffed. "I have three small children and a newborn. Of course I'm hiding in the bathroom. Hiding is my life."

I logged into my computer and finished my wine. The Siamese mewled and complained at my feet. One jumped onto the keyboard. "I'll trade you two kittens for your four kids."

"Do the kittens wear diapers or need constant supervision?"

"No to the first question, and I think yes to the second." I removed the kitty from my keyboard.

"Then no. I'm comfortable in my current chaos."

"Thanks for nothing." I typed Annie's name into the search engine. "How's Poppet doing?" Poppet was the newest addition to the Hawthorne brood.

"Good. She can sleep through anything, but I haven't slept in three months. Seven years if you want to be technical."

A chorus of little voices echoed through the line.

"Drat," Scarlet whispered. "They're calling for me through the keyhole and under the door." She groaned. "Mommy's in the shower. Daddy will help you."

"Daddy needs help changing the baby!" One voice rose above the others. "Now *he* needs a shower."

"Oh, lord," Scarlet said. "I'm not getting a shower tonight, am I? If you come over to visit soon, bring some of that powdered shower-in-a-can stuff that hippies use. And a poncho to cover the spit up stains on every dress I own."

"Hey. This will pass, and you've gotten an awesome little offspring out of the deal. Who cares if you smell funny for a few months? At least that'll keep Carter on his side of the bed."

"You'd be surprised."

I choked back a laugh. "Okay. Go. Take your shower. Carter doesn't need your help with anything no matter what the kids say. He's a big, powerful attorney. He can work it out while you take ten minutes for yourself. Tell him I said so."

"Okay. Stay out of trouble. I'm too tired to help, and I worry about you."

"I'm fine. I'll come over soon and watch the kids so you can nap."

"Bring wine."

"What are friends for?" I disconnected.

Cotton and Cashmere bit my ankles and pawed at my feet. "Meow."

"Come on." I loaded them into their crates and went back to the kitchen to clean my counters.

Twenty minutes later, there were pupcakes in the oven, and my timer was set. I stacked feathers on my couch in piles of green, gold, and purple. My Mardi Gras line would go on with or without Annie and all the blood-splattered pieces collected from the crime scene as evidence. Replacing the ruined items wouldn't be easy. The materials' cost alone was astronomical, not to mention the time involved and the fact that each piece was a Furry Godmother original creation. Then again, starting over was becoming my thing, and maybe without Annie, my work wouldn't be seen on a global scale, but it would still make local pets and owners happy, and I was okay with that.

I bundled feathers into threesomes as I scanned online articles with Annie's name and perused her social media accounts. Josie was right. Annie had a few haters. The faux fur line she'd presented as an alternative to the real thing had been an epic disaster. Commenters on blogs and message boards thought Annie should've taken a strong no-fur stance. No exceptions. They argued that her faux line continued to glorify the murder of innocents for fashion.

I researched a few of the angriest individuals and discovered that one going by the username PrettyCharlie86 lived in town. Charlie also had a blog dedicated to ethical treatment of animals, and his bio came complete with a photo of him and a friend outside his home. The house number was visible on the door, and I recognized the street. "Gotcha." I jotted the address down.

Next up was a YouTube video of Annie called "Choosing the Right Protégé."

I stilled my hands as Annie smiled for the camera and introduced an emaciated young man as Shannon Martin.

My heart skipped. I leaned closer to the screen. *Those were your designs on Annie's desk.* Why? Review and evaluation? Or something else. I wasn't convinced the weakling beside her could lift a fork, much less a crystal humanitarian award, but anyone working closely to Annie was worth an interview.

I focused on the screen, memorizing Shannon's face and imagining Annie's former protégé fighting for the rights to his designs. *I look forward to meeting you, Mr. Martin.*

The timer on my oven dinged, and I nearly had a stroke. I pushed the feathers and laptop aside and stretched to my feet.

Something moved outside my front window.

I spread one hand over my collarbone to calm my racing heart. I'd thought someone was out there before, and it had been nothing. I crept to the window again and peeked through the parted curtain panels.

A man stood on my lawn, facing my porch. He was anchored by the long shadows of my oak tree, wearing black coveralls and a giant papier-mâché cat head. Big white-and-green painted eyes watched my home.

I yanked the sheer curtain panels together and sprang away from the window. My back thumped against the wall.

Whoever he was, he was big and close enough to throw something and hit the house.

"Leave or I'm calling the police," I threatened through chattering teeth. I jammed shaky fingers against the number pad on my home security system and waited for my new favorite word to appear: "Secured."

I rubbed my face and exhaled slowly. I debated calling Jack, but I'd already gotten his feathers ruffled today. If anyone tried to open a door or window, the alarm company would send a car to check on me. I was probably safe. The stranger was probably a cast member from some Faux Real event going on in the city.

I crawled back to the window and peeped through a crack between the curtain and the wall.

Nothing but shadows.

Chapter Four

Furry Godmother's secret to success: More antiperspirant.

After a restless night of bad dreams and mewing kittens, I made quick work of my morning routine and tucked Penelope into her carrier. I'd checked my lawn a hundred times after going to bed, certain there was someone just beyond my window. There wasn't. I'd considered making an emergency appointment with my therapist, but I didn't have the money to waste. Following my mugging in Arlington, I'd imagined my attacker everywhere when I knew he was in jail. Minds under duress do crazy things. Still, given the choice between having imagined a cat-man on my lawn versus actually seeing one, I'd take door number one, which said a lot about where I was emotionally.

The short drive to work cleared my head by a fraction and relaxed my clenching muscles. Magazine Street was peppered with shop owners dragging displays onto the sidewalk and tourists toting cardboard trays filled with delectable beignets. The soft, yeasty dough and powdered sugar called to me as I unlocked Furry Godmother and jumped inside. I smacked my hand against the light switch panel and punched the code into the alarm. My tummy growled. The contents of my refrigerator were as thin as my bank account these days, save ingredients for my nightly baking. I did my best not to eat those. Despite my growing clientele, start-ups were expensive to maintain, and lease space on Magazine Street was Manhattan steep. Not to mention the money I'd spent on a home alarm system and high-end materials for the Mardi Gras proposal pieces I wanted to show Annie.

I freed Penelope from her crate, and she trotted away, swinging her tail in the air. I'd make a run to my house for the Siamese after Imogene arrived.

I shook my hands out at the wrists and pushed images of Annie and the cat-man from my mind. There was nothing I could do for Annie, and the cat-man was long gone.

I flipped the "Closed" sign to "Open" and went to put on some music. Bright morning sunlight glittered over wide oak flooring. The soft pink-and-green palette of Furry Godmother was accessorized with punches of yellow and a healthy sprinkle of fleur-de-lis.

The little bell over the door dinged. Imogene walked inside. Her clothes were askew, and her hair was wild. Dark glasses covered her eyes. "Good morning, sugar."

"Wow." I whistled. "Rough night trapping ghosts in the Quarter?"

She wrinkled her nose and pulled off her glasses. "I wasn't catching ghosts."

"Oh." I loaded fresh treats into the bakery display and puzzled over my misunderstanding. "I thought you were helping a friend with a ghost problem?"

"I was."

I shut the little glass doors and tossed old wax papers into the trash. "Were you exorcising it?"

"Heavens no."

Well, now that that's all cleared up. I dusted my palms and mentally moved on.

Imogene grabbed a dust wand and went to work on my shelves. "Have you fed Brad and Angelina?"

"Not yet." Brad and Angelina were my box turtles who lived in a beautiful habitat display against the far wall. Their lagoon was lined in blue rhinestones, and their shelters were hand stenciled by me. "There are fresh strawberries in my lunch sack under the counter." I powered up the register and double-checked that Spot had made it back to his charging station safely.

"Imogene?" I interrupted as she hummed her way through the dust in my shop. "I hate to leave so soon, but I'm watching Annie's kittens, and I need to run to the store."

Imogene fastened dimpled hands over curvy hips. "I heard all about that mess on the news this morning."

"Me too." I'd watched every minute of coverage, and the media was blowing everything out of proportion as usual. Luckily I'd escaped the scene without being caught on film. "The kittens need proper transports. The police shoved them in awful metal cages. I don't want their toes or whiskers getting caught in them." I grabbed my purse and keys. "I'm going to pick up two nice travel packs like Penelope's and bring Annie's kitties here for today."

"Go on." She flipped Brad and Angelina's UV light on. "I can handle things here."

"Thanks. I won't be long."

I ducked into the sun and waved to a magician on stilts outside the Frozen Banana smoothie shop next door. A trio of women in scanty burlesque ensembles weaved a crooked path up the sidewalk by my car, probably on their way home from last night.

I'd had nights like those once, though not dressed quite like that, and given a choice, I'd choose a good book and Penelope over whatever they'd gotten into.

I motored over to Fins, Feathers, and Fur, our local pet supply store, and dropped two cozy travel packs on the counter with my credit card. Mom called twice, and I rejected both calls. I wasn't ready to rehash my night, especially after the strange appearance of a possible stalker on my lawn.

I darted back Uptown and hurried into my house with the carriers and a bag of assorted cat foods. Annie's kittens didn't come to greet me. Hopefully they hadn't made a mess anywhere while I was away. I checked the metal cages sitting near my guest room, as if they'd willingly return to them. "Kitty kitty kitty," I called. *Please have chosen the litter box every time.*

I locked the door behind me and went in search of the kittens.

My shotgun home was long and narrow, a style synonymous with the old south. The structures were built to house local laborers, but time and sentiment had made them collectors' items. Pieces of the city. Parts of history. My place was in a mediocre section of the otherwise swanky Uptown. I'd painted the house yellow and accented with stark white trim. The interior was airy, inviting, and at the moment, eerily silent.

Fear for the kittens built in my gut as I opened the last door in my hallway. Empty.

I restarted my search, moving faster and calling for them more loudly. I peeked under beds and coffee tables, pillows and throws. Ugly metal crates aside, there were no signs of Cotton or Cashmere.

"Buttercup!" I cried to the fish tank. "You know where they are. Why can't you talk?"

I turned in a small circle, seeking something I'd missed. My back door came into view. I'd flown past it on my first trip through the house. This time I took a closer look. *Unlocked.*

I cursed.

Images of the cat-man making off with Annie's babies filled my head as I dialed the only number I could think of outside of 9-1-1. I suspected missing kittens weren't an acceptable cause to bring out the full cavalry.

"Detective Oliver." Jack answered on the first ring.

I rattled off every desperate thought I'd had for the last twelve hours without slowing for air. An engine growled on Jack's end of the call, while I shook my fist at the ceiling and bunny-trailed about a cat-man and feline snobs too fancy to eat my homemade treats.

"Answer the door," he said.

Fear rolled over me as I turned toward the front of my home. "Why?"

Someone knocked. "Open up," Jack demanded. "You've been talking since I got in my truck ten minutes ago. At least invite me in for coffee."

I deflated like a punctured balloon. "Good-bye." I disconnected and ran for the door. "Come in."

Jack stepped inside. "How long would you say it took you to lose our only witnesses?" His dark hair was damp from a shower and smelled of shampoo. His ghost-blue eyes were the color of rain on a windowpane.

Not that I noticed.

He moved closer, securing the door behind him. A slate-gray T-shirt clung to the planes and curves of his chest before disappearing into the waistline of low-slung jeans. "Eight? Ten hours?" He prompted.

"Twelve." I marched into the kitchen to make coffee. "They were here when I left for work."

"Where's Penelope?"

"With Imogene at Furry Godmother. I dropped her off and went to buy proper carriers for Annie's kittens. I planned to keep them with me today, but when I got back from the pet store, they were gone." I pointed to the back door.

Jack strode through the room and ran his fingers over the slightly splintered frame. "Someone broke in? Did they take anything else?"

"No. I don't think so."

He checked the alarm panel beside the door. "How'd they bypass the system?"

I pursed my lips.

He furrowed his brows. "Tell me you set the alarm."

"I always set it when I'm home."

"And when you go to work?"

I spun away from him and filled a coffeepot with water.

"Lacy."

"I don't have anything to steal. Everyone knows that. The alarm is for my safety, not because I think someone will rob me."

"Sure. No chance of that."

I grabbed two mugs from my dish rack. "Would you like your coffee in the blue mug or your lap?"

"Mug." He snapped pictures of the doorframe and tapped on his phone screen for several minutes. "I've got a guy from Crime Scene coming over to print the door. Not sure it'll do much good if the burglar only touched the cats. Probably wore gloves to break in."

"Great."

"Yeah. It's too bad you don't have an alarm." He dragged the final word for several syllables. "Probably doesn't help that the reporter on Annie's story listed your name in the morning paper. Made you sound like a true animal lover"—he poked the splintered frame—"but it sure didn't do you any favors."

Tears welled in my eyes, and I faked a yawn to cover. "Those poor kitties could be anywhere. How am I supposed to know where to start?"

He flipped the dead bolt and wiggled the frame to be sure it stayed put. "First things first. This isn't safe. I'm calling a guy over here to reinforce this."

I pulled my hair over one shoulder and twisted it in my trembling hand. "Okay, but get a quote."

"I'm sure he's reasonable."

Reasonable to Jack's vault of money and reasonable to my anorexic bank account were two different things. I was budgeting my electric consumption and refilling bottles of water from the sink, but I kept my mouth shut. We had plenty of other things to argue about.

"What about the kittens?" I pushed. "Can we put out an Amber Alert?" Was it selfish to hope that whoever came for them wouldn't be back for me? I released my hair and rubbed sweaty, shaky palms against my thighs.

He stared. "Amber Alerts are for humans. The police are pretty strict about that."

"Then what can we do? How can I find them?"

"I don't know. They're cats. Maybe they'll come back."

"Funny. Did you learn anything else from Josie last night? When I left, she was giving her statement." In those designer shoes, she was nearly as tall as the cop interviewing her. I had shorty syndrome and serious tall-girl envy. Being in the fashion industry had only made it worse.

Jack slid onto a stool at my island. "Between you and me, that girl's not the brightest. She seems more like a charity case than a professional assistant. She went to Annie's former high school and participated in an art show that Annie attended. The two of them hit it off. Annie took Josie under her wing, taught her about the fashion industry, and gave her a job running errands. Josie's a living example of what can happen if a person is in the right place at the right time. She's gotten paid to travel the world on someone else's dime."

"You sound unhappy about that."

He tapped his thumbs against the counter. "I'd hoped for more information from someone working so closely with Annie, but it sounds like Annie was a control freak and Josie was a glorified errand girl." He fixed me with a careful stare. "Tell me more about the guy in the cat suit."

"It wasn't a suit. It was black coveralls, I think, and a big papier-mâché cat head." I mimed the giant size with my arms. "The whole thing was black. There were pointy triangle ears on top and big white-and-green painted eyes."

Jack worked his jaw. "Where was he standing?"

"Out front. In the shadows from the tree." I struggled to swallow a brick of fear and emotion. "He was there, and then he was gone. Maybe he was coming from the festival, just walking home this way and stopped for some reason that has nothing to do with me."

"Maybe," Jack hedged. "He didn't attempt to make contact? Come near the steps or door?"

I shook my head. "No."

"He could've been staking out the place for today's intrusion. I'll have the team comb the lawn and general area before they go."

I poured coffee into the mugs. "I can't believe I lost Annie's kittens."

"We'll find them. With any luck, the burglar left prints on the door and it wasn't his first rodeo. If the prints are in the system, we'll have him in custody before lunch."

"If not?"

My doorbell rang, and Jack went to answer it.

I sucked down hot coffee until my eyes watered.

Jack returned a moment later with a short but handsome man in a thousand-dollar suit. "Lacy Crocker, this is Bryce Kenney, Annie's attorney."

I waved from my side of the kitchen island. "Hello, Mr. Kenney."

He scanned the room. "Call me Bryce. I understand you've opted to provide temporary care for Cotton and Cashmere."

I slid my gaze to Jack. "That was my intention, yes."

"The local police have sanctioned this?" he asked Jack.

Jack cast a look in my direction. "Yes."

Bryce set an envelope on the island. "This is payment for your services. If your care is needed for more than thirty days, another payment will be issued at that time. If the estate is settled in less than thirty days, you'll be expected to return a prorated portion."

Jack lifted the envelope and peeked inside. "This is ten thousand dollars."

My jaw dropped.

"Yes, sir," Bryce said. "Five thousand per cat, covering a time frame of thirty days. I'll need you to sign this document confirming payment and formally accepting temporary responsibility for the animals."

"I don't want that," I said.

Jack tapped the envelope on the island. "I guess we have a motive."

"For her murder?" Bryce gasped. "That's absurd."

"Not really." Jack swiped his phone to life and tapped the screen again. "It could also be the reason for her cats' abductions. Some idiot's probably holding them ransom."

Confusion creased Bryce's brow. "The kittens' trust can't be released willy-nilly. Even this temporary situation has to be properly documented." He moved his gaze to me. "Are you telling me Cotton and Cashmere aren't here? Someone's taken them?"

Jack stuffed his phone into one pocket and grabbed a pink colored pencil from a cup on my counter. "I'm going to need a list of everyone who knew about the cats' money."

I pushed a slip of paper to Bryce.

He removed a hundred-dollar pen from his jacket pocket, ignoring the pink pencil. "There's no list. Annie wanted assurances that her babies would receive the best care in the event of her death, but she didn't advertise it. The kittens were meant to go to Annie's great-aunt Katherine in Colorado Springs. Katherine was a true cat enthusiast and big fan of Annie's, but sadly, she passed away last month. Natural causes. The will hasn't been updated."

"And the money?" Jack asked.

"Nothing about that has changed. The trust will follow the pets to ease the financial burden of their caregiver."

"She must've told someone about this," Jack reasoned, impatience lowering his voice. "Who was Annie close to?"

Bryce seemed baffled. "I don't know. She keeps in touch with a few members of her family, some fellow designers, her assistant Josie." He shrugged. "This is a better question for someone else. Annie and I didn't talk about her personal life." He blanched. "What about her ex-husband, Dylan Latherope?"

"Is he in town?" I asked.

"I don't know about that, but Dylan . . . He's . . . something. Their separation was ugly, and he fought hard for custody of those kittens. If he's heard about Annie, he'll be here wanting Cotton and Cashmere turned over to him. You might want to reconsider your role as caregiver." Bryce turned to Jack. "She could become a target for his aggression. If you'd like, I can reassign the kittens' care until Annie's estate gets through probate. I'm filing with the courts Monday morning."

"Reassign their care?" I wiggled my hands in the air. "I don't even have them."

"Oh." Bryce slid a phone from his pocket and handed it to Jack. "Annie had the kittens tagged. You should be able to locate them with this app."

I frowned. "She put trackers on her kitties?" The sentiment was sweet, and the concept was interesting, but the idea of implanting Penelope with a tracking device bothered me. It went against my instincts about what was natural.

"She had to," Bryce answered. "Everyone knew how important the twins were to Annie, and that put them at risk."

Jack turned the phone to face me. Two little red dots pulsated on Esplanade Street. "Let's go." He returned the phone to Bryce.

I set the alarm and motioned the men onto my porch.

"*Now* you set it," Jack snarked.

I grabbed the new travel carriers and followed him outside. "You know who else lives on Esplanade?"

He beeped his truck doors unlocked. "Who?"

"PrettyCharlie86, a blogger with plenty of mean things to say about Annie online. I found him last night while I was baking." I brought up a picture of Charlie on my phone and turned the screen toward Jack.

"Nice work."

A black sedan pulled into the drive behind my VW.

Jack changed direction. "My guys are here. Give me your house key."

I wrenched it off the ring and tossed it to him. "Do you know the code?"

"Yeah. I just watched you punch it in. Give me five minutes." He spread the fingers on one hand and held them over his head as he marched away.

I climbed onto the passenger seat of Jack's truck and hung my elbow out the window.

He had a quiet conversation with two men in navy NOPD windbreakers before leading them into my house.

"Hurry up," I muttered.

Bryce shuffled into sight and handed me a business card. "Please don't hesitate to call if you need anything. I'll be in town for a week. Beyond that, I'm attainable by phone or e-mail, and I can be back here in twenty-four hours if you need me."

"What if we get to the address on Esplanade and the kittens aren't there?"

A fresh hint of desperation played on his brow. "Call. I'll give you an update if they've moved. If Detective Oliver is able to return the animals to your custody, how can you be sure this won't happen again?"

That was a good question. I didn't know how it'd happened this time. "I'll protect them," I promised. "Whatever it takes."

He seemed skeptical. "I hope you're right. If not, I'll be in touch to reclaim the money." He tipped an invisible hat and climbed into a rental car at the curb.

* * *

Jack parked outside a white two-story on Esplanade where teens jumped skateboards over crumbling curbs and a couple flipped burgers on a pint-sized charcoal grill. He unfastened his seat belt. "Wait here."

I opened my door. "Why would I wait here?"

"We're not exactly in the Garden District anymore."

A kid wearing a black hoodie and skinny jeans kicked his board into his fingertips and sauntered over to me. "Baby, you look like the kind of librarian who could make me read books."

I whipped my hand out and snatched his board. I tossed it onto the sidewalk behind me. "Go away."

The kid rounded his shoulders and stalked into my personal space, eyes narrowed into slits. "No one touches my board."

"I believe that."

Jack stepped between us and lifted his badge, effectively stopping the moron's next witty refrain. "NOPD. Do you know the guy who lives here? Shaggy brown hair, goatee, late twenties. Recently acquired two Siamese cats."

Hoodie moved back two big boy steps. "Man I don't know nothing."

I puffed air into my overgrown bangs. "Well, at least he's honest."

Jack snorted.

The kid released a slew of colorful phrases, flipped his discarded board onto its wheels, and rode away.

I climbed the steps to Charlie's house.

The front door opened before I reached the top. The angry blog commenter stepped outside. "Man I don't know," he barked into a cell phone. A rainbow knitted scarf circled his throat. The matching beanie hat stood erect on his puffy hair as if someone had filled it with air. A yellow T-shirt and maroon corduroys emphasized his gangly shape.

"PrettyCharlie86?" I asked.

His attention snapped to me, and he covered the phone with one palm. "Yeah?" A slow smile spread over his lips.

Jack pushed his badge into Charlie's face. "NOPD. I'm here to arrest you for breaking and entering and burglary."

"And murder," I added.

Charlie ended his call, eyes bulging. "Murder?" He lifted his hands up. "I've never hurt anyone in my life."

"Tell it to the judge," I said. "Where were you yesterday between two and four?"

Jack fixed me with a hard stare.

"Sorry." I motioned for him to take over.

He looked at Charlie. "Well? Answer the lady."

"I was working at the coffee house on Canal."

"Can anyone confirm that?"

"Sure. Yeah, everyone. Ask anyone you want. Check the security cameras or the fitness app on my phone. My steps are charted so I can set goals."

"I will," Jack said. "Now invite us inside to collect the cats you stole today."

"How do you know . . . ?" he trailed off.

"Tracker chips," I answered.

After a long moment of debate, he swore. "Fine. Come on."

Jack gave his truck a worried look before following Charlie inside and closing the door. He beeped his locks and antitheft system to life through the window.

"No one's going to bother your truck," I teased. "Who's uncomfortable in this neighborhood now?"

"I left the ten thousand dollars in there," he said.

"What?" Now I was worried. "When did you take the envelope?" I'd forgotten about the money once Bryce told us how to find Annie's kittens.

We moved slowly through the home. Jack kept one hand on his hip, ready to draw his sidearm. "I'm still deciding if you were brave or stupid with that kid."

"I needed to let off some steam, and I have enough at present to whistle like a teakettle." Plus I knew Jack would protect me.

Jack entered a small sitting room behind Charlie. "Listen."

Annie's kittens mewed and growled somewhere deep in the home. Jack followed Charlie down a long hall and returned with one kitty in each arm. "Here." He handed them to me.

"Turn around," he told Charlie. "You're coming with me to the station."

"Why?" Charlie backed against the wall. "I didn't kill anyone. Try one of her other haters. What about Gideon Fargas or some other blogger? Talk to them. It wasn't me. Hey!" He dragged his feet. "Stop! I gave you the cats."

I cuddled the noisy babies. "You stole them, and you broke my door!"

"What if I say I'm sorry?"

I marched away. "Unlock your truck, Jack. I'm going to put these girls in their travel packs."

Jack followed me outside, pushing Charlie along by cuffed hands. "Why'd you do it? Ransom? Anger?"

Charlie whined. "I'm not saying anything else without a lawyer."

A cruiser arrived moments later. Two uniformed women escorted Charlie to the back seat.

I belted the carriers into the back of Jack's cab and took my seat in front.

He spoke with the officers before returning to Charlie's home.

Ten minutes later, we pulled away from the curb. Jack gave me a look. "I checked every room. No signs of a big cat head. Do me a favor and set your house alarm tonight. If Charlie's alibi sticks, the killer's still out there, and we don't have any idea who might be after these cats and their money. In fact, that money might be the reason Annie was murdered."

I peeked at the passengers meowing behind us. Jack was right. Convoluted as it seemed, someone could've killed Annie to get custody of her kittens and their trust. If that was true, and I had the kittens, then I was in the killer's way.

Definitely not a place I wanted to be.

Chapter Five

Furry Godmother's friendly reminder:
Notoriety is lovely until the unwanted guests arrive.

By the time Jack returned me to Furry Godmother, the autumn sun was low on the horizon, poised like a massive fireball preparing to eviscerate the city. In reality, the temperature had dropped into the low seventies, and I longed for a sweater. Traffic was backed up by an emerging dinner crowd, and shoppers were moving slowly along the sidewalks, heavy-laden with bags from a successful day on Magazine Street.

I wrestled the cat carriers from Jack's truck and waded through a crowd waiting to cross the street. I smiled at a barkeep rolling her happy hour sign onto the sidewalk. The kittens wobbled and complained inside their packs as the hard plastic smacked my thighs.

Imogene met me at the door and pried a load from my aching hand. "Goodness." She set the container on the floor and unlatched the little door. One of Annie's kitties came screaming out.

The other carrier bounced recklessly on the ground at my feet.

Imogene jumped. "What have you got in there? A banshee?"

I opened the door and released the second Siamese. "They're Annie's kittens, and they're having a rough week. We should give them some slack."

She visually trailed their frantic paths around the room before reapplying her are-you-crazy look on me.

I rubbed the bunching muscles at the base of my neck. "They'll settle down once they acclimate."

A low hum drew my attention to the rear hall.

Imogene giggled.

Spot the vacuum-robot toted Penelope slowly in our direction. She sat proudly on top, squinting her eyes and feigning disinterest.

Imogene bent forward at the waist, still laughing. "I had to see it to believe it, and it's funny every time."

"How long's she been doing that?"

"Hours," she said through another round of laughter.

"What's she wearing?"

Imogene wiped her eyes. "Wings. She's a fairy princess."

Of course she is.

Annie's kitties spotted Penelope and attacked, pawing and gnawing as Spot crept by.

Penelope hissed and arched her back, vehemently defending her ride.

"On second thought, maybe they should acclimate somewhere else." I dropped my purse behind the counter and dialed my dad.

"Hello, angel." His jovial voice warmed my bones. "How are you holding up?"

I rested my head on the counter. I hated needing help. I despised asking for it. "I need a favor."

"Anything. Why don't you come over for dinner and we'll hash out the details."

I bit my lip. "Okay, but Dad . . . I need you to keep two Siamese kittens for a little while. They were Annie Lane's, and they're homeless until her estate goes through probate."

He sucked air. "I'd love to! Siamese are wonderful companions. Have I ever told you how much I enjoy the breed? Simply fantastic."

I glanced at the low-intensity catfight brewing at my feet.

Penelope shot me a look of betrayal as she defended the Roomba. "Yep. They're super."

"It's settled. Bring them over tonight and don't forget your appetite. Your mother's making gumbo. Wait until she hears about this."

I imagined smoke rolling out of my mother's ears. "Okay. See you soon." I disconnected and slid my gaze to Imogene. "Dad said he'd take them."

She pursed her lips. "Your mother's going to kill you."

"Yeah." I scooped Cotton and Cashmere into my arms and carried them to the stock room. "You ladies can hang out in there for a little while. No one will bother you, and I'll bring you something yummy to eat in just a minute." I made a quick trip to the bakery counter and ferried fresh water and salmon loaf to the stock room. "Voila. Dinner is served." I did a dramatic curtsy.

They overturned the bowls.

I closed the door with a grumble and went back up front. "They should be okay until closing." I grabbed a storage bin from behind the register and headed to the window. "I need to swap out this display before I miss the festival completely."

I removed pieces from my newest Furry Godmother line, Vive la France, and handed them to Imogene. "Was it busy while I was away?"

"Lots of reporters at first, but I put a stop to that with a keep-on-walking spell. It was slower then. I took some orders for baked goods and spoke to your mother about the mess you got into last night."

I forced myself to not implode. I was a new shop owner, and she'd put a spell on my place that caused people to *keep on walking*. Had she considered her spell might be the reason we hadn't had any customers all day? I wiggled my head. That reminded me. "How's your friend with the ghost problem doing?"

"Veda? She's okay, but she's getting old, and it's harder to be effective once you get into triple digits."

I did a slow blink and handed her a set of A-line skirts with poodle prints. "Your friend's one hundred?"

"Yeah," she sighed, "and she's getting tired."

"I'd imagine."

The door swung open, and a group of women wandered in, arms loaded with shopping bags. The spell must've worn off.

"Welcome to Furry Godmother," I said. "I design custom creations for pets and bake fresh organic treats daily."

The women didn't look like they cared.

Imogene arranged a stack of satin pet pillows embroidered with things like "Oh, la la" and "Oui! Oui! Cheri!" on a merchandising shelf near the register.

I carried a replica Eiffel Tower to the counter, stepping around Penelope as she cruised by. "This can go in the stock room." As soon as Annie's kittens were gone.

Imogene returned to the display window with glass spray and a roll of paper towels.

A woman with ivory skin and raven hair pounded through the door, spinning my little welcome bell in a tizzy. "These are pet supplies?" Her Gothic garb fell somewhere between dramatic teen and Count Dracula.

I smiled. "I make organic treats and custom couture for our furry loved ones. Is there something I can create for you?"

Thick liner circled her smoky eyes and black-painted lips. "I need a studded collar."

"Sure thing." I dusted my palms and spun an accessories rack. "Gems or rhinestones?"

"Spikes."

I leaned around the display for a look at the girl's face. "Color?"

"Black."

"Size?"

She wrapped her hands around her throat, then extended them to me as if her neck was still in the center.

I left the rack and went to stand by her. "You want Vamp Tramp on Royale. Take the St. Charles streetcar to the Quarter. It's cheaper than a cab and faster than walking. Vamp Tramp's prices are reasonable, and the workers are very knowledgeable."

The woman almost smiled, then left.

Imogene quirked an eyebrow. "Vamp Tramp?"

"I was Elvira for Halloween once."

She shook her head.

The shop phone rang, and I grabbed it to avoid further interrogation about my younger years. "Furry Godmother, where every pet is a princess and every day is a royal celebration."

I secured three orders for pet treats while Imogene cleaned the window.

"All set." Imogene returned the cleaning supplies. "What will it be this time?"

I went back to my window and absorbed the blank canvas. So many possibilities. I liked to coordinate my display with the time of year or a significant event in the city. This presentation needed to reflect the Faux Real Festival and all its magical fun. "I'm thinking this should be artsy and theatrical."

I began with a deck of cards, carefully fanning them out and gluing them in place. Next I hung individual playing cards from clear line, as if they floated over the deck. I fixed a white stuffed bunny in the corner and tied a black satin magician's cape around his neck, flipping the corner up to reveal a scarlet underside. Behind him, I strung a line of twinkle lights and hung pendant banners for the festival. I fetched top hats in every size and shade of felt.

I paused to admire my work.

The door whooshed open again, and a string of evening customers walked inside, holding their hats. Wind whipped lost flyers down the sidewalk.

Imogene greeted the newcomers, while I finished the display. Shops often grew crowded after dinner, when satiated guests stumbled from nearby restaurants, ready to walk off their meal.

I packed the leftover window display items into a labeled and lidded tote while absently pondering the reason Charlie would've stolen Annie's kittens. It wasn't to hurt her—she was already gone. It wasn't for the money—he had no way of collecting. Could Charlie have been a thief for hire? Was someone hoping to collect ransom? If he was, then someone besides Annie's attorney knew about the trust. Who?

The bell jingled, and a man wearing three-hundred dollar jeans and flip flops strode inside. He levered black aviators onto his forehead and scanned the room, apparently looking for someone. Maybe he hadn't noticed the sun had set.

I stretched upright and straightened my dress. "Can I help you?"

His red-rimmed eyes and grim expression worried me. I imagined his body in black coveralls with a big cat head on top.

"I want to talk to Lacy Crocker."

I waved.

His scowl deepened. "I believe you have something of mine."

A hush rolled through the cluster of lookie lous filtering around my shelves.

"I don't think so." I lowered my voice, hoping he'd take a hint and follow suit.

He extended a hand in my direction. "My name is Dylan Latherope. I'm Annie Lane's ex-husband. She stole my cats when we divorced." He produced a folded portion of newspaper from his back pocket. "According to this, you have them, and I want them back."

He wanted Annie's kittens? Bryce was right. Once word got out about Annie's death, he came to stake a claim. How would he treat her babies after he had the kittens and money? Were there measures in place to ensure their well-being? Would Bryce make sure the one collecting the cash didn't give the kittens to the pound once the money starting arriving monthly?

I squared my shoulders and faked bravery. "You'll have to discuss that with Bryce Kenney, Annie's attorney. He's in town for a week. *I* can't help you." I couldn't even keep my name out of the newspaper.

He stepped closer, jaw clenching. For a brief moment, I wondered what Dylan Latherope was capable of doing to get what he wanted.

"I think you should go."

Silence fell over the room, and the Siamese meowing seemed to gong from my backroom.

Mr. Latherope's scowl fell away. His eyes went round like saucers. His chin quivered. "Cotton? Cashmere?" He took long strides in the direction of my stock room with me on his heels.

"You can't go back there," I demanded, spinning my phone to call the police.

Imogene slid into the opening of my narrow rear hall. "Uh-uh," she said, arms crossed and feet wide. No one was getting past her in that disposition. Her sweet smile had a sinister edge. "I'm sorry, sir, but this area is for employees only."

He stopped as if he'd hit a wall. "I hear my babies." His pleading eyes had no effect on Imogene. "Daddy's here, darlings," he called.

Imogene's gray brows crowded low between her eyes. Sheer concentration changed her grandmotherly face to something fierce. Her lips moved silently.

Mr. Latherope pulled his head and shoulders back, leaning away from the sounds of his "darlings." He turned to face me on stiff legs.

I tipped my head toward the mob of openly staring customers. "I can call the police if you'd like. I'm sure they can answer your questions if you don't want to bother Annie's attorney right now."

Mr. Latherope followed my gaze to the gawkers. One lady raised her phone, and the flash went off. "Fine." He cast Imogene another glance. "I'll leave, but this isn't over." He jerked the door open and burst into the windy world. "Those are *my* cats!" he screamed into the sky.

I waited until he disappeared around the corner before releasing my breath. "Sorry about that," I said to no one in particular. I pressed a palm against my chest. My mouth was dry as sand. I hated bullies. Standing up to them made me want to collapse or vomit, but every fiber of my stubborn soul demanded I set them straight before letting them get away. I pulled my shoulders back and hefted the storage container off the floor. Not to pass judgment, but Mr. Latherope seemed a tad unstable. Definitely not the kind of person I wanted to cross any more than necessary.

The last bully I stood up to had invested in my store, only to pull his money when I was accused of murder. He'd had a big contract on the line with a local casino and refused to risk the opportunity because of his association with me. Loss of his financial support had been devastating. I thought I'd lose the shop without him, but I overcame. I ate granola bars for dinner some nights, but I'd persevered. The shop was still afloat. I was tougher than I looked.

I took several more phone orders for baked goods and crossed my fingers that the revenue would be enough to put a little extra aside this month. My home kitchen was in dire need of several upgrades to maintain my increasing nightly production demands.

By seven, live band music and the lure of cheap drinks had pulled shoppers away. Imogene and I closed up shop in companionable silence, though I felt her gaze on me through every motion. I hugged her good-bye and packed three cat carriers into my VW, snapping their seat belts and ignoring loud Siamese protests.

"Time for dinner at my parents' house," I told them. "You girls will be safer there than you are with me." I checked my mirror and eased into traffic. No signs of cat-men or Annie's angry ex-husband.

I hooked a right away from Magazine Street and cringed at the sound of meowling kittens. I'd survived a mugger, a carjacker, and an abduction, but when my mother saw what I had in those travel packs, she might be the one to finish me off.

Chapter Six

Furry Godmother's fun fact:
A bird in a sash is worth two in the nude.

I parked my car in the driveway behind my parents' house and said silent prayers for sanity. With any luck, Jack was able to get enough information from Charlie to make an arrest for Annie's murder. Even if he wasn't the killer, he could have information that would lead us to the guilty party. I wriggled the carriers from my car and set them on the driveway. I was out of breath before I got the door shut. "Good grief." I straightened my dress and formulated a plan to get three cats in travel packs to the house without leaving one behind. "Ladies I think I need a wagon."

I inhaled the sweetly scented air of a brewing autumn storm, and a smile bloomed on my face. The gentle bouquet of Mom's meticulously tended flower garden sent me back twenty years. Warm wind tossed frazzled hair against my cheek, and nostalgia swept through me in dizzying waves.

Dad's office door swung open across the lawn. His veterinary practice was a Garden District success, operated from a converted barn in their yard. "Hello!" He waved a hand overhead from his place on the welcome mat. His usual white lab coat topped a pinstriped button-down and marvelous navy tie. His expression was childlike as he honed in on the line of travel packs in the driveway. "Let me get a look at those sweethearts." He strode across the lawn and crouched before the carriers. "Gorgeous."

The Siamese hissed and growled.

He laughed and slapped his palms together. "Splendid. Here we go." He grabbed their carriers and headed for his office.

I followed with Penelope. "I really appreciate this, Dad. Annie set her kittens up with a trust, and Jack thinks it could have been the motive for her murder. They were abducted from my place this morning, but they have microchips, so we tracked them. Jack has the guy who took them in custody, but I don't think I can keep them safe if people keep coming for them."

"I see," he said. Worry creased his brow. "Anything else I should know about your day or these lovely ladies?"

I picked flaking polish off my thumbnail. "Annie's ex-husband came to my shop looking for them, but Imogene gave him *the look*, and he left."

"Well, he's probably lucky he walked away. I'm not sure what happens if someone ignores the look."

I added that to the growing list of things I didn't want to think about.

Dad flipped his tie over one shoulder and opened the kittens' carriers. Cotton and Cashmere trotted out. They rubbed their faces on his pant legs and purred. No animal had ever seen him without falling immediately in love, and they were no exception. He stroked their coats as I blathered every detail of my day, cocking an eyebrow once or twice without interrupting.

"If I'm being honest, they're kind of mean to Penelope," I continued, "and they hate my baking. They're a little loud, and the fear they could be abducted again is more than I can stand."

Dad rubbed the bridge of his nose beneath his glasses. "It's no problem."

No problem for him maybe. "Have you talked to Mom?"

He stood with a smile. "Yes, and she's glad you're coming for dinner."

I watched Cotton and Cashmere knock Dad's things from his desk. "What about the kittens?"

He lifted Penelope's carrier. "I told her they were coming, but let's not mention there's a bounty on their heads."

I wanted to argue his word choice, but bounty felt right given the day's events. "Sorry I missed drinks with the new neighbor."

Dad motioned me outside. "Don't worry about that. Your mother has a bunch of suggestions on ways you can make it up to her." He placed a hand between my shoulder blades, steering me across the yard and through the back door of the Crocker family homestead. A humble little Victorian with twenty-plus impeccably decorated rooms.

Voodoo, the family cat, wrapped herself around dad's legs when we arrived. Voodoo was the latest in a long line of black cats owned by Dad's family. It was a long-standing Crocker tradition to rescue a replica cat when the reigning Voodoo grew old or ill, giving neighbors the impression she was ageless or that Dad was Dr. Frankenstein by night.

I was never quite sure if the stunt was mean or quite clever, but it was definitely amusing.

Mom arrived from the kitchen on the click-clack of designer heels. "There you are. Come in. There's wine."

I stooped to release Penelope from her carrier.

The spicy scents of Mom's gumbo wafted into the room behind her, clearing my sinuses and exciting my tummy. She used the best, freshest ingredients, plus a tub of garlic and the Louisianan holy trinity: bell pepper, onion, and celery. To me, Mom's chicken-and-sausage gumbo was evidence heaven existed. Surely, the recipe had come from there.

I followed her into the dining room on a cloud of hunger and anticipation. Her black dress pants and ivory wrap blouse were stunning, perfectly paired with a pearl necklace and earrings. The pieces elongated her neck and emphasized her youthful shape. Mom and I looked alike from the chin up, except I was usually smiling.

She poured a half glass of her favorite Pinot and set it in front of me. "You're having a rough couple of days." She didn't say it like she meant it. She said it like it was my fault. "Your hair is lovely."

"Thank you."

"The dress is a dab dowdy."

There it was. A compliment shooter with an insult chaser. "Dowdy?"

"You're young and vibrant. Why not show off a little personality with your fashion choices? Invite people to know you."

"I do." I looked at my outfit. "What's wrong with this outfit?"

She lifted and dropped one shoulder. "You need a more approachable look in your line of work. My stylist could change your life."

I was approachable. Wasn't I? "I don't need help from your stylist. I have a fashion degree."

Dad took the seat across from Mom. "I think you both look beautiful."

Mom rested twined fingers on the table. "Moving on then. We need a few things from you."

"Me?" I asked. "What kinds of things?"

"There's a Faux Real event in need of another judge Saturday night, so I volunteered you. Don't bother arguing. It's a done deal and a Crocker's civic responsibility to support the community."

I knew I should've gone to more of her parties last week. "What kind of event?"

She frowned. "Something nouveau and artsy. I can't recall the details, but you're due for another board position, and I know you hate those, so this will suffice. People will see you're involved again, and they won't expect you to help with anything else for a while. I'm buying you time. It's a favor to you, really."

"I'm going to need more information."

"I'll text you."

I counted silently and sampled my wine. "What else?"

Dad cleared his throat. "The next favor is mine. Commander's Palace is hosting a cooking competition for the festival on Monday night. Every seat requires a ticket, and all the monies go to our local culinary school, so I bought six seats at the speaker's table. The event's at seven. I'd love for you to join us. It'd be a shame to have empty seats at the speaker's table."

"Commander's Palace? Yes, please. I'd love to."

Mom scoffed. "Why doesn't he get any sass?"

"He told me where, when, and what. For all I know, you've volunteered me to judge a burlesque competition."

She looked concerned. "I don't think it's a burlesque competition."

I had another sample of wine. "I'm judging an event with no name on Saturday and having dinner at Commander's on Monday. Anything else?"

"Yes." Mom produced a purple folder from the empty seat beside her. "The Jazzy Chicks need sashes. Something dazzling, like Miss America, not plain like those little cookie sellers."

"Sashes for chickens." I pulled the folder closer with one fingertip. "Jazzy Chicks Confidential" was written in block letters across the top.

The Jazzy Chicks were a group of funny-haired chickens from the county fair. Mom and a few of the ladies in her social circle owned them and toted them around the parish for a small fee, raising poultry awareness and donating the earnings to charity. The plans were probably confidential because the Jazzy Chicks had an ongoing battle with a group of wealthy landowners from a few plantations on the bayou who called themselves Llama Mamas. The two groups spent a levee full of time, money, and effort trying to outdo one another in the donation department. It was a little silly, but it made Mom happy and fulfilled her genetic need to argue.

In keeping with the parameters of my overly complicated life, I worked for both groups.

A series of brown-and-yellow ovals were sketched on copy paper inside the folder. Each oval had an orange triangle, presumably a beak. She pointed to the drawings. "We want green, purple, and gold sashes, all blinged out but nothing too heavy. Chickens aren't very strong. Use sequins."

I traced the pictures with my fingertip. "The ovals are the chickens, right?"

She ignored me and continued with a line of extremely specific instructions until I thought I'd die of hunger.

"Got it," I said. "If I had some hot gumbo, I could probably start on these tonight."

"Done." She wrenched upright and swept dramatically into the kitchen, returning moments later with a tray and three bowls of gumbo.

Dad dug in with gusto. "I'm glad to hear you'll attend the cooking competition and whatever your mom volunteered you for, Lacy. It's good to have you back, representing the Crocker name."

I slid a spoonful of delicious sausage and peppers between my lips. A little sigh escaped. It was good to be home.

Mom opened a napkin over her knees. "I agree. It's also nice to see you putting your 'fashion degree' to use."

I rested my spoon in the bowl. "There's no reason to make air quotes when you say fashion degree. Fashion is a legitimate course of study."

"Well." She tipped her head left and right as if I might be wrong.

71

Mom had made medical school plans for me before I left her womb. She had sent me to her fancy college alma mater after high school, where I majored in molecular, cell, and developmental biology for two years. I defected junior year to a state school. I did finish the degree, but I skipped medical school in favor of design school. We tried not to talk about it. "At least your time wasn't completely wasted," she said. "The Jazzy Chicks truly appreciate your work."

"As do the shoppers at my store on Magazine Street," I reminded her. "I've only been open for eight months, and I've already gained recognition." Partly because I was wrapped up in another murder investigation, but mostly because I worked hard. I closed her folder. "I'll make delightful sashes for your Chicks."

"I know you will." She smiled sadly.

I spooned another hunk of sausage into my mouth to avoid grinding my teeth.

Mom blew ripples over the surface of her dinner with dim interest. "You'll need to keep our sash designs on the DL. That means down low." She gave me an odd look, as if I might not be fully following. "That means to keep them quiet."

"I'm aware."

"Good. We can't allow word of our new costumes to make it back to Margaret Hams and those damned Llama Mamas." She leaned in, conspiratorially, and gave me a cat-that-ate-the-canary smile. "Since we started our poultry education tour, we've spoken to twelve 4-H groups, seven FFA organizations, and nine schools. We've raised over twenty thousand dollars between donations made at the events and fund-matching pledges within the group."

Dad sat back in his seat. "That's fantastic. All the money goes to St. Jude?"

"Yes. We're donating one big check at Christmas." Her eyes sparkled. "We're doing so well, we made a bet with the Llama Mamas. Whichever group raises the most money by the end of this month has to wear the other group's pin on their coat until Christmas." She hid her smile behind steepled fingers. "So we also need you to design the ugliest pins on earth. Can you do that? Anything you'd like. You have free rein, as long as they're awful. I can't wait to see those Mamas wearing them for a month."

"Okeydokey." My bowl was empty, and my dress was tight. I wished I could change into sweat pants and make room for more.

Dad cleared the table while I mentally cursed my love of structured clothing. He set my bowl on the tray. "Have you seen Chase Hawthorne lately?"

"Not since the summer, no." I hated the pang of regret that hit with the thought. Chase was a rich kid, like me, who'd devastated his family by deviating from their plan, also like me. Instead of joining the prestigious Hawthorne law firm after college, Chase had moved to Miami and become a professional volleyball player. If that career ever fell through, I had a feeling there was solid work for him in underwear modeling.

My parents exchanged a long look.

"What?" I asked. "Is he okay?" He'd seemed fine the last time he called to chat. Though, that had been several weeks ago.

Dad hurried to the kitchen.

I locked my attention on Mom. "What was that look?"

"Nothing? What?" She shrugged innocently. "Chase is fine. Better than fine. Is it wrong if your father and I want the best for you? We saw a little spark between you two this summer and hoped it might've kindled a fire."

She wanted me to find happiness with Chase? It probably didn't hurt that the Hawthornes' money was as old as Mom's family money, or that the Hawthornes owned the most powerful law firm in the state—possibly the entire south.

"Chase and I are just friends. Also I don't like it when you talk about kindling my fire. I know what you mean by that."

She dotted the corners of her mouth with a napkin. "It's basic biology and logic. Chase is a wealthy, educated, handsome, and strapping young man. No woman in her right mind would turn him down."

"Jeez. Don't say it like you've noticed." My gumbo threatened to make a reappearance.

She guffawed. "Honey I'm old, not dead."

"And married. Old and married."

"Anyway," she brushed over my silly complaint. "Your union would overthrow every local grab for power. You'd be royalty."

"Don't say union."

"His family put a stop to that awful lawsuit last summer. You remember? When you ran over that stranger's foot."

"That man tried to carjack me!" I folded my hands in my lap and crossed my ankles under my chair. "I agree. Chase is a good catch, and I liked him, but he left again, and that can't be helped. Also I'm not trying to catch anyone." End of weird discussion.

Mom resumed her smug face. "Did you know that if you and Chase hit it off, you and Scarlet could be real sisters like you've always wanted?"

Scarlet's husband was Chase's older brother, Carter. "Yes. We'd be sisters-in-law." The thought had crossed my mind, stupidly, back in high school when I was a senior and far too cool to talk to a lowly sophomore. No matter how hot I'd thought he was.

My phone buzzed to life, and I scrounged it out of my bag. Jack's face lit the screen. Speaking of handsome heartbreakers. "Hello?"

"Lacy? Where are you?" He was out of breath and uncharacteristically worked up. "Are you okay?"

"I was, but now I'm a little worried." I flopped my napkin onto the table and stood to pace the room. "What's happening?"

"Where are you?"

"I'm at my parents' house. I brought Annie's kittens here for safekeeping. Her ex-husband came to the shop today looking for them."

He swore under his breath.

"Talk," I said. "You never call unless something's wrong. What is it?" I sorted through a ready list of possible worst-case scenarios. "Are you hurt?" I looked around me. My parents, Penelope, Annie's kittens, and I were safe. "Is it Imogene? Scarlet?" Oh, my goodness! Pain radiated through my chest. "Did something happen to Scarlet or the kids?"

"No. No. No." He slowed his speech into the easy southern drawl I recognized as cop mode. Emotions were locked safely away. "Nothing like that. I just needed to know you were safe."

"Why?" He might've gotten his stuff together, but my emotions were climbing the charts. "Am I in danger? Was there a threat made on me? My family? The kittens?"

There was a long stretch of silence.

"No threats, but there was an attempted break-in at your house."

I closed the distance to Mom's table and fell back into my seat. "Again? Was it Charlie?"

"No. We set him loose around five, but he went to work from there. His boss confirmed that he hasn't left since he clocked in. His alibi for Annie's death holds up too."

"How's my house?"

Mom froze. She turned wide blue eyes on me.

Jack exhaled deeply. "Fine, as far as I can tell. The door's still secure. A little dinged up, but we can fix that. A neighbor walking her dog called in a report of strange behavior. She saw a man she didn't recognize trying to get in through your back door. I heard it on the scanner, recognized your address, and came over."

"I'll be there in a minute. Don't leave, okay?" I kissed Mom's cheek and took her folder.

She caught my hand in hers. "What's happening?"

"I'm not sure. Jack's at my place. I'll call and fill you in as soon as I know more."

I stuffed Penelope into her carrier. "Who needs sleep when I can have fear and anxiety instead?" I mumbled on my way out to the car.

Chapter Seven

Furry Godmother's life lesson:
When playing cat and mouse, don't be the mouse.

By midnight, I was curled under a blanket on my couch, freezing. Two break-ins in two days. Sure, one attempt hadn't been successful, but that didn't make me feel any more secure. In fact, it made me feel like whoever tried and failed would be back to finish what he started. My teeth rattled together. My body's unfortunate response to extreme emotional circumstances.

Jack lowered his powerful frame onto the cushion beside me and set a steaming mug on the coffee table. "I made tea. Decaf so you can rest. I considered adding a shot of bourbon for good measure, but you don't have any."

I pulled the blanket tighter around my shoulders. "I can't get warm."

"It's the anxiety. Your body is preparing for fight or flight, redistributing blood flow and otherwise dealing with your day."

I lifted the tea and inhaled bitter tendrils of steam. "I know how the human body works," I crabbed.

"Then why'd you ask?"

"I didn't." I frowned over the top of my mug.

Jack's expression was grim. "I'm sorry this is happening to you."

I swallowed more tea, and the chill slowly faded from my bones. "You're sure it wasn't Charlie?"

"Yes."

"Then who? Why?"

Jack untucked his shirt and exhaled. "I don't know. Charlie said he took the cats as some sort of statement to his online world. He was saving the poor abused and neglected felines. He was going to be a hero."

"Dumb."

"Yep. I doubt another activist would attempt the same crime on the same day, and he hadn't posted about his plan yet. He wanted to make a surprise announcement."

I twisted a loose blanket thread between my fingertips. "I'm glad your guy was so quick to fix my door. No one else would've gotten it done already, and the second burglar could've walked right in." A pang of shame coursed through me. "I didn't get to thank him properly."

Jack toed off his boots and kicked back. "I thanked him plenty."

"Maybe I can send him a card." My teeth cracked and bounced against one another, jumbling the words.

"Do not send a thank-you card. Try to relax before you have a panic attack and scare yourself half to death."

"That would make me twice as lucky as Annie."

Jack adjusted a throw pillow behind his head and ignored me.

"Charlie has an alibi for her death, but are you looking at all her other online haters?"

"Yes."

I doubted that was possible, but I lost steam and changed direction. "Should we assume whoever tried to break in tonight was after the kittens?" As long as the burglar wasn't after me, he could have anything he wanted, besides Penelope and Buttercup.

"I don't assume anything." He checked his watch.

"Will you stay with me tonight?" The words were through my lips as quickly as they came to mind. So much for finding a casual way to deliver the invitation.

He rolled his head in my direction and tented his brows.

I backpedaled. "You don't have to. I mean, I understand if you can't. You're obviously under no obligation to babysit me, and you probably have to work in the morning. My spare bedroom only has a squeaky twin pullout." Nothing like I imagined the master suite at the Smacker mansion. He probably had a king-sized bed on a pedestal, smothered in black satin sheets and loaded with puffy pillows in shams that matched his pajamas. I stole a sideways glance at him. He didn't strike me as the sort to wear pajamas.

"I don't."

"What?" I jerked my chin in his direction.

"I don't have to work in the morning. I go in at eleven." He hitched his cheek into a lazy half smile. "What did you think I meant?"

I shook my head in the negative and finished my tea.

"For what it's worth, I don't think the latest break-in attempt was about you. I think someone is looking for something."

I made a face. "What? The kittens?"

Jack stretched long legs out before us. "I don't know yet."

"Well, what do you know?"

"I should've put liquor in your tea."

I hoisted myself off the couch and sloughed the blanket onto the empty space behind me. "I have to bake. It helps me think. Plus, the oven will heat the house." I rubbed my gooseflesh-covered arms. "You don't have to spend the night. I'm going to cook instead of sleep." I punched the buttons on my stove, preheating it to a toasty three-fifty.

Jack followed me to the kitchen and dropped a bit of dried bloodworm into Buttercup's tank. Penelope watched, ever protective of her little sister.

I filled cupcake tins with paper liners and wished my pajamas didn't have peaches all over them.

Jack checked the back door. "My guy did good work." He trailed his fingers down the new doorframe and over the replacement locks. "It'd take a battering ram to get through here now."

I tied an apron around my pajama pants and refocused my erratic emotions. "You haven't told me what I owe you for that."

He cast me a strange look. "Let me think about it."

I wasn't sure if the electricity zipping over my skin was dread or excitement.

I released a controlled breath and rolled my shoulders, loosening knots of tension that had been collecting since yesterday. "Doggy Divas placed an order for twenty dozen peanut butter pupcakes. They're including one in every party bag at their spa event this week. A reporter from *Devoted to Dogs* magazine will be there, and I'm hoping to get some good press for Furry Godmother."

Jack made a noncommittal noise. Much like the ones I made when Mom prattled on and I wasn't listening. He checked his phone for the fortieth time.

"What's wrong?" I slouched. "Don't say nothing because there's something."

He gave me a face.

"What? I'm nosy. Maybe you were right to avoid me these last few months. I want to know what's bothering you. I can tell it's not about this case, so don't try to misdirect me."

He set his phone on the island. "I'm pursuing a personal thing. It isn't relevant to Annie's investigation."

I lined bags and bottles on the counter beside a pile of measuring cups and spoons. "Go on." Two hundred and forty pupcakes would take me two hours to complete, and it was already twelve thirty. I dumped measured ingredients into a deep bowl and gave it a shake. Whole wheat flour, rolled oats, baking powder, baking soda . . .

"Don't you need a recipe?" Jack asked.

"Not anymore. I could make these in my sleep. Sometimes I think I do." Eggs. Applesauce. Vanilla. Peanut butter and bananas. "Don't change the subject." I slid the bowl under my mixer and plugged the beaters in. "I'm not going to stop asking you what you're up to, so you might as well fess up. I'll give you three to five minutes to decide." I rocked the beaters forward, plunging them into the bowl, and powered the mixer on. The machine whirred to life, spinning the bowl's contents into a delicious-smelling batter. I drove my gaze in a steady circuit from the clock, to the batter, to Jack. "Time's up." I clicked the mixer off and removed the bowl. "What's it going to be?"

He rested his forearms on the counter in a move of clear indecision.

I scooped batter into paper liners. "If you tell me your problem, maybe it will take my mind off this day for a while. No promises, but maybe."

He joined his hands and bobbed them against the island several times. "I'm looking into my grandpa's death."

I stopped midscoop. Grandpa Smacker had died a year ago. Why look into it now? What had changed? I raced mentally backward through my time with Jack. One thing came to mind. His grandpa's live-in girlfriend. "You think Tabitha had something to do with what happened. That's why you didn't make her move out when you moved in. You're keeping tabs on her." I recalled the kiss Jack had planted on my cheek at the Animal Elegance Gala, when he pretended to be my boyfriend for two minutes while she watched. I filled the last row of pupcake liners and slid the trays into the oven. "Are you going to fill in the blanks, or should I continue speculating?"

He didn't answer.

I repeated the batter-making process for batch number two, giving him a few minutes of my silence as I measured and scooped.

"You only make two trays at a time? No wonder this takes all night. You need a bigger kitchen."

"I might have a double oven installed when I remodel." In my dreams, I'd also buy a pony.

"Why not bake at your parents' house? Their kitchen is massive."

I wiped the dusting of flour off my countertop. "I'm going to pretend you didn't ask me that."

Penelope leapt onto Jack's lap and purred. He rubbed her head. "Have you heard any more from your ex?"

"No. He sent a couple nasty e-mails and texts after I picked Penelope up from the airport, but I ignored them, and he lost interest." I beat the next batch of batter and covered it with plastic wrap until the first round finished in the oven. "You were saying something about your grandpa's death," I prompted. "You might as well tell me willingly."

Jack laughed. "Fine. Grandpa was in good health when he died. He was seventy-eight and incredibly fit. He walked every morning. He ate well. Had regular checkups and no history of heart disease. Yet he had a heart attack."

"Heart attacks happen all the time to people without a history of heart problems. Most attacks come without warning. When there are warning signs, people ignore them—especially people who are otherwise healthy."

His gaze drifted away. "Do medical examiners usually find traces of GHB in the blood of healthy heart attack victims?"

"Your grandpa was roofied?"

"Yeah. Not an overdose, but there was evidence of the drug along with dinner and red wine." His voice was crisp and clear. A recitation of fact. A small vein pulsed in his neck, betraying his careful expression.

I couldn't imagine what he was feeling. I ached to comfort him, but what could I say? "Go on."

"The medical examiner said there was evidence of ongoing use, but my grandpa would never have taken drugs intentionally. The examiner knew it. I know it. So what was going on?"

"I hate to play the devil's advocate, but how well did you know him when he passed?"

Jack's cool blue eyes turned fierce. "Well enough to know he didn't do drugs."

"Right. Sorry." I removed the first round of pupcakes from the oven and turned them over on a wire rack. I righted them with quick fingers. "How'd you keep this out of the papers?" Allegations of drug use would've flattened the Smacker empire like one of my soufflés.

"The medical examiner was a friend of Grandpa's. I promised to look into the GHB, and he agreed to keep the details under wraps for as long as he could. I've been searching for breadcrumbs for months, and all I know for sure is that Tabitha was Grandpa's main companion. According to his friends, neighbors, and board members at Grandpa Smacker, they were inseparable. Grandpa told me about their walks and rituals. They baked together. Traveled. They had a glass of red wine in the courtyard every night before bed. Normal stuff. Aside from the huge age difference, they were a regular couple."

So that explained the wine in his stomach. "Do you think Tabitha was drugging him? Why GHB? That's a date rape drug."

Jack looked lost. "I don't know." He covered his face with one hand. "He loved her. I'm sure their relationship was consensual. Nothing weird like that."

"Okay." I filled the muffin tins with fresh papers and batter. "What do you know about Tabitha?" I reset my timer and pushed the pans into the oven.

"Not much. I know she's only forty-five. Just ten years older than me. More than thirty years younger than Grandpa. She has no job but never needs money, and she's about as high maintenance as women can get. Weekly nail and massage appointments. Facials. Hair appointments. An expensive gym membership. I can't get into her financials without a warrant, so I don't know where the money comes from, but she never runs out. Could be extensive credit card debt, but I'm not convinced. The only details I found online were past phone numbers and addresses. She's a ghost. No social media. No arrests. Not even a parking ticket. I went to her old addresses and asked about her. The few neighbors who remembered she existed didn't know anything about her. They all thought she seemed like a nice lady."

"Maybe she is." I whipped plain cream cheese, peanut butter, and extra-virgin olive oil in a bowl for pupcake frosting. "Someone else could've slipped him the GHB earlier in the day. It lasts several hours. Maybe you're on the wrong path."

"No way. She was with him all the time. She put the drug in his wine. I know it. What I don't know is why." He dragged heavy hands through dark hair before resting them on the back of his neck.

"Oh, yuck." I stuck out my tongue in a faux gag. "She sent food to my shop after the break-in this summer. Would I know if she drugged me?"

Jack made a face. "You? Probably not."

"Ha. Ha." I pushed the conversation around my crowded head a moment longer. "What if she used small doses of GHB? Not enough for him to feel drugged. Just enough to loosen his tongue. GHB would lower his inhibitions, so she could prod into his business affairs. Your grandpa's trade secrets could bring in a lot of money. I'll bet the right inside information would sell for a fortune to a rag magazine." I dropped my spatula and snapped my fingers. "I could help you gather intel. I can make friends with her, maybe spy." There was a hopeful note in my voice I hadn't expected.

Jack washed up at the sink. "I think your life is full enough without adding any of my burdens. Besides I think Tabitha is on to me. She started talking about moving out."

That was interesting. After a year, she was ready to leave? "Maybe she's finished whatever she was up to, and she's ready to go."

He turned, palms up like a surgeon prepping for an operation, and bumped his hip to mine. "I've never been any good at watching people work. Tell me what to do, and we'll knock this out."

I laughed. "Now you sound like Imogene. She can't stand to be idle."

"I never thought I'd be compared to her. How's she doing?"

I turned to face him with a bright smile. I had information guaranteed to lift his mood. "She's helping a friend in the Quarter with a ghost problem." I waited while that sunk in.

His lips parted. A moment later, he laughed. "Is that so?"

"Yes. Her friend, who is over one hundred years old, has this ghost problem, and Imogene seems very put out by the whole thing, but she's being coy and won't tell me exactly what they're up to."

Jack arched his back and expelled a loud belly laugh. "You're not going to believe this. I think I know her friend."

"You know a one-hundred-year-old woman in the French Quarter with a ghost problem? Who are you?"

He settled into a charming smile. "I've never met her, but I've heard plenty. Her name's Veda, right?"

"Yeah," I said, utterly baffled.

"My former partner, Henri LaSalle, works homicide in the Quarter. He's always ranting about this nutty old lady and going on about her magic cookie shop. Now that I'm thinking about it, it seems fitting she and Imogene are friends. Wait until I tell Henri."

I paused. "Are her cookies magical, or is it the shop?"

"I have no idea, but that woman drives Henri to drink. He says she's always in the middle of a big mess. Kind of like you." He ran a delighted gaze over me, slowing in key places before looking into my eyes. "Lucky for him that lady's a hundred and not thirty."

"What's that supposed to mean?"

He opened a carton of eggs and cracked one into my bowl. "Nothing."

I stepped closer, bringing our torsos within a few inches of one another. "Are you suggesting I'm a pain in your backside? Maybe you should be thankful I don't have any ghost problems."

"A lack of ghosts hasn't made you less kooky." His smile reached his eyes for the first time all night. He leaned a hip against my counter and watched me.

My heart burst into a fresh frenzy.

I forced myself back from the heat of his body and powerful pull of his stare.

It was hard not to believe in magic when Jack Oliver had so obviously put a spell on me.

Chapter Eight

Furry Godmother's advice for lonely ladies: Get a cat.

I sipped iced coffee and puttered through my shop the next morning, tidying and nitpicking, while shoppers glided past the window in packs. Sunlight glinted off passing cabs and designer glasses. Saturdays on Magazine Street were the busiest of the week. I was thankful for the distraction and potential income.

Jack left at dawn, after I insisted he go home and get some sleep. We'd played cards and watched old movies when the baking was done.

Hard to believe that just two days ago, I'd come to work in a cold sweat, terrified to meet my hero. Afraid she wouldn't like me or that she'd think my designs were junk. If only that was the worst thing that had happened. I'd prefer Annie Lane hate me and be alive than this macabre alternative.

I flipped through the local paper on my counter. Annie had made front-page news today. Pictures of her life were scattered around paragraphs describing her success and untimely death. I would have preferred if I hadn't been named as the one to find her and the first person questioned in her murder.

Penelope climbed aboard Spot the vacuum and pawed the start button.

"Sorry, sugar. I powered him down for the day. I can't have you tripping customers and causing a fall." I'd purchased my shopkeeper's insurance from a guy in a denim jacket and button flies. I suspected the coverage was flimsy.

She absorbed the information and climbed down, disgusted.

Shoppers trickled in throughout the morning. Some asked about my designs, but no one placed an order. A suspicious number of people entering the shop had a morning paper under their arm or poking out from their purse.

A woman in dark glasses and matching cliché trench coat marched through my door and headed straight for me at the register. "Lacy Crocker?"

I put my hands behind my back in case she wanted to hand me a subpoena or handcuff me. "May I help you?" I answered with a question, to be safe.

She pulled the glasses off her oval face. "Are you Lacy Crocker? Yes or no?"

I narrowed my eyes in warning. My extensive debutante training had ingrained in me that the stink eye was a lady's most appropriate form of defense. Anything I said or did beyond that was admissible in court and could besmirch my good name. Depending on who this woman was, I could also apply heavy sass. "What can I do for you?"

She huffed an indignant breath. "I'll take that as a yes. You're Lacy Crocker, and I'm Clary Blare, lead reporter for *AAH Magazine*."

"AAH?" I scrambled to recall the acronym. Was it a political publication?

"*Animals Are Humans*," she said smartly, as if it was impossible I hadn't heard of it before. "We're a national magazine out of Albuquerque. I assume you're making that face because you disagree? You don't believe animals are people."

"You said your magazine is called *Animals Are Humans*. No, I don't agree that's true."

She smiled and pulled a notebook from her purse. "I figured as much. You operate a fancy, overpriced pet shop and don't think pets are humans? Why on earth does anyone shop here?"

People stilled at the racks, ears turned casually in my direction.

"I suppose you could ask a client, but I'd guess it's my great attention to detail and passion for what I do. I don't think animals are humans. Animals are animals, and there's no shame in letting them be what they are. Cats are cats. Dogs are dogs, and you, well I'm not sure about you, but I have an idea."

A small gasp fluttered through the silence. Someone raised their cell phone in my periphery.

I kept my eyes on the moronic reporter. "I think animal lovers and responsible pet owners should embrace their furry babies and enjoy them for who they are. At Furry Godmother I take great care to ensure every treat I bake and every item I sell is the best, safest, healthiest option for our pets." I tipped my head. "Surely you understand. I run on coffee, and that's okay because I'm human. I'd never dream of giving coffee to an animal. Would you?" I made a horrified face. "Oh, my goodness, you would, wouldn't you? You think animals need to have human things, or they aren't being treated fairly." I shook my head. "That's a very dangerous way to think, Ms. Blare. Anthropomorphism is fun, but it is a fallacy. Animals have emotions and opinions, but they aren't human. Your pet might beg you for the last bite of pecan pie or a sip of your sweet-smelling cocktail, but you can't give it to him so that you feel better. Human food can kill your pets or cause anemia, diarrhea, or poisoning. Would you do that to your fur baby so his life seems fair to you? So you can pretend he's a human? As if what he truly is isn't enough on its own?"

The little crowd turned angry faces on Clary Blare.

Her red cheeks darkened to eggplant. "Of course not."

"Then you agree? Animals aren't humans. Now I'm confused. What's the name of your magazine again?"

She pressed her lips into a hard white line.

Penelope jumped onto the counter between us and nudged my hand with her nose.

I stroked her back and tickled her ears while Clary decided on her next move.

She bounced back quickly. "Is this your cat?"

I didn't answer. Stupid questions and all.

"Aren't you also caring for Annie Lane's cats? Where are they?"

"Someplace safe. Being loved and treated as kittens." I smirked. Immature, but I couldn't help it.

"Have you locked her kittens in your house all day while you bring your cat here for show? Is that why Charlie stole Cotton and Cashmere two days ago? Was that who broke into your home again last night? Did he come back again to save them?"

I lifted Penelope into my arms for moral support. "I don't know who broke in. I wasn't home."

"Well," she said, casting her gaze over the growing audience, "that's convenient."

"None of this has been convenient."

She pressed her hot palms on my counter and leaned toward me. "You've had a tough couple of days, Ms. Crocker, so why are you here, playing shop and behaving as if nothing has happened?"

I bit the insides of my cheeks and reminded myself to watch my words. I had an audience with Internet access. "I realize you're not from around here, but in New Orleans, the show goes on. We never stop. We celebrate life, and we mourn death, probably to degrees you can't imagine back in Albuquerque. I'm endlessly sorry for what's happened to Annie, and frankly, you're ignorant to think otherwise. If opening my shop today seems wrong to you, then go home—no one invited you—but I'm charging onward because New Orleanians keep going. Furthermore, the only true insult to Annie that I see is the fact you're here chasing smoke instead of reporting on her incredible life. Do you think she wanted to be remembered for dying?" My temper cooled, and I stepped away from the counter. "Kindly leave—I'm finished talking with you."

The gathering of silent shoppers began a slow clap.

"Annie had her share of enemies, Ms. Crocker. If you care as much as you pretend to, the least you can do is keep her cats closer than she did. Take care of them." She whipped herself around and strode away.

The store burst back to life. Shoppers chatted rapidly into cell phones and excitedly at one another, likely replaying my verbal smackdown. Hopefully none of it would wind up on YouTube. I kissed Penelope and set her on the floor. Why couldn't I win more word battles? I knew lots of words, but they were never ready when I needed them. That New Orleans speech was the best I'd done in years, and I still couldn't shake the feeling that Clary Blare had gotten the best of me.

The front door burst open, and Imogene bustled inside. She rounded the counter and grabbed my wrists. "Your mother just told me about what happened last night." Her eyes slid shut for a long beat before she released me. "Are you still carrying the Chilean I gave you?"

"Yes." I turned for my purse, tucked snugly beneath the counter, so she wouldn't see my eyes roll. A Chilean was a little three-legged pig. Imogene had given me the figurine to remedy my bad juju this summer. I knew she'd check up on it eventually, so I kept it close. "Here."

She snatched him up and stuffed him into her overflowing quilted shoulder bag. "This fellow can't cure what you've got."

"Okay. What else do you have?"

She cocked an eyebrow. "You never turn down my help. Strange behavior for someone who doesn't believe."

I slid my arm around her back. "I accept your help because I love you. I'd wear garlic to ward off vampires. Stir my coffee with chicken bones. Whatever you want. *You* believe, and that's good enough for me."

"Vampires would like garlic if they had any sense. Garlic's delicious. Now here." She dropped a small hunk of brown paper in my hand. "This'll keep you safe until I can get your juju cleaned up." She folded my fingers over the little thing. "No one can put a spell on you while you have this in your possession."

"What is it?"

"That's a dime, covered in red pepper and rolled in brown paper. It's for protection. You put it in your shoe." She stared at my feet.

"Oh-kay," I drawled. I wiggled one ankle boot off my foot and balanced on the other. I dropped the dime inside my empty boot. "See? Anything for you." I slid my toes back inside the shoe.

Imogene shook her head. "The dime goes under your heel."

I tilted my foot and let the dime slide beneath my heel. "There. How's that?"

She dusted her palms. "That'll help."

"Great." I glanced at the sprinkling of shoppers who'd lost interest when Clary left and went to wash my hands in the little sink behind the bakery counter. The dime bit into my heel with every step. "I have to make a delivery to Doggy Divas soon. Do you mind taking over while I'm gone?"

"Not at all."

I lined boxes of fresh treats on the counter, then shimmied them into logoed shopping bags. Clary's words plucked at my skin. She was right—Charlie wasn't the only activist who hated Annie. In fact, Charlie had mentioned Gideon Fargas by name when we rescued the kittens. That had to be significant. I excused myself to the stock room and took a seat at my desktop computer.

A few keystrokes later, I found Gideon Fargas, also known as Gideon the Guardian. He was a middle-aged man with a bald head and Harry Potter glasses who'd established the Heart to Heart animal shelter after Hurricane Katrina. He took strays in and fed them, gave them a safe place to sleep. Many families were forced to abandon their pets during the storm. Gideon matched the strays with new families, many who'd lost their pets in the storm. I tugged the soft material of my dress hem. Gideon seemed like a dedicated humanitarian, but would his love of pets have pushed him to do something as irrational as murder Annie? Just because she made a faux-fur line? I clicked a few more times and got an address for the shelter.

I collected my purse and pupcakes for Doggie Divas. I said good-bye to Imogene and leaned my hip against the shop door, pushing it wide.

Imogene waved absently and smiled as Penelope rode by on Spot.

I made a mental note to get better shop owners' insurance.

Traffic was thick when I pulled away from the curb and stopped almost immediately at the light on my corner. Smiling people crossed the street in droves, pushing strollers and sucking on cold drinks. I powered down my window to enjoy the spunky sounds of a jazz band while I waited for the light.

As the final crush of bodies entered the crosswalk, a dark form appeared on the empty corner. A man wearing black coveralls and a giant papier-mâché cat head faced my car. The man lifted a big fuzzy paw and moved his arm slowly, left and right at the elbow. I blinked long and slow. Did other people see him?

Horns honked behind me, and I jumped in my seat. The light was green. The car in front of me was nothing but taillights in the distance.

I willed my foot to release the brake and press the gas in steady acceleration. I caught the red light at the next intersection and fumbled for my hands-free headset. I hooked the thing around my ear. My wobbling voice demanded, "Call Jack."

"Call back," said the automated response. The useless technology repeated the last number who'd called my phone.

"No." My mother had called this morning. I hadn't answered. Jack was still at my place, and I didn't want to get something started with her. "Hang up," I instructed the phone. The call connected and rang. My heart lurched. I didn't want to talk to my mother. I needed to tell Jack about the cat-man. "Disconnect!"

People outside my open window stared as I yelled and slapped the stupid phone until it ceased to ring, giving only half my attention to the crawling traffic ahead of me. I tossed the earpiece into the passenger seat and vowed never again to make a call while driving. Maybe I'd even return the hands-free device. I was definitely removing the app from my phone. My nerves couldn't take it.

I worked to slow my breaths. It wasn't night this time. There were no shadows to confuse for something else. A grown man dressed as a cat had stared me down on the busiest street in the district. Was it Charlie in disguise? Had he been staking out my place before nabbing Annie's kittens? If so, why was he watching me now? If it wasn't Charlie wearing the cat head, then who? Annie's ex-husband? Given a choice between stalkers, I'd have preferred Charlie to Dylan Latherope. Latherope was off-balance and quick-tempered. It terrified me to think of what he might do to me—the stranger denying him access to his beloved darlings—given the chance.

I needed to dial Jack manually as soon as I arrived at the animal shelter. If I had any extra money, my second call would be the therapist.

The light turned green, and I inched forward with traffic.

I swallowed shards of terror and double-checked my rearview mirror. In the distance, the cat-man continued to wave.

Chapter Nine

Furry Godmother's lesson from a stalker: Take more pictures.

I motored into the small lot outside Heart to Heart animal rescue and triple-checked my power-door locks before dialing Jack. As if the cat-man sighting wasn't enough to ruin my day, I'd spotted an SUV in my rearview mirror on Napoleon Avenue, and despite horrendous traffic, was unable to put it more than two bumpers behind me. I'd hoped the vehicle would peel away, be absorbed in the allure of a French Quarter Saturday, but it pulled into the lot behind me.

"Oliver," Jack barked.

"You answered!"

"Kind of how phones work. Do you need something?"

"Yes. I need help. I'm at the Heart to Heart animal shelter in the Quarter. I was followed here by a big SUV. Before that, I saw the cat-man again on Magazine. He waved. I feel like that was a threat." I considered my confession. "Maybe not a threat-threat, but definitely an escalation, like he's saying, 'I see you, and I know you see me.'"

"And you think he's in the parking lot with you?"

I gave the SUV another look. I couldn't see a driver through the dark tinted glass, but I imagined he wore a giant cat head and waved like a Stephen King character. "Maybe. Whoever's in there hasn't gotten out."

"Sit tight. I'm going to call you back."

My emotions went haywire. "Wait!" On the one hand, Jack answered, and I was saved! On the other hand, who was in the SUV, and why wasn't anyone getting out? What did the driver have planned? How fast could Jack get to me? Traffic was horrible. "What should I do? Should I go into the rescue or wait in the car?"

"Are you not familiar with the expression, 'sit tight'?"

I hung up on him. I didn't have time for sarcasm. I was in a car. I could drive away and save myself. I restarted the car, overwhelmed by indecision. My gaze traveled to the SUV parked across the lot. Who was in there? Why?

Curiosity clawed through me. I imagined marching over and knocking on the tinted glass. What if the glass slid down and a gun poked out? Maybe leaving was a better idea. I could visit Heart to Heart another time. The police station wasn't far. I was willing to bet the SUV wouldn't follow me into that lot. I forced my curious thoughts away in favor of survival.

Unfortunately, the Quarter streets and sidewalks teemed with traffic and pedestrians, making travel nearly impossible. I could cut into the mix, but it would take time, and I wasn't sure how my tail would react. And Jack had told me to sit tight. A Segway tour glided through the mess like ducklings after their mama, wearing little yellow helmets and fierce expressions of concentration. A little smile tugged my mouth. Segways were a lot of fun as long as they weren't driven while under the influence, like goofy Chase Hawthorne had many years ago. I shook off the happy feeling. I had serious problems to deal with. Anyway, it was a good thing Chase had left town again, because I owed him a kiss for his assistance in Penelope's safe return, and I wasn't ready for kissing Chase. I'd never be ready. He was too smooth, and I was a sucker for good looks and confidence. Honestly I should steer clear of all handsome men.

I breathed hot, stale air, afraid to roll my windows down despite the greenhouse effect on my skin.

I cast a guilty look at the bags on my passenger seat and imagined peanut butter frosting dripping from my pretty pupcakes onto their papers. I cranked the air conditioning and flicked a vent in their direction. "I will deliver you soon," I promised. "Do me a favor and try not to melt first. Do we have a deal?"

A siren barked.

"Good grief!" I jumped.

A sleek black Camaro parted the pedestrians like a shark through the sea. Custom red-and-white lights flashed behind the grill. Undercover cop. Someone was busted. I looked around for trouble.

The car stopped behind me.

Was he here to rescue me? Excitement coursed through me.

The Camaro's door swung open, and a man in black jeans, black boots, and a clingy black T-shirt slid out. His hair was long enough to put fingers through, and his cheeks were lined in stubble. He headed straight for the SUV.

"Yes!" I spun around like a child peeking into the next booth during dinner.

He rapped his knuckles against the glass and braced his free palm against the blatantly visible sidearm at his back. "New Orleans PD." His deep voice cut through the distance between us. "Roll this down. Now."

The window powered down a few inches, not enough for me to see the driver.

I cracked my window for better acoustics and dialed Jack. "Oliver."

"There's a cop talking to the SUV guy. I can't see who's behind the wheel, but there's definitely a cop. Should I go over there and talk to them?"

"Yeah. I'll go with you." Jack's truck swung into view and parked on the sidewalk across the street. People stared a moment, then went around.

Jack loped into the lot and headed for the SUV.

I jumped out and followed.

The SUV's door opened slowly. Jack and Undercover Cop dragged Dylan Latherope, Annie's ex-husband, from the vehicle.

I stumbled back a step.

"There she is!" He lunged toward me as the other men held his arms. "You have my cats, and I want them back!"

Jack cuffed Mr. Latherope and pressed his face against the truck's hood.

Undercover Cop gave me a curious look before poking his head inside the SUV.

I inched closer, uncertain how close I wanted to be if Latherope hulked out or exploded.

He struggled against Jack's grip. The skin of his cheek stretched and contorted against the SUV's hood. He glared at me with bulging eyes. "What are you doing here?" he demanded. "You already have one cat and two of mine! Are you getting more? Are you planning to leave mine here while you go on collecting their trust? Did you lock them in a car on a day like this?" He wiggled and lifted his feet, trying to kick Jack away.

Undercover Cop pulled out of Latherope's car. "No weapons. No contraband. Car's clean." He extended his hand to me.

I accepted.

"Detective Henri LaSalle, New Orleans Homicide." He squeezed once and turned to Jack. "This guy's stalking your girl over a pair of cats? Like kitty cats?"

Jack lifted his chin. "Yep."

Henri flicked Latherope's forehead. "Man, don't be stupid. You want to go to jail over cats?"

I tried not to focus on how easily Jack had allowed Henri to call me Jack's girl. Juvenile as the term was, I liked it. *Dumb. Dumb. Dumb.* "Did you happen to see a cat head in there?" I pointed to the SUV. "And coveralls?" Mr. Latherope was currently in faded denim and a Saints shirt.

"Cat overalls?" Henri asked.

"Coveralls," Jack answered for me. "Black ones and a big papier-mâché head. A black cat face with pointy ears." He gave Latherope a long look. "Nah, car's clean."

Latherope stopped fighting. "What?"

Henri clapped Jack's shoulder and anchored Mr. Latherope off the car by his cuffs. "I'll have a talk with this one for you." He unlocked the cuffs.

Latherope rubbed his wrists.

I stepped back and bumped into Jack. I hadn't noticed him move behind me.

He set a wide palm on my arm. "Latherope." His breath blew against the top of my head. "I want you to pretend I just issued a restraining order, because if I catch you within a mile of Lacy again, I'm going to serve you up a hot Louisiana butt whooping."

"Whooo-hooo!" Henri hollered. He crossed his arms and smiled. "You don't want none of that, sir. I've had some. It's no good. Now start by telling me why you're stalking that nice woman."

Jack spun me in his direction. "You okay?"

I nodded stiffly, straining to hear Latherope's answer. "Why aren't you talking to him?"

"I'm pissed off. Henri's here. Better to let the cool guy ask the questions."

I gave his blank face a careful exam. "This is you mad?"

One stiff dip of his chin confirmed.

"Okay then. Moving on. If Latherope wasn't the cat-man, then he's still out there." Unless I'd finally gone around the bend. "What's the point? To wave and stare? Why the costume?"

He crossed his arms and widened his stance. "Is your ex mad enough to come down here and try to upset you?"

"Pete?" I tried to picture it, but anytime I thought his name, I remembered the look on his face when I'd come to surprise him during his night shift. As it turned out, he wasn't working that night as much as getting to know a coworker. Biblically. "No. Even if he was mad enough to think about coming to New Orleans, he's too lazy to do more than angry text. Plus, he was a cheater, not a psychopath. What kind of person does stuff like this?"

Jack shifted his attention in the direction of Henri and Latherope. "I dispatched a pair of uniforms to Magazine when you called. They're asking around about a guy in a cat head."

"Then you called Henri."

"I knew Henri was closer to you than I was." He dropped his gaze back on me. "I called him first."

The statement felt weighted, and I didn't like what that did to my pulse.

"What are you doing here, anyway?"

"I came to talk to Gideon Fargas. Charlie mentioned him. Gideon runs this place."

"I'm aware." He tapped a finger to the shiny badge on his belt. "My guys talked to him already. He's harmless."

I raised my brows. "He writes a blog on the health and safety of animals in New Orleans, and the guy who mentioned him by name was arrested for stealing my kittens. I think those facts make him relevant—at least enough to provide a new lead. I'd like to talk to him." I took a step toward the rescue and turned back. "Did you hear Latherope? He knew those kittens came with a trust." I squinted against the brilliant midday sun, unable to bring Jack's face into view without my sunglasses.

"I heard that, and I plan to hear more about it when I'm done with you. Meanwhile, you're wasting your time—this Heart to Heart guy's not a killer."

"How do you know?" I shaded my eyes with one hand. "You weren't even the one who talked to him."

The rescue door flung open and smacked shut. A man in a ball cap and glasses barreled onto the sidewalk. His shoulders were hunched forward as if he'd robbed the place.

Instinct kicked me into gear. "Mr. Fargas?" I followed him down the crowded street. "Mr. Gideon Fargas?"

He stopped. "Yes?" A look that resembled hope crossed his face. He pulled earbuds from his ears and smiled.

"I was just on my way to the rescue." I pointed behind us.

"Oh." His smile widened. "I'm probably not going to catch a cab anytime soon in this mess, am I?"

"Probably not."

He nodded and turned toward the rescue with me at his side. Khaki cargo pants sagged around his drooping tummy, where a black canvas belt was failing its job. His wrinkled polo shirt had a logo over the pocket and a coating of animal hairs. He pushed round-rimmed glasses up his nose with the side of his index finger. "What kind of pet are you looking to adopt?"

Jack fell into step beside us. "Actually," he butted in, flashing his badge, "we'd like to talk to you about Annie Lane."

Gideon stopped. "What?" The hope in his eyes extinguished. A sad smile tugged his mouth. "That's a chubby guy's luck, right?"

"I don't know what you're talking about," I said. "Did you know PrettyCharlie86?"

He groaned. "Yes, of course. I read about what he did to Annie's kittens. What a loser. Always trying to pull some stunt for new followers. I've already spoken with the police. I can't help you, but maybe the lady caring for the kittens can. Have you spoken with her?" He looked at the sky.

"Her name's on the tip of my tongue. It was in the paper. Lucy Cracker."

"Lacy Crocker," I corrected.

He dropped his gaze to mine. "I think it was Cracker."

"No, it wasn't. And yes, we did. We've concluded that she's a lovely person and completely innocent. Is there somewhere we can speak privately? Your office, perhaps."

Gideon's expression blanked. "No. I don't think that's a good idea. Why don't we talk here?"

Jack glared at the side of Gideon's head. "Any particular reason we can't see your office?"

"No. Why would you ask me that?" The words jumbled out in a near stutter.

"Because you're acting squirrely," I said.

"Come on." Jack opened the rescue's door and waved us inside. "Let's take a look at the office."

I followed Gideon. Jack followed me.

Both sides of the main room were fenced off. Cats on one side. Dogs on the other. Some in cages, some romping through narrow play centers. Barking morphed into a low yodel when a hound dog took notice of our arrival.

I stopped to rub behind its ears. "What was your problem with Annie anyway?" I asked Gideon. "All those nasty allegations about mistreatment of her kittens were completely unfounded. Her kittens are in perfect health. They've seen a top-tier veterinarian who will confirm my statement. See how that works? I consulted a relevant professional and reported facts to you, but you go online and slander based on hearsay and speculation. Don't bloggers have a code of ethics?"

"I am not a blogger," he nearly puked the word. "I founded this shelter. I'm the sole proprietor. I write an ongoing essay about the state of our city's orphaned pets. I'm a professional, Miss——?" He hung on for my name.

"Lacy Crocker," I deadpanned.

He arched his brows. "Of course. The lovely and completely innocent woman recently questioned for murder?"

"Correct."

He opened his office door with a stage sigh and motioned us inside.

Covering the entire wall opposite his desk was a detailed, megacreepy Annie shrine. Memorabilia. Selfies from the Internet. Professional photos of her and the kittens. Surveillance pics of her PA, house staff, moving trucks, delivery men . . .

"You were stalking her?" I guffawed. "Are you serious?"

"No." He flopped into his cracked leather office chair. "I tracked her. It's my job to monitor the safety of local pets."

"By whose authority?" I asked.

"Mine. The community's. Guardians everywhere."

I circled one wrist to keep him moving along and rubbed my aching forehead with my free hand.

"When a local pet owner has multiple online accusations of animal mistreatment, I have to dig for the truth. Either to confirm or dispel the rumors. If I confirm them, then I need proof of the animal's endangerment before I can request a removal or have the owner fined. What I do isn't stalking, Miss Completely Innocent. It's called due diligence. The cop understands me, right?"

Jack snapped pictures of Gideon's stalker wall. "I'm not supporting this. Stalking is illegal."

Gideon lifted his desk phone. "Fine. I can see you don't believe me. I'm calling my lawyer." He pressed an old-fashioned receiver to his ear. "For what it's worth, I'm sorry about Annie's death, but maybe something good will come from it. If someone killed her for mistreatment of those cats, then maybe the next person will think twice before harming their pet. It sets a good example in a complicated way, you know? At least she's protecting animals in death."

I turned to Jack. "Can I kick him?"

"No." He snapped another photo. "I think he's got the right idea. I'd call my lawyer too if I was him." Jack turned his phone around and sent a text.

I surveyed the crazy. Gideon's wall was all kinds of disconcerting. He must have followed Annie every day since she'd returned to the city. He had a dozen shots of movers hauling boxes to her home and every step of her life since then.

I leaned closer for a look at a young man in basketball shorts and a sleeveless shirt. He carried a box with a big *X* on it, like the one filled with little pillows in Annie's office. The one Annie's assistant had returned for. I tracked my finger over the pictures. The movers wore navy work pants and red polo shirts. "This guy is the only one carrying boxes with an *X*, and he's not with the company."

Gideon hung up, walked to the office door, and whipped it open. "My lawyer says he can meet us at the station to answer questions. Otherwise, you need to leave me alone."

Jack nodded. "Detective Henri LaSalle will meet you there." He went into the hallway, and I followed. "It's been . . . eye-opening."

Gideon shut the door in our faces.

"You barely spoke to him," I whispered as we hurried back through the rescue and out the front door. "How did your guys think he was harmless? Did you see that crazy shrine? What should we do now?"

"My guys spoke with him at his home. Speaking of homes, you need to go to yours. I'm going to meet Henri at the station."

I beeped my car unlocked and dropped behind the wheel.

Jack caught the door before I could pull it shut. "Where are you really going?"

"I want to know who that guy in the pictures is and what was in the boxes no one else was allowed to carry."

Jack rolled his head back and made a disgusted sound. "If I go to the station, are you going to break into Annie's house and dig through the box of pillows in her office?"

We settled into a staring contest.

"Five minutes," he said finally. "And you aren't allowed to touch anything."

"You're a good man, Detective Oliver."

"You're a big pain in my—" He shut my door, snuffing out the rest of that thought.

I gunned my VW to life and smiled. I was a big pain with a new clue and finally getting my way on something.

Chapter Ten

Furry Godmother's warning for your ovaries:
Newborns don't always smell like powder and lotion.

I followed Jack onto the porch at Annie's and kept watch for nosy neighbors while he unlocked the door. I definitely didn't want to show up in the morning paper again. My mom would have ten consecutive strokes.

"Wait here." Jack walked inside and closed the door.

I counted silently to ten and let myself in. The home was eerily silent. Strips of well-trodden plastic formed a path from front door to kitchen.

I crept onto the steps, careful not to alert Jack. Halfway up the stairs, something thumped in the kitchen. I leaned over the handrail and listened harder. This time it sounded like the door opening. "Jack?" I whispered. What would have made him go in the front door and out the back? "Jack?" I crept down two steps, debating whether or not to run up and check on the box in Annie's office before he caught me.

"What are you doing?" Jack's voice boomed from the top of the steps.

I spun fast enough to lose my footing and fall back against the sturdy railing.

"I thought I told you to wait on the porch."

"You!" I pointed a trembling finger at him. Words bottlenecked in my mind and throat. *You don't tell me what to do! You nearly scared the coffee out of me! You are downstairs! I heard you!* I wobbled upright and gripped the railing. If he wasn't downstairs, then who was? "I thought I heard the back door."

Jack sprinted past me, lithely taking the steps two at a time.

I sat where I was and wished for a paper bag to breathe into. This wasn't how my day was supposed to go. Or my life for that matter, but opening the scope of my complaint that wide was asking for trouble. I rubbed my hands on the soft knit of my dress and shoved myself upright. There was plenty of time for a breakdown later. At the moment, I had unsupervised access to Annie's office.

I sped down the hall and into the room where the box of pillows had been. The blinds were shut, making it difficult to see without turning on a light, and I didn't want to leave fingerprints on the switch. Annie's rich color scheme added to my troubles. Shades of hunter and navy paired with dark-stained woodwork until I thought my eyes would bleed from effort.

I shuffled across the floor, careful not to step or trip on anything, and peered into the box in the corner. Pashminas. What? I crouched to inspect the box. No *X*.

Where were the pillows?

I scooted back to the light switch and flipped it with my elbow. None of the boxes stacked near her desk had *X*s. Someone had taken the pillows, but who? Someone with access to Annie's home. Someone who'd promised Annie to mail them on Thursday? Like Josie Fresca, Annie's personal assistant.

I knocked the light switch to off with my arm and tore through the office door, smacking headlong into a wall of muscle, pheromones, and frustration.

Jack gripped my arms until I stopped swaying. "What were you doing in there?"

"Same thing you were. I wanted another look at the boxes from Thursday night."

"They're gone."

"I know."

He released his grip on me slowly. "The back door was unlocked, and the rear gate was open. Whoever was here is long gone, probably with those boxes."

I folded my arms, careful to place my hands over the spots where his had been. "You know who probably has a key to this house? Josie."

He moved down the steps. "Yes, and I've requested a cruiser to pick her up."

Jack locked Annie's doors, and we parted ways on the sidewalk where I'd parked behind his truck.

He opened his driver's side door but paused before climbing in. "I'm going to the station. Can you stay out of trouble if I leave you on your own for a few hours?"

I had pupcakes to deliver and just about enough of his sass. I climbed inside my car and drove away.

The lot at Doggy Divas was full. An enormous banner rippled in the breeze. Two cartoon pilgrims bookended the words: *Give Thanks for your Pets by Pampering their Paws.*

I saddled myself with logoed Furry Godmother bags and headed for the door. I must've missed lunch, because I could smell the peanut butter on the pupcakes, and my mouth watered. The waiting room was wall-to-wall pets and their humans.

No one was behind the welcome desk.

A woman in a navy pantsuit rushed to my side and relieved me of my bags. "You're Lacy Crocker from Furry Godmother?"

"Yes." I stretched and curled my fingers to recirculate blood flow.

"I'm so glad you're here. It's lovely to finally meet you." She set the bags on the welcome desk and unloaded the boxes from inside.

I said a silent prayer the pupcakes weren't a mess when she opened the lids. Traditionally, my treats tolerated heat and humidity well, but I'd never intentionally kept them in the car so long. "I'm sorry I wasn't here sooner. I'm happy to wait while you take a look at the product."

"No need," she said.

I offered a tight smile. "I'd feel better if I knew you were satisfied with the product before I left. I'm happy to replace any units that didn't arrive as expected."

"I'm sure they're delicious."

Delicious? Was she speaking from a canine perspective, or did she intend to try one?

"How are you doing?" she asked. "I've got to be honest. I'm surprised to see you out today after what you've been through this week."

A man playing with his phone looked up.

"I'm sorry," I said, realizing my error. "You don't work here, do you?"

She blushed. "No. I guess not, though I am technically working. I'm from *Pamper Your Paws* magazine."

"Yeesh." I rang the little silver bell on the welcome desk. "Is every pet magazine in America here this week?" I muttered.

"You can hardly blame us," she said. "Annie Lane's death has been a huge loss to the animal advocacy community."

I dinged the bell again.

"Any idea if the rumors were true?"

I conjured a flimsy thread of calm. Every onlooker in the waiting room was a potential customer of mine. "Annie Lane didn't mistreat her animals. Her kittens were examined last night by a respected local veterinarian"—known to me as Dad—"and determined to be healthy and in good spirits. No signs of previous or current abuse. The lies posted online about her were exactly that. Lies. Furthermore, Annie's faux-fur line was an attempt to show that there are humane and reasonable ways to enjoy the look of fur in fashion. Twisting and perverting her intent in an effort to create blog traffic or sell magazines is low and shameful. Annie Lane was a local hero, and I'm running short on patience this week for people who say otherwise."

"Amen!" a woman called from her seat in the waiting room. "Hear, hear!" voices echoed.

The reporter opened and shut her mouth like a fish out of water.

I dinged the bell once more. This time a young lady appeared. "Sorry for your wait. How can I help you?"

I handed off the pupcakes after inspecting them myself. Some of the frosting swirls had lost their shape and become a tad gooey-looking, but a little light refrigeration would remedy that in an hour. I left a stack of business cards on the counter and went back to work.

* * *

At six, I closed up shop, grabbed a large pineapple-coconut smoothie from Frozen Banana, and headed to Scarlet's house. Carter and his dad were taking her three older children to a ball game. I was recruited to hold Poppet while Scarlet had an hour-long, steaming-hot shower with no one crying outside the bathroom door.

I pulled smoothly onto her wide cement drive and sighed in relief. Nothing bad ever happened at Scarlet's house. She welcomed me inside with a look of excitement and gratitude. "Thank you so much for coming. I won't really take an hour," she said.

I scooped a sleeping Poppet into my arms and smiled. "Take as long as you want."

"Bless you."

I eased into Scarlet's glider and put my feet up. Poppet was snuggled in a blanket and making nursing movements with her mouth. She and I were bound to be fast friends one day. I, too, dreamt of food.

I lifted my sweating smoothie and took a long drag. Frozen Banana made the best smoothies on the planet, and they never judged when you asked for a shot of rum.

Poppet didn't like the fact that I couldn't rock and suck a straw at the same time. She puckered her brow into a frown, and her lips quivered. I kissed the wrinkles on her forehead until they smoothed. "Shhhhh. You're okay," I whispered. She went back to her imaginary meal.

I lifted her tiny fingers in mine and stroked her impossibly soft skin. "It's hard to believe you're real." Imogene believed in magic she couldn't see, but I'd grown up watching life occur. I'd seen Mom grow fifty tomatoes from one small seed and watched Dad deliver litters of pups and kittens. I'd seen chicks hatch from eggs with no help at all. Now my best friend had four babies, all from her womb and yet each totally different from the next. Born completely helpless but full of desires and opinions. That was my kind of magic. The remarkable, unbelievable things I *could* see.

Scarlet probably thought she was taking advantage by leaving me unattended after inviting me over, but she had it backward. Rocking Poppet was exactly what I needed after the last few days I'd had. Thick emotion bubbled in my chest. I closed my eyes and concentrated on the sweet scents of baby powder on Poppet's skin and the fabric softener in her blanket. Would the tides turn one day? Would Scarlet rock my baby while I escaped to a hot shower? The idea seemed so peculiar that I didn't know how to proceed. Who could I trust enough to start a family? Jack's face came to mind, and sure, he'd probably take a bullet to save me or a complete stranger, but heroic cop moments were here and gone. Over in a heartbeat. Heroic love kept going. Through prolonged illnesses, unfathomable losses, despair, failure, and worse. Heroic love kept its boots on the ground even when its partner wanted to quit and run. The cynic in me insisted not many were capable of love like that.

Scarlet reappeared with wet hair and a fresh gleam in her eyes. "Tell me everything I've missed."

I filled her in, quietly, while she scrubbed a thick white towel over her head.

"Where do you think the box with the pillows went?"

I smiled at her fuzzy pink slippers and cozy cotton pajamas. Scarlet wasn't the type to be seen without makeup or with wet hair this side of Rio. "I don't know. I'm not even sure who had keys to the house. I assume Josie the assistant did, but beyond that, I couldn't even guess. A cook? A maid? I don't know. Jack's talking to Josie, so maybe he'll get better information this time around. She was pretty useless the last time they spoke."

"I don't understand what was so important about the pillows." She scrunched her hair in a towel. "Maybe something was buried under them."

"Maybe." How far had Jack dug when he looked through them Thursday night?

"Or!" Scarlet snapped her fingers, and Poppet winced. "Or," she lowered her voice, "they were the last thing Annie was working on, so they're worth a ton of money now? Collector's items?"

"Maybe." Honestly, nothing about stealing a big box of small pillows made sense to me. Literally everything in Annie's house was worth more than those pillows. Scarlet was right about one thing. The pillows made a good hiding spot.

"I'm going upstairs to blow-dry my hair. If the doorbell rings, answer it. I ordered dinner. There was no way I was cooking."

"Deal."

Poppet fussed again, trying and failing to leave the Land of Nod.

I rearranged her in my arms and stood, hyperaware of a raging blow-dryer somewhere on the second floor. I swayed gently as I moved through the rooms. Eventually, the blow-dryer quieted, and Poppet stilled.

The doorbell rang.

Scarlet pounded down the steps. "Food!"

I loved this family.

She'd swapped her pajamas for navy leggings and a green V-neck tunic. Her wild red hair was doubly thick and two inches longer after a year of prenatal vitamins. The happy glow in her cheeks had been there since we met. She wrenched the giant wooden door open. "Come in!"

The man who stepped inside nearly buckled my knees. I made a strange, incoherent sound.

"Nice to see you too," he said.

"What are you doing here?" I whispered.

Before me, Chase Hawthorne wore a fitted Armani suit over six-plus feet of sexy. He towered over Scarlet as he planted a kiss on her head. "Good evening, gorgeous wife of my brother." He handed her a large bag from Acme Oyster Company and a bottle of red wine. "Lacy." He put the full force of his eyes to work on me.

Scarlet nearly skipped into the kitchen with her bounty.

Chase moved in on me until our toes touched. "There you are, my beautiful princess." He lifted his niece from my arms and cradled her to his face.

I scanned the cheerful room for a place to collapse. "I thought you went back to volleyballing?"

"I did. I finished the season, then I came home." He jiggled Poppet and did a little bounce step. She was so tiny in his arms, barely longer than the space between his wrist and elbow.

"Why?" The word took shape, breathlessly, on my tongue. I was a moron.

Chase smiled, a grand television-worthy smile. "Inspiration."

"Come on," Scarlet called from the kitchen, where she'd spread open food containers on her table and uncorked the wine. She removed Poppet from his arms. "Eat. Drink. Thank you so much. Both of you."

Chase poured a glass of wine and handed it to me.

"I can't," I said. "I already had rum in my smoothie."

He moved the glass farther in my direction. "If you need a ride home later, I'll gladly drive you."

I took the glass. "So how long are you staying? When do they need you back on the court?"

"Technically I retired." He poured a glass of wine for himself. "Though I'll still spend plenty of time in court."

"Why?" The notion dumbfounded me. "Why stop doing something you love?" Why abandon a dream he'd crossed his family to go after? "Were you injured?"

"No." He loaded a plate with fries and po' boy halves. Grilled onions and mushrooms toppled onto the table.

"Oops." He pinched them between his thumb and first finger, then shoved them in his mouth.

I looked away, plucking the material of my knit dress off my collarbone. Maybe it was the rum, but the room seemed warmer than necessary.

"Coming home this summer was the best thing I could've done," he said. "I left feeling inspired."

I angled toward him, careful to leave a little distance. "Yeah?"

"Yeah. I had fun writing that bogus letter to your ex. It stayed on my mind. I wanted to do that again. Then I remembered I have a law degree. My family owns a law firm. They wanted me here. I wanted to be here." He shifted out of his suit jacket and dropped it over the back of his chair. "So here I am."

"There you are."

He winked and tossed a shrimp into his mouth. "I saw you making a place for yourself in the world we both escaped yet somehow both belong to, and it inspired me. You inspired me. I'm hoping you'll let me lean on you for moral support, and if I screw up a little at first, I can call you for advice on setting my path straight again. What do you think?"

Scarlet hid her smile behind Poppet's sleeping face.

"Okay."

"Okay?" he parroted. "So that's a yes? I can call you?"

I looked at Scarlet.

Chase reached his long arm out and grabbed my fingertips. He pulled me closer to the table. "What can I get you?" He dusted his palms. "I bought one of everything. What'll it be?"

I stared into his happy green eyes. "You're home for good?"

"Yeah. Working at the family firm. The change is still new, but I'm adjusting."

"Uh-huh." Chase was back? I'd only allowed myself a few indulgent fantasies because I was unlikely to see him again. Now here he was, plying me with wine and greasy foods.

He sucked sauce off the tip of his thumb. "They've kept me pretty swamped at the office, but I swung by your store today. I missed you. Imogene said you were having a tough week, so I asked Scarlet to invite you here for dinner, then I gave Dad and Carter tickets to take the kids to the game and voilà."

I stole a loose shrimp off his plate, unable to hide my smile. "So this was a conspiracy? That's a lot of work to surprise me with dinner."

He shrugged. "I also got to make my dad happy and kiss my niece, so I'm winning all around. What do you think?"

"I think you're greatly appreciated." I took a seat beside Chase, instantly at ease. "Thank you."

"You're welcome."

I looked up to thank Scarlet, but she was gone, so I helped myself to half a po' boy and bit into the French bread with enthusiasm. I savored the lettuce and tabasco-infused mayo as breaded shrimp and oysters tried to roll free. Too bad for them, this wasn't my first po' boy. I popped the runaways into my mouth with a moan.

Chase watched with a grin, presumably amused by my mess.

I washed the bite of heaven down with another sip of wine. A goofy smile parted my lips. I blamed the alcohol. "I'm glad you're back."

"Me too."

I went to the refrigerator for a bottle of water. No more wine for me. "And you're here to stay?" I repeated.

He nodded slowly. "Everything I want is right here. I'd be crazy to go anywhere else."

"Aww," Scarlet cooed from her hiding spot.

And it was my turn to blush.

Chapter Eleven

Furry Godmother's hard truth:
If the award fits, it's probably the murder weapon.

Two hours later, I was stuffed with good food and compli-
ments, courtesy of Chase Hawthorne. Poppet had woken,
nursed, and conked out in Chase's arms while Scarlet and I
gossiped on the couch. Her eyes fluttered a few times, and
her head bobbed twice before she fell asleep midsentence.
Exhausted as she was, a small smile curved her lips. I covered her with a blanket and put the game on television for
Chase. "Thank you for dinner," I whispered to him as I
kissed Poppet good-bye.

"See you soon?" he asked.

I nodded and slipped through the front door.

The night was brisk and blustery, but I wasn't ready to
go home. I idled at a stop sign and made an impromptu
decision. Scarlet lived in my parents' neighborhood. The
clock on my dashboard indicated it wasn't quite ten. It
would be rude of me to be so close to my parents and not

say hello. Plus I should check on Cotton and Cashmere. Give Dad another round of thanks for taking the kittens in, especially knowing how Mom felt about the proposition. As a bonus, I'd score points with her for coming over without any prodding.

I made a hasty right and headed for the Crocker slice of paradise. I bounced my little car down the rear drive, enjoying a familiar jostle over earth long ago displaced by roots of historic oak trees.

Every light in the house was on, but thankfully a party wasn't in motion. I knocked on the back door and took in the beautiful starry night. It felt like just yesterday I'd made daisy chains on that porch and covered books in lollipop-stained fingerprints. Standing there made it hard to believe the world was a scary place, and for a moment, I let myself pretend.

The little porch light flamed into being. Dad opened the door with a broad smile. "Lacy!" He kissed my head and pulled me inside. "You look beautiful. Come in. Your mother will be so pleased to see you."

Cotton and Cashmere trotted into view wearing two of Voodoo's old collars. The rhinestones glistened, and the little bells jingled. They sang their happy song as loudly as ever.

Mom arrived behind them with a sigh. Her black silk pajamas looked as elegant as anything she wore. Her blonde-and-silver hair was down and tucked behind one ear. "Have I thanked you for leaving these precious animals at my house indefinitely?"

I stooped to greet the purring kittens. "They seem happy. What does Voodoo think?"

"She hates them," Mom said. "She barely leaves our room."

Dad scooped Annie's babies into his arms and laughed. "I think they're magnificent." He rubbed them against his cheeks and set them free. "I also think you're just in time for coffee and dessert."

Mom curled her finger at me. "Come along."

Dad broke away in the opposite direction. "I'll grab another place setting."

I followed Mom dutifully to the parlor, over antique rugs, past ornate tapestries that had been in her family since they left France in the late eighteenth century. Mom's pedigree was a masterpiece in itself, and there was no end to her family pride. Blue-and-gold flames danced in the gas fireplace. A carafe perched on the sideboard with a pair of cups, saucers, and a cream-and-sugar set. A plate of chocolate-covered strawberries finished the spread.

I took a seat in my favorite Queen Anne chair.

Mom glared parentally. "Are you going to tell me about the most recent break-in attempt, or are we going to pretend that didn't happen?"

I puffed my cheeks. "The important thing is that I wasn't home, and I was never in danger."

She didn't look convinced.

"No threats have been made against me. None of this has anything to do with me."

"Nor me," she said. "Funny how my name isn't in the paper every morning, according to your logic."

Dad appeared with a cup and saucer. "I know I've said it once, but I'm so glad you stopped by. It's a wonderful feeling, having you back in town. I can't seem to get used to it. Tell us. How was your day?"

I shot Mom a look and ran mentally backward in search of something I could discuss without her head falling off. "I had dinner at Scarlet's. Guess who delivered our Acme Oyster House po' boys."

Mom made a throaty sound. "Do you know how many calories are in those? Breaded everything. And the mayo," she said, swinging a limp hand in the air. "It's one thing to enjoy our local flavor and wholly another to pollute the body God gave you. You'll have three zits by morning."

I gave her a look. "You didn't guess."

Dad ferried coffees to Mom and I. "I give up. Who delivered your po' boys?"

"Chase Hawthorne." I looked from Dad's face to Mom's for some sign of surprise.

Nothing.

Recognition dawned. "You both knew Chase was back?"

Mom made a sour face, as if the question was personally insulting. Of course she knew. She knew everything that went on in the district.

"Why didn't you tell me?" I asked.

"We tried," she said, "but you're always too busy. When was the last time we had a decent conversation?"

I bit the insides of my cheeks and lifted the cup to my lips. No one had a "decent conversation" with my mother unless they'd confessed their sins over a two-hour lunch and multiple mint juleps.

Dad took his position beside Mom on the love seat and balanced his saucer in one hand. "So, young Hawthorne is back in New Orleans delivering sandwiches?" His easy smile pushed away my frustration.

"Yes, but apparently the pay stinks, so he took a second job as a lawyer."

Dad nodded approvingly. "That makes two district families finally reunited."

I smiled. "I guess a little time away was all the clarity we needed."

"Ten years," Mom said.

I forced a tight smile. "Right." The word "sorry" formed in my mind frequently but rarely made it to my lips. I owed her more than an apology for breaking her heart and making her worry. "I'm looking forward to dinner at Commander's Palace Monday."

She arched a perfectly sculpted eyebrow. "I'm glad you haven't forgotten. Chase agreed to sit at our table when I spoke with him yesterday. Wasn't that nice? The Hawthornes have a table of their own, but he seemed quite content to sit at ours."

The Hawthornes probably had several tables. I sipped my coffee and thought of the photos lining Scarlet's mantle. "How many Hawthornes are there now? At least twenty in the district. Probably more than fifty in the city. They're getting to be a small army."

Dad chuckled. "Lucky ducks."

"Indeed." Mom crossed her ankles. "Do you know what you're going to wear?"

"Yes. My black backless Givenchy. I've got a matching clutch and heels, but I need a decent wrap."

"I'll buy you a wrap. Wear your hair up. It's not a prom."

"Sure." I pulled the length of my pale curls over one shoulder and checked for dead ends. "I'm overdue for a trim."

Mom fidgeted, probably desperate to offer a day pass to her spa, where I could get myself together. "You look lovely in that dress. The tights were a nice touch."

I leaned back. A compliment. "Thank you—my mother chose it for me."

Her well-practiced look of nonchalance crumbled. "What do you think about it?"

I gave the material over my thighs a long stroke. "It's soft, warm, and comfy. I think it's very fashionable and figure flattering."

"You like it?"

I nodded. "Very much."

She bit back a smile. "Fine. I'll send more."

I opened my mouth to protest but thought better of it. For thirty years, she'd tried to dress me up. Maybe it was time I stopped protesting and let her. She had access to more couture than I could dream of, and it made her happy. Plus, free clothes. Triple win. "Maybe a few pieces."

"I'll let my stylist know. Tell me more about your visit with Chase," she prompted.

"We didn't talk much. We ate and helped Scarlet with Poppet. It was nice but brief."

"Well, the dinner will give you two another chance to talk."

I liked the sound of that.

"How are my chicks' sashes coming?" Mom asked.

I flicked my gaze to her. I hadn't given them ten seconds of thought since she asked for them. "Almost done. In fact, if I get going now, I can probably finish them tonight." I carried my empty cup to the sideboard. "Thank you for the coffee. Penelope's probably livid. I left her at Furry Godmother after work." I checked my watch. "That was more than three hours ago."

Dad popped onto his feet. "Don't leave empty-handed." He rushed to the kitchen and returned with a plastic container. He piled strawberries inside. "A little treat to keep you company while you finish those sashes."

"Thanks, Dad." I lifted onto my toes and kissed his cheek.

"I ordered the strawberries from Sucre," Mom said.

"Thank you." I wrapped her in a hug. "For everything." My eyes misted for no good reason. Probably lack of sleep or overstimulation. I shook off the unease. *Sure I could ask to spend the night, but then what? A second night? A week?* I couldn't explain the fierce need to live life on my terms, but I was certain it evolved from eighteen years of not being able to pick out my own friends, clothes, and schools. *And I agreed ten minutes ago to let her dress me again.* I suppressed the urge to groan. There was a fine line between bonding with my mom and letting her take over. I hadn't found it yet, and I wouldn't find it tonight. No, for now, my home had an excellent alarm system, and I had an NOPD detective on speed dial. That was good enough for me. "I'll see you Monday night."

I stopped on Magazine Street and picked up Penelope, then drove home slowly, avoiding the inevitable. I examined every passing car and shadow for a creeping cat-man or other yet-to-be-identified danger. When we got to my driveway, I couldn't pull in. "What do you think?" I asked

Penelope. "We need to go inside and feed Buttercup, but there could be a lunatic in the bushes. We need to have those removed."

She rubbed her face against the mesh of her travel crate.

"You're exactly right. We should get backup." I drove through the district on autopilot, passing and circling Jack's house twice before admitting defeat and taking a spot in his drive. I could've bugged my dad or Chase, but Jack seemed the obvious choice. If he found someone in my bushes, he could shoot him.

I hauled Penelope's carrier from the car and wedged the container of strawberries in the top of my purse. It was rude to show up unannounced, but bringing a gift would soften the blow. Thank the stars for southern laws of hospitality, where all anyone needed was a casserole and a finger to push the doorbell. Whoever answered was obligated to invite the visitor inside. Show up without food, and the sign at the property line, *Trespassers may be shot*, was in effect.

A wrought-iron gate creaked open on my right before I made it to the door. Jack padded over brick pavers in bare feet and board shorts. His hair was wet. His chest was bare, and a towel was thrown over one shoulder. "What are you doing here?"

"I have strawberries." I shifted Penelope's carrier into my left hand and pulled the plastic container from my purse. "My parents sent them," I lied.

"Everything okay?"

"Mm-hmm." I nodded, unsure where to look. "You're swimming?"

He freed the towel from his shoulder and rubbed it on his head. "Laps. Sometimes repetitive motions help me relax."

Heat rose from my core to my cheeks. "How did it go with Josie and Gideon?"

He took Penelope's carrier and held the gate for me. "As well as could be expected. She's either coy or well trained in verbal evasion. I doubt the latter. Gideon's lawyer wouldn't let him answer ninety percent of our questions." I followed a side path around the front of his house to the grand courtyard in back, complete with flower garden, cobblestone patio, and heated pool. Steam hovered over the water like an apparition, and moonlight reflected on the surface.

He grabbed a shirt from the pool's edge and pulled it over his chest. "Can I let Penelope out in the house? We can talk out here."

"Sure."

"Can I get you anything?"

"No, thank you."

He disappeared into the house with Penelope and returned with a hooded sweat shirt and a leather coat I'd never seen him wear. He pulled the sweat shirt on and handed me the jacket. "Here. The air's gotten chilly."

"Thanks." I threaded my arms into too-large holes and settled on a white Adirondack near the water. "I think I'll have a talk with Josie. It seems like she was the closest person to Annie. She has to know something useful, even if she doesn't realize the information is useful."

"I think you should stay out of this." He pulled a red chair next to mine and lowered himself onto it. "You nearly got yourself killed last time, and call me a buzzkill, but I can't handle seeing you go through something like that again."

"I'm not getting involved."

He shot me a tired look.

"What if I just ask her a few questions about the day of the murder? She might be more inclined to open up to a woman—especially one who isn't a cop." He didn't answer, so I kept going.

"I think she was in shock when we spoke to her at Annie's house. She'd come home to find her friend murdered and the house teeming with emergency crews. That had to be overwhelming. Then today, she was hunted down and carried to the police station for an interrogation." I handed him the strawberry container. "That had to be scary, plus you can be a little intimidating."

He popped the lid on the container and held it out to me. He frowned. "You think I'm intimidating?"

"Yes." I plucked a small berry from the top and admired its chocolate cocoon. "Then again, I was afraid to go home tonight. I'm a chicken. That's why I'm here." I shoved the strawberry into my mouth before I admitted something else I'd regret.

"I'll drive you home when you're ready, walk you inside, and check the house before I go." He stared across the surface of his pool. "You're welcome to stay here as long as you want. I have a bunch of spare rooms." He snorted a humorless laugh. "I don't even know how many."

For the first time since we'd met, I got the feeling Jack was lonely, and my chest ached for him. His mom had handed him off to his grandfather to raise. Grandpa Smacker was more businessman than child-rearer, so Jack was sent to school abroad until graduation. He had joined the military from there and had come back to New Orleans for the detective position about three years ago. He had lived and worked in the Quarter until his Grandpa passed. He had no real ties to anyone now. His mom was estranged from him, and he'd never mentioned a dad. Jack said his mom had gotten pregnant young, so I supposed there was a chance he didn't know his father. If that didn't make someone lonely, I wasn't sure what would.

"You know, if you're not comfortable sleeping here and you don't want to go home, I can take you to your parents' house and see you inside."

"Negative." I bit into another waiting strawberry and suppressed a moan. "How's the personal investigation going?"

His jaw clenched. "Awful. I'm hitting dead end after dead end, partially because I don't know what I'm looking for and partially because I can't come out and ask what I want to know. This isn't a formal investigation, and I don't want the papers getting wind of my inquiries until I have something to tell them."

"Got it." He didn't want the medical examiner's full report to make national headlines. *Seventy-eight-year-old grandpa-to-America died with drugs and alcohol in his system.* Grandpa Smacker stocks would plummet. The company he'd worked all those decades to create would be irreparably wounded by actions completely outside his knowledge. People would lose jobs. Families would lose homes. "You know who can ask anything she wants because she's never on an official investigation?" I asked.

He laughed.

"I'm serious. I could reprise my role as your girlfriend and invite Tabitha out for coffee or drinks. A little girl talk could loosen her lips, maybe even produce a fresh lead."

"I'll think about it."

"Good." I was impressed. Jack was probably the only person on earth who hated asking for help more than I did. The fact that he'd consider letting me get involved said a lot, either about his situation or his trust in me. I chose to think it was the latter. "If there's anyone you want me to unofficially bump into tomorrow and ask about my old pal Tabitha, let me know. I think I can fit them into my schedule."

His smile reached his eyes, lifting his cheeks high and revealing a line of perfect white teeth. "I'll think about it."

"Okay. So tell me more about Josie so I can prepare for my chat with her."

"There isn't much to tell. The only new information she had was a collection of funeral details. Annie's family is flying her body back to Manhattan for a service that will be aired on the Fashion Channel. There's a public memorial there today."

"A televised memorial. Gross." I set the strawberry top on the arm of my chair.

"Very," he agreed.

"What's wrong with people?"

"Money." He turned serious eyes on me. "Someone's probably making a fortune from signing off on the coverage, and they aren't above exploiting a dead family member to make a buck."

I rested my hands on my tummy. "Yuck."

"It's probably the reason she's dead, too. Someone knew about the cats' trust and wanted a quick payday. Kill Annie. Save the cats. Collect the money."

I wrinkled my nose. "I don't know. I'm not seeing a big play for the kittens. Charlie was on some kind of activist mission that had nothing to do with the money. Latherope thinks the kitties belong to him, so he's on a power trip. No one else has mentioned them."

Jack gave me a weary look. "Latherope knew about the trust, and I guarantee that's what it will come down to in the end. It's always about money, Lacy. Every time. Money or jealousy, but Annie wasn't married or seeing anyone, and that leaves money."

I made a mental note to call her attorney and ask who would inherit Annie's estate. She was close to her parents, or at least she'd seemed to be. I'd connected to her emotionally as I watched her rise from local fashion icon to the cover of magazines abroad. She was my hero through high school and college. We were cut from the same cloth, both products of New Orleans, only children, creative hearts with a passion for fashion. The glaring difference between us was money. Annie's family was blue collar with little to give financially, but they told her to chase her dreams. She mentioned that in every interview I'd read. My family had everything to give, and my mom still tried to mold me into something I wasn't. Something she preferred. Any success I'd had in fashion felt vaguely like disappointment.

Jack pinched a strawberry between his fingertips. "I did some more research today. Annie wasn't as big of a star as you made her out to be."

"She was big to me." Bigger than most aspiring designers ever got.

He nodded. "Fair enough. It looks like her mom waited tables and her dad worked on cars until a few years ago, when Annie bought them a home near their extended family in New York."

"She made it in a cutthroat industry with no contacts or money to cheat the system. She got there with hard work and chutzpah."

"I can see why you liked her." He fixed a sincere gaze on me. "What would it be like to do something remarkable for our families? You and I may never know, but I think it would be great."

He wished he could do something grand for his family. "Me too." A sense of camaraderie settled in my chest. Despite how opposite Jack and I sometimes seemed, he knew what it was like to be showered in affluence and choose to make his own path anyway. A little smile caught my lips. What had his grandfather, who raised him in elite European boarding schools, thought when Jack joined the military? Or when he'd chosen blue blood over running the family's billion-dollar empire?

"What?"

My smile fell as something new registered. "If the medical examiner's releasing the body, he must have confirmed the cause of death."

"Blunt-force trauma to the head. He confirmed the Crystal Saxophone award as the murder weapon."

A whack on the head with something heavy from the home. No skill necessary. "Anyone could have done it."

"Anyone she'd let inside. There were no signs of forced entry or a struggle."

I rested my head against the wide wooden slats of my chair. "One sweep of the arm and an entire life ends."

"Yep."

"Seems unfair." I studied the stars, nestled in their inky black sky. How insignificant were we if one fraction of a second could wipe out decades of our existence? I turned my eyes to his. "We work so hard at living. It shouldn't be so easy to take that from us."

"I guess we should remember how precious our time is and live accordingly." The enigmatic color of his irises was barely visible in the dim patio lighting.

"Do you?" I asked.

"What?"

"Live accordingly."

He stared into my eyes. An emotion I couldn't fathom played on his features. "Not often enough."

Chapter Twelve

Furry Godmother's advice for autumn attire:
Layers. You never know when things are going to heat up.

I woke feeling rested for the first time in four days. Jack had followed me home when the strawberries were gone. He walked me inside, as promised, and double-checked all the doors and windows. He even checked under my bed, where I ended up crashing, accidentally. I'd planned to watch the street all night for stalkers, but wine and sleep deprivation were a powerful combination. When I finally peeled my eyes open, it was after seven.

I showered and dressed in a hurry, then finished Mom's sequined sashes alongside a pot of coffee. By nine thirty, the little wraps were folded in squares of white tissue paper and packed lovingly into a logoed box. Her sketches were a great source of inspiration for a rested mind. She was going to love the finished product.

I dropped some freeze-dried bloodworms into Butter-cup's tank and admired her personal oasis. "It's time for the mammals to go to work, sweetie. I hope you have a great day. Guard the house for us." I drew a heart on her tank with a red dry-erase marker and blew her a kiss.

Penelope rolled on my feet and purred.

"Looks like you're ready." I packed her into her carrier and grabbed my black backless Givenchy. "We need to make a quick stop at Grandma's hoity dry cleaner, then you can play with Spot until the shop gets busy."

I buckled her carrier into the back seat and hung the gown on the little hanger peg by the window. We made the trip to Bon Cherie Cleaners in under ten minutes with the windows down and radio up. Sunday mornings were lazy, and I loved them.

The woman behind the counter at Bon Cherie looked like a movie star from old Hollywood. She gave the cat carrier in my hand a long look but didn't ask. Instead, she took the dress and painstakingly wrote a receipt with fingernails too long to be functional. According to the slip, my Givenchy would be cleaned, steamed, and ready for pickup in twenty-four hours.

I took the ticket and saw myself out.

The sunlight was glorious and somewhat blinding, but I recognized Josie immediately. She paced on the corner two blocks down, staring at her cell phone. Long dark hair waved over her long narrow frame. Her fitted teal top and plaid skirt were sugary cute with black knee socks and Mary Janes. The girl definitely had style.

"We've got her," I told Penelope. I tiptoe ran along the sidewalk in Josie's direction with Penelope's carrier clutched to my chest. I closed the distance at a clip, waiting for the right moment to call her name.

She swung her arm overhead, trying to get the attention of a distant cabbie.

"Josie!" I hurried my pace and gripped Penelope tighter, trying not to rattle her half silly. "Josie Fresca!"

She spun in my direction and gasped.

"Hi!" I smiled brightly before slowing at her side and panting. "Hello."

"Are you okay?" She shifted away from me. "Is that a cat?"

I bobbed my head, catching my breath. "Mm-hmm. We're good. I'm Lacy. This is Penelope."

Josie narrowed her eyes. "Hey I know you. You were at the house when they found Annie." Alarm lit in her eyes. "I told the cops to talk to you. They keep dragging me in, but you're the one who found her. What were you even doing there? Who are you?" She stepped backward into the street. "Stay away from me."

"No." I held my palm out like a traffic cop. "Be careful, cars fly down that street."

She gave the empty road behind her a cursory gaze. Her large black glasses slid slightly down her nose.

"I swear. Locals know it's barely traveled, and they use it to cut across the district." I inched back. "Please come out of the street."

"I called a cab."

"Okay, great." My time was limited, and something told me she wasn't exactly going to jump on an offer to go somewhere alone and talk. "You're right. I was the one who found Annie. We had an appointment that day. The door was unlocked. I went inside when no one answered.

I thought maybe she treated the house like an office and I should let myself in."

She gave me another skeptical look.

"It's true. Annie and I were in discussions about a companion line for her Mardi Gras collection. She really didn't tell you who I am?"

"You make clothes for pets." She moved out of the street and balanced on the curb.

"Right. I own Furry Godmother on Magazine Street."

"I thought you'd be old. I mean, older."

I tried not to dwell on her distinction. "Are you staying at Annie's house?" Did she still have access? Had she been the one to take the boxes?

"No. The cops took my key."

"Bummer. So where are you staying? In the district somewhere?"

"With friends. I grew up in the city. I live with Annie now—lived," she corrected, "but it's not the only place I can stay. It was just more convenient when she was working. I didn't have to race to her side. I was already there."

I nodded. "So you don't have your own apartment here?"

She furrowed her brows. "No."

Had Jack tainted my opinion, or was he right? She was more evasive than my mother at a silent auction.

I switched gears. "This must be really hard for you. I've barely slept since it happened, and I didn't know her. You and Annie must've been close."

"Yeah." She opened her patent leather clutch and unraveled the paper from a roll of peppermints.

"Did you ever get those little pillows mailed out?" I put on a lighter smile. *You remember, the ones you tried to take five seconds after Annie died? The ones that are now mysteriously missing.*

Josie's face went slack. "No."

I was losing her, and I didn't have any new information. Her cab had to be close by now. "Do you have any idea who'd want to hurt her? I've been trying to figure it out, and I'm stumped. There are a lot of people online who seem pretty mad but not enough to act on it. Was there someone in her life that she might've fought with that day?"

"No. She didn't have a life. Work was her life, and everyone hated her for it. In a good way, though."

I puzzled. "Hated in a good way? Do you mean all publicity is good publicity?"

"No, I mean their hate validated her truth. Annie made it. If she wasn't on her way to massive stardom, then no one would care if she wore live mice for hats and talked to her mailbox. Haters hated her because they weren't her. You haven't truly succeeded until everyone hates you."

Well, that seemed ominous. "What about you?"

"What about me?"

"Does anyone hate you?" Moving from poor-city-kid status to famous fashion designer's personal assistant had to solicit a little jealousy from someone.

She curved her mouth into a small, emotionless smile. "No one knows I exist." A Black & White cab rolled into view, and she groaned. "Finally." She turned on her heels and walked away.

"Wait!" I followed her toward the slowing cab. "One more thing."

She kept moving.

"I met a guy with a ton of pictures of you and Annie."

"Me?" She stopped outside the cab.

"Yes. There were several shots of Annie moving back to town. I saw a guy in basketball shorts carrying boxes like the one from her office filled with pillows. Do you remember who that was?"

She wagged her chin left and right. "There were about a hundred people helping that day." She wrenched the cab door open and dropped inside, immediately shutting me out.

Not exactly the warm tête-à-tête I'd imagined us having.

The cab's taillights blinked out of existence as it motored away.

I hauled Penelope back to my car and strapped her carrier in. "Jack was right. There's no way Josie's that useless."

Furry Godmother opened late on Sundays. Shoppers were usually light until lunch, which made Sunday the perfect day to clean, restock inventory, and organize. I washed windows, dusted shelves, rearranged store displays, and worked up a priority list for the week's orders. I accomplished more before noon than I had in days. Imogene took Sundays off for church. She rarely went but insisted it was the Lord's day and liked to remind me that shops were never open on Sundays when she was a girl. I liked to remind her it wasn't the 1960s.

When I stopped for a sip of water, a familiar face cut through the clumps of shoppers outside my window. Bryce Kenney, Annie's attorney, bypassed lackadaisical window-shoppers and headed my way. He crossed at the corner and blew through Furry Godmother's door with purpose.

"Good morning." There was a note of uncertainty in my voice. I hadn't expected to see Bryce again without an appointment.

He stopped inside the door and stared through the front window, scanning the view in both directions.

"Bryce?" I poked his arm gently. "Something wrong?"

"What?" He blinked bright-blue eyes. "No. Well, yes. Maybe. I've come to check on Cotton and Cashmere." He dug into his pockets with sudden gusto.

"I don't want any more money." I wished he'd take back what he'd already given me.

He produced his cell phone and turned it to face me. "Have you seen this man?"

I certainly had. "Sure, that's Mr. Latherope. I've seen him more times than I'd prefer. Why?"

"How many times? Where did you see him? Has he been in contact?" The low hum of Spot the vacuum drew his attention. "What's that?"

Penelope rode into view a moment later, chin held high. Spot bumped into a display and headed back the way he'd come.

"That's my cat, Penelope, unless you meant the vacuum. We call him Spot."

"Where are Cotton and Cashmere?" Bryce straightened to his full height of not much and dashed around the displays, checking the floor and shelves. "Oh, no! They're gone!" He returned to me in a minipanic. "When was the last time you saw them? Has Mr. Latherope been here this morning?" He produced his phone and began tapping the screen.

"They're fine. Everything is fine. You don't have to check their trackers, if that's what you're doing." I went to the minifridge behind my counter and grabbed him a bottle of water. I hadn't thought to call Bryce before taking the kittens to my dad. Hopefully that wasn't against the law. "Annie's kittens are in good hands. I took your advice and shifted them into the care of someone unrelated to any of this. I visited them last night. They're really happy, I think."

"What about Latherope?" He accepted the bottle and cracked the lid.

"He's part of the reason I decided to delegate the kittens' care to someone else. He came here acting like a maniac. He's even followed me through the city looking for them."

Bryce lowered his shoulders a bit as he sipped. "He's been to visit me too. Several times. He's trying to make me change the estate paperwork before submitting it to the courts tomorrow."

Gooseflesh raised on my arms. "What does he want changed?"

"Everything." Bryce shook his weary head. "He thinks Annie's family is collectively the devil. He wants an intervention on their crazy plan for a televised memorial. He wants the kittens' existence eliminated from the paperwork and the kittens returned to him. He wants half of everything because he feels entitled." He did a dramatic eye roll. "He supported her financially when she was a starving artist, paid for design school, funded her life and career for many years during their marriage."

"Shouldn't those claims have all been settled during the divorce?"

A guilty smile played on his lips. "Latherope refused a lawyer. He assumed he could manipulate her until the end, convince her to come back to him, and sway her decisions on the split."

"No attorney for a divorce this big? That's bizarre."

"He's bizarre. And dumb. He lost his shirt in those proceedings. Literally. Annie was awarded rights to everything in their household, right down to his closet contents, which, of course, she graciously returned."

I tried to recall the media coverage of their divorce and couldn't. I'd stopped keeping tabs on Annie's life after college, when I'd traded the dream of launching a fashion line for obsessive wedding planning with Pete the Cheat. "Why did they split up? They always seemed so happy in front of the cameras."

Bryce screwed the little lid onto his water. "That's not my place to say."

"Right. Sorry."

"It's okay. Nothing you can't read about online. Well I came to warn you about Latherope, but I see you're ahead of me there." He checked the street again. "I'll let you get back to your work. If you change your mind about the kittens . . ."—he trailed off briefly—"if he finds where you're hiding them or the situation becomes too much for you to deal with, my offer stands. I can assign a legal guardian outside the city until the estate settles."

I absently arranged a row of bagged treats on the counter, half hearing the offer and half choosing my next words. "I'm fine, really. You know, you mentioned Latherope's play for Annie's estate, and I realized I've been so preoccupied with the fact her kittens have a trust that I haven't thought to ask who gets everything else." Maybe no one cared about the piddly cat trust when there was an entire estate to gain.

Bryce made a strained face. "I'm not at liberty to discuss her legal matters, but some of this will become a matter of public record soon. If you're still interested when things come out of probate, you'll be able to see the title changes on her homes and possessions. Sorry again for not being more up front."

"Comes with the job?" I smiled.

He puffed a sigh of relief. "Very much."

"It's fine. I understand."

A fresh trickle of shoppers wandered into the store and spread out.

Bryce made a move for the exit. "I should go. Please don't hesitate to call if anything changes with Cotton and Cashmere. I'll be in town until Thursday, then I'm flying to New York, but like I said, I can be here in no time if something goes grossly awry." He cast his gaze through the room. "Be careful with Mr. Latherope. He's in no condition for reason."

"Got it."

Bryce left, but shoppers kept coming. With the festival in full swing and Thanksgiving on the way, it was my busiest Sunday of the season. If every day were as busy as this one, I'd make the store's lease payment on pupcakes and turkey-inspired-tutu sales alone. My thoughts wandered to the people in Annie's life who might be desperate to make their own lease payments. Josie was currently homeless, as far as I knew, and strangely tight-lipped about where she was staying until Annie's house stopped being a crime scene. Did it matter? She had to move eventually now that Annie was gone.

I dialed the sandwich shop across the street and ordered a lunch delivery. I couldn't think with a noisy tummy, and my eyelids were getting heavier by the minute.

Penelope weaved around my legs, obviously disappointed. Spot had redocked himself for a battery charge, and she didn't approve. "It's for the best," I told her. "The shop's too busy for a cat on a Roomba. Think about my insurance."

"Good, you're here." A familiar voice turned me toward the front door. Margaret Hams, the leader of the Llama Mamas, scuttled to the counter on stumpy legs and orthopedic sneakers. She wore a fanny pack embroidered with a big red heart beside the words "Your Llama." Her gauchos and wide-brimmed hat were practical for plantation living but always looked a little out of place on Magazine Street.

"Hello, Mrs. Hams. You look happy."

A grinchy grin had split her face. "I am," she purred. "I've stopped in several times this week. You never seem to be here."

"Really? Imogene hasn't mentioned it, or I would've given you a call." I regretted the comment immediately. Maybe there was a reason Imogene hadn't mentioned it.

She crossed her eyes and stuck out her tongue. "Do I look crazy to you?"

A little, if she was asking.

She righted her face and narrowed her eyes. "I know your mother and that woman are tight as spandex. I checked the block for your car, peeked in the windows, and kept moving. I started to think you had sold the place and taken off again."

Burn. "No, Mrs. Hams. I'm here to stay. For the record, I left to go to college."

"Took you ten years?"

Jeez. For being Mom's archenemy, they certainly sounded alike. I centered myself and waited to hear what she wanted.

She lifted a bagged treat off my counter to her snub nose and sniffed. "I assume the money I pay to keep you on retainer is still satisfactory."

"It is, thank you." More than enough, actually. She rarely asked for anything, though when she did, she wanted miracles. "You're very generous."

"I'm aware."

Humble, she was not.

"Then let's get down to business." She rested her forearms on my counter and laced her fingers. "I need you to work your magic for my girls."

"No problem." I dug through my drawer for a sketch pad and pencil. "What will it be?"

"We need matching hats and scarves. They should be festive, shimmery, and theatrical. Something that can be seen from blocks away." She spread her fingers and wiggled them beside her face. "I want them to steal the show."

Uh-oh. Mom and the chicks hadn't booked a show, and I was in charge of making the ugly pins for the Llamas to wear when the Chicks raised more money this month.

"The show?" I feigned disinterest as I sketched a charcoal llama and prepared to dress it.

She waited until I looked up before speaking. Her stout body fizzed with excitement and victory. "The Llama Mamas have secured a spot in the district's Thanksgiving Day Parade, and we're taking sponsors for a new project. Donations will go to the maintenance and upkeep of historic bayou plantations. When folks invest in the Llama

Mamas this month, they're supporting a piece of our country's history."

I fumbled with the awful news. "You're going to be in the Thanksgiving Day parade?" Mom was going to lose her mind. That kind of exposure was priceless.

"That's right, we're walking the entire Magazine Street leg." She leveled me with a no-nonsense expression. "Don't breathe a word of this to your mother, or she'll be angling for a spot too."

I doodled in the corner of my paper. Anything I learned from Mrs. Hams was confidential. I offered the feature as a courtesy and basic good business practice where fashion was concerned. Imagine if celebrities' Oscar gowns were leaked before the show. Why would anyone tune in? The whole thing would be ruined.

Mrs. Hams fidgeted with her wild salt-and-pepper hair. "I'd like to see those squatty chickens march six miles."

I found a new page on my sketchpad and concentrated on the problem at hand. Mrs. Hams wanted custom hats and scarves for her llamas. They needed to be fabulous and fit for a New Orleans parade. I outlined several loose concepts. "Are you thinking about basic knits, something outlandish and feathered, or somewhere in between? What do you think of these?"

She shrugged one shoulder.

I continued to doodle. "Do you have a specific color scheme in mind?"

"I'd like them to look like candy corn."

"Candy corn?" I grabbed my gum eraser and vanquished all the little graphite feathers. "Candy corn." I let the words take root.

"The little triangle sweets. Everyone loves candy corn, and this is the only time of the year that we can enjoy it. Isn't that clever? I want the hats to stand up like that deal the pope wears, no disrespect."

"None taken."

"They should be white, yellow, and orange." She pointed to the air over her head at three different heights. "Use sequins or rhinestones, something shimmery to catch the sun."

I made a trio of rough outlines based on her description and turned the pad toward her. "Any of these?"

She pulled the paper off the counter in one hand and raised the glasses on her silver necklace with the other. She squinted at the drawings. "Not the first one. My heavens. The llamas are ladies."

I had no idea what that meant. "Of course."

"This!" She dropped the paper with a clap. "The one in the middle. Make those."

I turned the pad back to face me.

"Chop chop." She clapped twice. "We need them for dress rehearsal in two weeks."

"Yes, ma'am." I transferred her chosen designs onto the llama drawing and colored the accessories with my pencils. I made a few quick notes on the paper's edge and reminded myself to find the file with her llamas' measurements. The scarves needed to be long enough to dazzle without dragging on the ground or tangling around their feet. The hats needed to be loose enough for comfort and tight enough to stay put. "Would you like a work order for your records?"

"No need." She flipped her chin up. "I know where to find you."

That was true enough for now, but once Mom found out I had information this big about her archenemy and couldn't share it with her, *no one* would know where to find me.

Chapter Thirteen

Furry Godmother's words of wisdom:
Facing fears is best done in daylight, preferably with witnesses.

I ate my lunch at the counter, mulling over ways to tell my mom about the parade without breaking Mrs. Hams's confidence, which of course was impossible. Shoppers came and went in a steady stream of enthusiasm I couldn't quite muster. Though, the muffaletta salad in front of me was helping. What I really wanted was a muffaletta sandwich, but that was the size of my head, so this was a happy compromise. Muffaletta was authentic New Orleans comfort food. I skewered stacks of baby lettuce, julienne prosciutto, and bits of provolone with increasing fervor. Diced-olive salad and homemade vinaigrette dripped from each bite. The combination of rich, salty flavors slowly washed my cares away. Too soon, the bottom of my disposable container came into view. "Sad."

"Hello." A woman dressed like a French clown strode through the shop with a giant pink standard poodle on a black velvet leash.

I froze, startled senseless. My parents had taken me to the circus while we were in Paris many years ago. I discovered many things during that trip—a passionate interest in fashion, for example. I also learned I hated the circus. A dozen painted-face monsters had ensnared me at the request of my mother, lifting me into their arms and encasing me in the stench of stale popcorn and makeup. A quiver ran along my limbs with the memory. A lifelong distrust of clowns glued my sandals to the floor.

Her baggy white jumper had big black pom-pom buttons and a shimmering black ruff collar that protruded several inches from her neck. Her white face was marked with black-and-red diamonds on her eyelids and cheeks. "Yoo-hoo," she cooed in a thick French accent.

"Hi." I moved my attention to the dog and perked. "She's pink." I dashed to her side like a child who'd seen a unicorn and crouched for a look into the pretty poodle's eyes, careful to keep the furry sweetheart between myself and the clown. I dug my fingers into the puff of cotton-candy-colored hair on the dog's head. "Why are you pink, my little sweetie, cutie, baby?" My voice morphed into a high soprano. Baby talk poured from my lips. "What's your name, pretty princess? Huh?"

"*He* is Magnus the Conqueror," the dog's clown said with unfettered French disdain.

"Oh." I stood gracelessly. "He's beautiful."

"It's food coloring." She pointed to his bouffant.

"Lovely." I smiled. "And nontoxic."

"*Oui.* This is important. You have nontoxic treats?"

I got the distinct impression nontoxic wasn't the exact phrase she was looking for, but I got the gist. I ran around the bakery display and made a sample tray. "You're in luck, Magnus. Everything I bake is nontoxic." I arranged a few treat bits in a row and lowered the tray on my palm for Magnus's inspection. "This is a peanut butter and banana pupcake." I pointed to the first selection with my free hand. "This is a pawline. It's made with bacon fat and lots of crispy bacon bits. This last one is a carrot cake."

Magnus tilted his head as I spoke, absorbing the words.

"Would you like to try one?" I asked.

He sniffed the samples, then looked at me. His giant paw landed beside choice number one, nearly toppling my tray.

"He wants a pupcake," the clown explained.

"Of course." I held the bit in my palm. Magnus swept it off with his tongue.

The clown watched him lick his chops. "Fine. We take forty-seven."

I straightened. "What?" Was that also lost translation? I dug through foggy memories of prep school French for the names of numbers. "*Quarante-sept?*"

"*Oui. Quarante-sept.* I will treat the team."

All righty, then. I washed my hands before sliding on a pair of clear plastic gloves. "Are you and Magnus performing this week?"

The clown did a deep side-lunge bow number.

I jumped back.

Her black beret barely moved as she whipped herself into a normal stance. "We are members of the Tulane University Theater Troupe. Tonight we perform 'A Dog's Day in Paris' at the Monteleone. This is a hotel in the French Quarter."

"How exciting." I emptied an entire shelf of pupcakes into a large bakery box prelined with teal paper. My heart hammered as I sealed the box with a monogrammed sticker and set the treats on the counter. "Ninety-nine dollars and sixty-four cents."

"*Bon.*" She handed me her Visa as payment. A little picture of a college student was tucked in the corner of the personalized card. Under all that makeup was a rather plain-looking beauty. Not scary at all.

I returned her card and the receipt. "Thank you. Enjoy your pupcakes! Bye-bye, Magnus the Conqueror."

Look at me, facing my clown fears.

I wiped my counter down and smiled at the pink poodle and strange clown as they passed my window on the sidewalk, off to practice "A Dog's Day in Paris," whatever that was.

The store phone rang, and I lifted the receiver to my ear. "Furry Godmother Pet Boutique, where every pet is royalty and every day is a celebration."

The chords of a bass guitar thrummed in my ear.

"Hello?"

A scratchy indie-band voice joined the creepy bass. "You follow me. I'll follow you," the voice crooned. "You follow me. I'll follow you. You're never alone. Not at work. Not at home. I'm outside your door. Watching you. Forever more."

I hung up. Fear pooled in my gut as I scanned the scene outside my shop window. Nothing seemed amiss, but ice fingers slid down my spine anyway. I swept overgrown bangs off my forehead and shook away the desire to close the blinds. "Good grief," I whispered, "woman up." I was from New Orleans. It should take more than a wrong number and some creepy indie rock to upset me. Clearly, the week was taking a toll. I grabbed a box of sequins and dumped them on the counter. As long as the store was dead, I could sort and inventory the colors I needed for Mrs. Hams's order. Orange. Yellow. Silver. White wouldn't be shiny enough for the effect she wanted. I didn't have enough sequins for one llama-sized scarf, let alone a whole troop. "Shoot," I muttered. I darted into the stock room to assess my bolts of fabric. Llamas were big, and there were seven Llama Mamas. "I've got to buy more of everything," I muttered to myself. A trip to the store would keep me from starting right away.

The phone rang as I dragged myself back to the front. "Furry Godmother Pet Boutique, where every pet is royalty and every day is a celebration."

The weird music began again. "You follow me. I follow you. You follow me."

I hung up. "Listen," I told the silent phone. "I'm not following you, and if you want to follow me, you've got to get in line."

The phone rang again, and fine hairs on my neck rose to attention. Beyond my shop window stood a cat-man with a cell phone pressed to his ear.

"Ah-ha!" I bolted through the room and out the door. "Hey!" I called, racing between cars to the other side of the road, no time for stoplights and crosswalks. "You! Stop!" I yelled at the big head with the tiny phone. "Stop!"

The cat turned to face me. Its blank, painted expression stole my verve.

"Take off that mask." I lifted my phone and dialed 9-1-1, then hovered my thumb over the Send button. "Take it off or I'm calling the police."

The cat made a rude hand gesture.

Throngs of people passed us, splitting as if we were a fork in the river, an obstacle of no consequence. Meanwhile I faced off with a madman.

"Hey." A woman's voice drew my attention. She marched our way in matching black coveralls, a big cat head tucked under one arm. "What's wrong? Why are you yelling at him?"

A pack of cat-men emerged from a restaurant not far from where she'd magically appeared.

I stepped back, counting cat-people and burning with confusion and embarrassment under a hot afternoon sun. Why had I assumed, especially during an arts festival, that there was only one man in town with a cat costume? My mouth dried and my head swam. I forced my stubborn jaw to move. "Will you take off your masks?"

Everyone removed their heads, except the one in front of me.

Concern lined their collective expression.

My tummy seemed to bottom out. I didn't recognize anyone, and I regretted the heavy lunch.

"Are you all right?" The woman reached for me.

I moved back. "No. I'm not." I felt off-balance. Woozy. "I'm being followed by someone dressed like you. Why are there so many of you?" My throat caught on the words, choking me. Was this a panic attack?

"We're performing all week around the city," the woman said. She smacked the big faux head on the person in front of me. "This is Nick. He's a pain, but he's been too busy working with us to be stalking you. Take your head off, for cat's sake."

Nick wiggled the head lose and made a mean face at me. I'd never seen him before either.

"Sorry," I whispered. "I got a weird call, and I saw you with the phone." I scooted away from the mass of cat-people. "Sorry."

"Hey," the woman said. "They're selling these at the market in the Quarter, you know. Some artist is making them. Demonstrating papier-mâché. Anyone can buy one."

"Thanks." I turned and jogged back to my store. Anyone could buy one. *Anyone could be the cat-man.*

I entered Furry Godmother with new fear in my heart. No shoppers. Anyone could have entered and hidden while I was outside. No. That was paranoid thinking. Wasn't it? I mentally cursed my impulsivity and grabbed a broom for self-defense. Shop owner rule number one: never leave the store unattended. *Duh.*

I peeked behind the counters. No one.

I crept down the hall and kicked the bathroom door open. No one. Closet. No one.

I was essentially the stupid girl in every horror film. *There could be danger nearby; I think I'll check it out.*

Penelope sat on Spot in his dock beside my desk in the stock room.

"Is anyone hiding back here?" I asked her.

She pressed Spot's button with her paw. Nothing.

"I'll power him on if you answer me."

She stared at my broom.

"Why can't animals talk?" I circled the room and sighed in relief. No one.

The bell rang out front. I set the broom aside and went to fake sanity for a few more hours.

I chatted with tourists and shoppers for the remainder of the afternoon while keeping an eye on the people outside my window. No one stopped to stare. No one else called to play scary songs. My racing heart settled into a more reasonable state of excitement as I made mental plans to visit the market after work. I sold magician capes for bunnies to a grandma from Oregon, who said her grandkids were going to love dressing their darlings. I entertained a toddler with my turtles while her dad tried hats on the family cat as a surprise for his wife. I used Penelope as a fashion model for a young woman with her first cat, unsure how to dress it without making it mad. *Good luck with that.*

PrettyCharlie86 wandered in minutes before closing time. "Hey." His hands were shoved deep in his pockets. His head drooped forward. "I'm sorry about what I did. In hindsight it was really stupid."

My guard dropped by a fraction. "Okay."

He pulled one hand from his pocket and set his cell phone on my counter. "I wrote a public apology to you this morning, and I wanted to tell you in person. I heard you defending animals, and it got me here." He pressed a fist to his heart.

"You heard me defending animals? When?"

He pressed his finger to the little screen, and my face appeared. Amateur footage of my verbal spar with the rude *Animals Are Humans* reporter wobbled on the screen.

"Someone put this online?"

He nodded. "You're an okay lady. I shouldn't have messed up your door or tried to make some grand statement about Annie Lane. It was all in the heat of the moment, you know?"

Not really, but I nodded anyway.

He gave me a limp smile, collected his phone, and left. Maybe he was an okay guy, too, under all that self-importance and misappropriated anger.

I locked up promptly at five and set off for the Quarter. Penelope volunteered to keep an eye on Spot after I powered him up. I made the usual twenty-minute drive in thirty, thanks to an unprecedented number of horse-drawn carriages outside Jackson Square. The steady clip-clop of hooves and soft whinny of the stallions helped ease my mind as I crept closer to my destination. People of every size, shape, and color filled the narrow sidewalks of the Quarter, snapping pictures and making memories. I admired them for the thrill it must be, seeing New Orleans for the first time. The soft sounds of a bagpipe's lament droned unseen near the river, offset by the ever-peppy calliope music piped from the Natchez riverboat nearby.

I patted my steering wheel and hoped the papier-mâché artist kept good records of his recent customers. Then again, even if he had, what was I going to do? Demand copies and run down every person who'd made a purchase in the last four days? What if the stalker had borrowed his cat head from a friend or bought it at another festival?

I gave up car travel and parked several blocks away from the French Market. I donned my sunglasses and grabbed my trusty water bottle. Time to find my man. The market overflowed with people in town for the festival. I trudged through mobs of tourists and vendors in search of one artist selling cat heads. Even the usual street performers had relocated closer to the market. *Go where the action is*, I guessed.

An hour later, I'd bought a bag of bell peppers for a salad later and a fresh bottle of water. Humidity was ever-present in my city, as real as the aging sax player on an overturned bucket by the sidewalk.

When the papier-mâché stand came into view, I could've cheered. I'd begun to think he'd relocated to another part of the city or gone home for the day. His little demonstration table was set up in a grassy area behind the market. Huge crafted animal heads were stacked in piles. Creepy as the cat heads were, the Easter Bunny ones were worse. I approached slowly. "Excuse me."

A string-bean-shaped man crouched in the grass behind a box filled with newspapers. His jeans were skinny, and his feet were bare. He poured water from a gallon jug over his hands.

"Sir?"

He twisted at the waist, squinting against the sun. "What do you need?"

I tried not to stare at his beard or tiny man bun. "I'm interested in one of your masks. A black cat."

He made a disgusted sound. "I don't make those anymore."

"What? Why?"

"Because I've made forty in seven days. I can't look at any more cats." He rubbed his face with wet hands. "Let me make you something else. What's your spirit animal? Wait. Don't tell me." He snapped his fingers. "A sloth."

I made a stink face. "No it's not. I'm more like a white stallion or a powerful lioness."

"Nah." He tipped his head over one ear, obviously not seeing it. "Maybe a penguin."

"All right," I said. "That's enough. I'm not here to commission a mask. I want to ask you about the people who bought black cat heads. I'm being stalked by a guy wearing one, and I want to find him so I can have him arrested."

Man Bun looked everywhere but at my face. "Is this a joke?"

"No. Do you keep any records of your sales?"

He flopped into his pop-up chair and laughed. "Why would I do that? People pay cash. No returns."

"How do you claim the income for your taxes?"

He looked around again.

"Right. Silly me." I turned my phone on the vendor and snapped his picture. Four days had passed since Annie's death, and I knew nothing more about her killer than I had the moment I found her body. Maybe I needed a big stalker wall, too. A place where I could see everything at one time and connect the dots.

I sucked down cold water and headed back to my car with nothing but fresh irritation and a bag of peppers for my time.

And time was marching on.

Chapter Fourteen

Furry Godmother's quick tip for stopping on a dime:
Keep one in your shoe.

Imogene and I worked in companionable silence Monday morning. She handled the customers and phone calls. I worked on llama scarves. The early morning expedition to my favorite craft store had been a bank-draining success. Luckily, the new window display drew a steady stream of walk-ins. No one was buying me out, but few people left empty-handed. Imogene put a business card in every hand she saw. If nothing else, we were planting seeds for a harvest.

Despite my best effort to be rational, I held my breath every time the phone rang. Two random misdials did not constitute a threat. In fact, if the last few days hadn't been so strange, I'd have dismissed the calls immediately.

Imogene took another call. She smiled against the receiver and chatted several minutes before moseying across the room to me. "How's your project coming along?"

"What do you think?" I lifted the scarf for her inspection, draping the soft underside over my forearm. "When I finish adding sequins, I'll sew the ends and make them infinity scarves."

"You're going to blow Margaret Hams's tiny mind with these. How'd you get so far so quickly?"

"Prestrung sequins." I fished a fresh line from my supply bag. "Ta-da. I only have to arrange them and sew them down where they belong. Easy peasy."

"For you, maybe. I've seen your mama donate five-hundred-dollar blouses because a button fell off."

I blanched. "She donates things with missing pieces? That's awful."

"What's awful is that she never learned to sew a button."

I set the scarf back onto the counter, unable to drive yesterday's strange phone calls from my mind any longer. "Have we gotten any prank calls today on the shop's line?"

"Someone wanted size-thirteen peep toes. I guess they thought Furry Godmother was a drag queen company." She clucked her tongue and popped a hip. "When was the last time anyone saw a furry drag queen? Those ladies are better waxed than Madame Tussauds."

"Did anyone call and play music instead of speaking?"

She furrowed her brows. "What kind of music?"

"I don't know. Any kind."

She looked me over. "You're up to something."

"No I'm not."

"Then you're hiding something."

I corrected my posture.

The phone rang, and I grabbed it without thinking. "Furry Godmother, where pets are royalty and every day is a celebration."

"Your gown is ready," a snooty voice reported. "We close at four."

"Excuse me?"

A loud huff blew through the receiver. "This is Bon Cherie Cleaners. Someone dropped off a wrinkled mess yesterday and left this number. A black Givenchy gown with perfume and champagne spots on the collar. It looked like it was kept in a shoe box."

"That's me."

"It's ready." She disconnected.

I dropped the phone onto the base. "Mom's dry cleaner is a snot."

Imogene laughed. "Yeah, but she's good."

"Are you coming to dinner at Commander's Palace tonight? Dad bought a whole table."

"Not me. I promised to help Veda again."

I smiled. "Another ghost problem?"

"No. She's looking for her next of kin. Veda's fading and the cookie shop has to go to someone in her lineage, or all hell will break loose."

I waited for more information. She sounded a little too literal on that last part for my comfort. "Anything I can do to help?"

She pulled her chin back and flung a palm up between us like a traffic cop. "No, thank you, Miss Lacy. You're a nice girl, but we don't need any of what you've got." She circled the palm. "Your juju could tear up an anvil."

"I've never liked that saying." I'd heard it from her all my life. Apparently I was born under a blood moon, and my juju was doomed from the start. Convenient. "I think I'm doing pretty well for a cursed woman."

"Do you still have your dime?"

"Yes."

"Let me see it." She presented an open hand.

"What do you mean?"

"You said you have it. So it must be in your shoe where it belongs. Right?"

"Yep." Nope. I turned my wrist over for a look at my watch. "I'd better get over to Bon Cherie before the owner calls my mother and tells her I won't pick up my dress."

"You'd better stop at home and get that dime."

I grabbed my bag and headed for the door. "Yes, ma'am."

The drive to Bon Cherie wasn't bad, and though afternoon traffic was a pain in the butt anywhere in the city, at least I was moving against traffic instead of stuck in it. I parked across the street from the cleaners and dug through my glove compartment for the claim ticket.

I waved to the members of a walking tour headed for the cemetery, then dashed inside the cleaners for my gown.

The woman behind the counter was tall and thin in the extreme. Her sleeveless white sheath adhered to her narrow body like the paper on a drinking straw. "Yes?" she asked before I'd closed the door behind me. Her green eyes bulged, probably a result of the French twist she wore as a facelift.

I handed her my ticket. "I'm here for the black Givenchy."

She positioned frameless glasses on her nose and walked away.

A zippy number from Cabaret piped through hidden speakers. I tapped my toe along with the beat. I'd seen the musical in New York with friends and imagined myself onstage, confident and gorgeous like the six-foot models in fishnets. It had been a wild night full of firsts and lasts. I'd promised myself to go back, but somehow I imagined the trip wouldn't be the same at thirty.

The woman returned on the click-clack of stilettos, a garment bag over one arm. She draped the bag over the counter and dragged the zipper from top to bottom, freeing the gown for my approval.

We yelped in unison.

My floor-length gown was shredded into ragged strips. "What did you do to my dress?" I squeaked.

Her big green eyes protruded from her sunken face. "I don't know. I did nothing. This was perfect when I arrived." She ran her hands, unbelieving, through the jagged layers of chiffon and silk. "It's like a tiger," she said, making her hand into a claw and swiping.

I exhaled long and slow. "Or a cat." This was a message. A threat. Like the calls were a threat. I fumbled to the nearest chair and sat. "I need to make a call." I brought up the dial pad on my phone with trembling fingers.

The phone rang before I could send my call.

"Hello?" I warbled, hoping to unload the disaster on anyone who'd listen. Scarlet, Mom, Dad—I didn't care.

"You follow me. I follow you." The low, droning bass and eerie voice barged into my ear. "You're not alone. Not at work. Not at home."

I jammed my finger against the red disconnect button fifty times. A tear hit the screen. I wiped my face and the phone, then dialed Jack.

"Detective Oliver."

"Jack?"

"Lacy?" Alarm cut through his voice. "What's wrong?"

"I'm at Bon Cherie Cleaners. Someone clawed my gown into bits, and I'm getting phone calls with musical stalker connotations at work." I swallowed a hard lump of panic. "This time the call came on my cell phone." Calling the shop was one thing. That number was listed. That number was painted on the front window. My cell number was not.

"Stay inside the cleaners. Give me fifteen minutes."

I nodded to no one and disconnected.

The woman behind the counter fixated on my dress, stroking the tattered material and mumbling, "I'm the only one here. I don't understand."

I forced myself onto wobbly legs and turned my camera on the dress. Another shot for my future crime board. "It's not your fault. This was a message meant for me. Can you recover it with the bag? A detective is on his way."

The flash of my phone's camera startled her into motion. She lowered the bag over the ruined couture and zipped it shut. "I'm so sorry."

"May I?" I walked to the edge of her counter. "I'd like to take a look in the back, make sure we're alone."

"Of course." Her voice was soft and breathless, the hoity attitude gone. "You think someone else is here?" She clung to the front desk as I passed. "Who? Why? What kind of person ruins something so beautiful?"

I ignored her questions. She knew the answers. Someone unhinged and dangerous. Sane people didn't sneak around destroying things. I grabbed her broom when it came into view and wielded it like a baseball bat. I poked the racks of bagged clothing and checked her stock and bathrooms. No one.

"Where does this go?" I gripped the handle to an aluminum door. "Outside?"

"Yes," she called, still stuck to the safety of her counter.

I shoved it open and stepped into the sun, careful to keep my broom handle in the door. "Does it lock automatically when you close it?"

"No."

I let the door close to test her word. The rear courtyard was small but delightful—and accessible from every side. A pile of crushed cigarettes gathered in a planter. I tugged the door handle and swung the barrier wide. Anyone could walk inside unseen. "You need to lock the door behind you after cigarette breaks." I returned her broom and left my gown. "The detective will be here in a few minutes. Show him the gown and the courtyard. Tell him I went back to work."

I wanted my shop and my Imogene. I wanted to pet Penelope and bury my thoughts in sequined llama accessories. I didn't want to sit idly, waiting for something else to happen.

Imogene met me at the door. "What happened?"

My splotchy face must've given me away. I blurted the whole ugly scenario. My dress, the calls, the cat-man. I typed as much of the music's creepy lyrics as I could remember into my phone and found several matches on YouTube.

Imogene gripped my hand in hers. "I'm going to contact Veda. Maybe we can get in touch with Annie's ghost and get right to the bottom of all this."

I wiggled free. "No, thank you. Jack and I will get to the bottom of this. You and Veda worry about finding her next of kin. This is going to be okay." I repeated the last part, silently, a few times for good measure. I didn't believe in ghosts, but if I was one, I'd want to be left alone.

I played the video results on YouTube until I found the one from my phone calls.

Jack arrived twenty minutes later with a scowl. "I asked you to stay at the cleaners."

"Well I needed to be somewhere I felt safe."

Imogene whistled soft and low. "I'm going to check on your turtles," she whispered.

Jack shifted his weight, leaning one hip against the counter between us. "I took the dress as evidence. Checked the store and the rear lot. No signs of forced entry. No footprints or tire marks out back."

"I know." I turned my phone to him and pressed play. "Someone called here twice yesterday and played this song."

"The one you heard today on your cell phone?"

I nodded, focusing on the dreary lyrics to a blatant obsession song.

Jack stopped the music. "You need to stay with your parents tonight."

"No."

He grimaced.

I crossed my arms and stared back.

He jerked his buzzing phone to his ear. "Oliver," he barked. His clear-blue eyes pierced mine. His expression flattened. "On my way."

He hitched a thumb over his shoulder. "Let's go," he told me. "Miss Imogene, can you take care of things here if I borrow Lacy for a while?"

"Take as long as you need." She waved from the register, where a group of ladies cooed over silk headscarves and beaded collars.

I jogged onto the sidewalk, attempting to keep pace with Jack. "Where are we going? Who called?"

"Henri called. We've got a situation in the Quarter." He opened the passenger door of his truck and nearly tossed me inside. He appeared behind the wheel a moment later. "You're going with me because you can't be left alone."

I didn't argue. If I attracted lunatics, Jack was better prepared to handle them than Imogene or my folks.

We barreled through town, running yellow lights and weaving past indecisive drivers. His custom lights flashed behind the big silver grill on his truck. He pumped his siren to whoop and holler at every intersection. The districts blurred outside my window. My hair whipped in the thick Louisiana wind. The wide, reaching branches of ancient oaks gave way to a cluttered skyline, woven with historic buildings and punctuated by millennial high rises. My nerves balled into knots as I anticipated what we were in such a hurry to see.

A trio of New Orleans police cars blocked the street ahead. Lights from an ambulance circled outside Heart to Heart animal shelter.

Jack pulled his truck half onto the walk. "Folks heard a commotion, followed by what sounded like gunshots. Police came and found your guy Gideon unconscious."

"Will he be okay?"

Jack climbed down from his seat without an answer.

I jumped onto the sidewalk and raced in his direction. "Was he shot? Will he live? Just tell me so I can freak out over here in private."

"He's not dead." He reached for my hand and dragged me like a toddler behind him.

Henri stood in the doorway, dressed in all black again and still unshaven. He tipped his ball cap when he saw us. "Jack. Lacy."

"What do we know?" Jack asked.

"Not much new since we spoke. Operators got a call from the victim, reporting an intruder. Someone came through the back door instead of the public entrance. A passerby called several minutes later. She reported hearing an argument but couldn't make out the words. Lots of thumping and bumping, dogs going crazy, and a couple of loud pops. She called the police. Responding officers found Gideon knocked out cold."

EMTs pushed the door wide, shoving us out of the way. Gideon was strapped to a gurney, wearing an oxygen mask.

"Was he shot?" I asked.

"Blanks." Henri rubbed a heavy hand through his hair and slapped the ball cap back in place. "And that isn't the weirdest thing. I've got a guy two blocks down that says he saw a man dressed as a cat hopping fences. He claims the cat had a gun, so we took the guy in for more questions. No sign of the cat-man. That's nuts, right? A guy dressed like a cat holds up an animal shelter?"

Jack gave me a look. "I want to talk with the guy who saw the cat-man. How about Gideon? Anyone spoken to him yet?"

"He hasn't woken up, but the hospital has orders to give us a call when he's able to answer questions."

I followed Jack and Henri into Heart to Heart. We went straight for Gideon's office. I stopped short. Every picture on his crime wall was missing. Who would do that? Why? Was Gideon embarrassed that we'd seen and photographed it? I took a few pictures while Jack and Henri rehashed details I'd already heard.

Forty minutes later, Jack returned me to Furry Godmother.

"I'm headed to the station. I want to talk with the guy who saw the cat-man before he's released." He leveled me with an icy stare. "Stay out of trouble until I can catch up with you again later. I'm serious about staying with your folks tonight."

"Can't," I said. I popped the passenger door open and slid onto the sidewalk outside my shop. "I've got a schmancy dinner to attend in less than three hours, and I have to find a new dress."

Chapter Fifteen

Furry Godmother supports and enforces
a strict no-beignet-left-behind policy.

I spooned dinner into Penelope's bowl. "You're a lucky girl. You get to eat dinner in the privacy of your home and lay around all night. I've got to get dolled up and pretend I'm a proper lady."

She gave me a sympathetic look and chowed down.

I patted her head. "I'm extra jealous because you always have a good hair day."

I checked the locks on my doors and windows, dropped food pellets in Buttercup's tank, then went to my room for a depressing look at my closet. The Givenchy had been the perfect dress for tonight, and it was one of my last high-end numbers that were still in style. I'd sold several for rent and tuition in Virginia. These days my ensembles were comprised of ten-year-old things my parents had bought and others I'd found more recently at thrift shops. I heated the curling iron while I jumped in the shower and had a quick pity party. There wasn't a forgotten Cinderella gown in my wardrobe waiting to be rediscovered. I had work clothes, comfy clothes, and a few cocktail dresses. There wasn't time to call Mom or Scarlet for help. I was in an actual fashion emergency.

I made a wish while I blow-dried my hair, but nothing new appeared in my closet. I rolled endless blonde hair into barrel curls and pinned them in a pageant-worthy updo, then applied my makeup as if my life depended in it. After another critical review of my wardrobe, I had three possible contenders. None were right for the event. Option one was a red beaded minidress I'd worn for salsa night on a cruise last year. Fancy and fun. Probably a little too much of the latter. Option two was a black, retro-chic, fitted wrap dress with a deep-V front and little white polka dots. It was a personal favorite of mine, though admittedly better suited to a business dinner than a festival food competition. My last choice was a silver strapless number I'd made in college for something my professor called the "Red Carpet Challenge." I'd created a form-fitting formal by twisting layers of shimmering satin for the bodice and cinching them tightly at the waist. Strategically placed rhinestones were supposed to add subtle drama and sparkle. The material followed the curve of my silhouette from hips to heels and split on the left side to my knee. I loved the look, but I'd never been pretentious enough to wear one of my own designs to something so public.

I started with the salsa gown and held my breath. Cleavage inched toward my chin as I zipped myself in. The hemline made cheerleaders' skirts seem prudish. My mother would die a thousand deaths if I showed up like this. She'd probably make me go home and change. I peeled option one off and started again. The retro dress was lovely, and I could breathe while wearing it, but it was undeniably wrong for the occasion.

I held the silver dress against my collarbone and looked at my reflection in the mirror. "This is going to be a disaster."

* * *

Dad sent a car for me at seven and left my name at the venue's door. I bypassed the line and headed right to the front of the room, where dad waved to me with a smile. The words "Speaker's Table" were painted in fancy silver script on a small black canvas supported by a tiny white easel at the table's center. An array of glimmering silver sticks shot through a beautifully dramatic bouquet of white roses and black feathers. The soft silver tablecloth matched my dress.

Dad kissed my cheek. "You look stunning."

"So do you."

Everyone did. The crowd was ostentatiously dressed, vying for the attention of their peers. I was instantly thankful I hadn't worn either of my other dress choices. As long as no one asked who made my dress, I couldn't be cast as a snob who thought her designs were superior to everything on the market.

Mom arrived at our table with an empty glass. From the look in her eyes, probably not her first of the night. "Lacy." She opened her arms and beckoned me. "You look spectacular."

I kissed her cheek and returned the compliment.

Recognition dawned in her face. "What happened to the Givenchy?"

"It was torn." I formed a small smile. "I had to find something in a pinch. There was hardly any time."

"You could've come to me. You know I have a hundred dresses, and I would've called my stylist. She could get you anything you'd like in an instant. Who are you wearing, anyway? It's very good. Turn around."

I pressed my lips together and turned slowly.

"I like it. It accentuates your figure without showing off your assets, if you know what I mean."

"Everyone knows what you mean."

She laughed. "Who did you say this is?" She moved her keen gaze over my seams and hemline.

Wearing my own gown was borderline obnoxious, but if someone like Annie had picked it up for her line, I would have been famous. A pang of selfish regret pinched my chest. The file from her desk rushed to mind. Her protégé had a lot to lose when Annie died. Maybe Shannon Martin knew something about his mentor that could help Jack find Annie's killer. Had Jack spoken to Shannon yet?

Someone grabbed my waist. "Hello, gorgeous."

I spun in the small space and peered up at a delightfully familiar face. "Hello, Chase." I hated myself for the onslaught of lascivious thoughts.

He stepped back an inch and shook my parents' hands.

"I still can't believe you're here," I said, mystified by my luck at gaining his company for the second time this week.

He stretched a long arm toward the room's center, where a string band played a waltz and the district's upper echelon swayed to each magical note. "How about a spin around the dance floor?"

"I'd love to." I followed him into the cloud of moving couples and placed a hand on his shoulder. "You look quite dashing."

"Why, thank you, Miss Crocker," he said in a deliciously slow southern drawl. He took my free hand in his. Soft lighting threw long shadows across his gently rounded cheeks and danced in his playful green eyes. His other hand slid over the curve of my hip.

"Watch it, Mr. Hawthorne, unless you aren't very fond of those fingers."

He reset them in the dip of my waist. "You're right. That was mischievous, and I should be on my best behavior when I'm with you."

"Correct."

He lowered his lips to my ear and hovered while a shiver rocked down my spine. "Have you given any more thought to the thank-you kiss you promised me?"

I pulled back, cheeks burning, and failed to wipe the smile off my face. "This is your best behavior? Whispering in my ear and asking me to kiss you?"

He straightened to his full and ridiculous height. "You're absolutely right. Begging your pardon." He wrapped his arms around my back and drew me into a tight embrace. "We should keep a respectable distance."

I leaned my cheek to his chest and giggled softly. "This is not how you waltz."

"It's scandalous. You're such a clingy woman."

I pried my face off him. "I'm not clingy."

"Oh, no?" He opened his arms, leaving me flat against him.

I stumbled back with a laugh and shoved his chest. "You're going to get me in trouble." I dared a look at my parents' table. Mom, Dad, and several others were staring at Chase and me, whispering behind their hands and smiling. "Now you've done it. They're all watching."

He grabbed me again and swung me effortlessly into a graceful box step. "Ignore them. We're having fun."

"They're gawking. And gossiping."

He dipped me low and took his time righting me. "Let them talk." Our bodies moved seamlessly together over the smooth dance floor. "How's your investigation going? Anything new?"

I let my head roll back. "I finally had my mind off it for five minutes."

He paused as the tune ended and another much slower number began. "You know, I can take your mind off everything for a lot longer than five minutes if you'd just ask."

I released him on instinct. "You're killing me, Chase Hawthorne."

"My apologies, miss." There was no hint of apology in his tone—more like shameless amusement.

I fanned my face and headed for the bar. I felt his gaze on me as I walked away. The heat of his hands lingered on my skin. That man could ruin a lady's reputation without leaving the dance floor. "Ice water, please."

Feedback from the speaker's microphone quieted the room.

I gathered my water, napkin, and remaining wits, then returned to our table. Chase pulled a chair out for me.

The announcer began with a preplanned spiel on cue cards while the rest of the room found their seats. Chase sat beside me and locked me in his gaze. "You didn't answer me. Anything new with the investigation?"

I leaned in, overcome with the need to unload. "Everything's become so convoluted. Strange things keep happening. They feel unrelated, but the timing suggests they can't be."

He bent his head to mine and quieted his voice, a secret between only us. "Let me look into something for you. I'm excellent at research and bored at work. As it turns out, lawyering is a bit dull most of the time. I could use something fun to keep me occupied."

I typed Annie's protégé's name into a search engine on my phone and turned my screen toward Chase. "This is Shannon Martin. I found a file of his designs on Annie's desk, and I think I should talk to him."

"Do you think he knows something about what happened to her?"

I shrugged to keep my speech to a minimum.

Chase took my phone and searched for Shannon on social media. We bowed our heads together and trolled his Instagram while the announcer traded the microphone off to the night's featured speaker.

"He doesn't look too broken up," I whispered. Shannon had taken dozens of party pics at multiple Faux Real venues throughout the week.

Chase lowered my phone to his lap. "We should go find him. We can use his selfie obsession to our advantage, track him down, and ambush him while he's been drinking. We'll learn all sort of good information that way."

I lit up at the shamefully brilliant idea.

"Good evening." A low, gravelly voice caressed the microphone. "My name is Jack Oliver."

I whipped around to face the podium. Jack stood in the spotlight, wearing a custom-fit tux, hands shoved deep inside his pockets. My idiotic heart went bonkers.

His jaw worked as he stood there, silently.

"What's he doing?" I asked.

Chase swigged his drink. "He's the speaker."

My jaw dropped.

"You all knew my grandpa," Jack finally said. "Grandpa Smacker. I suppose, in a way, he was everyone's grandpa. To me, he was family. An honorable and upright man. A thinker. An entrepreneur and a philanthropist. This competition was his favorite event of the festival. He never missed a year." His Adam's apple bobbed slowly.

My life seemed to hang in the pause.

"Grandpa was supposed to speak tonight. He's had it on his books for nearly two years, and I wanted to honor that, so I agreed to stand in his absence. I'm not nearly as eloquent as my grandfather, or as business minded, but I love this city like he did, maybe more, and I'm proud to stand here tonight and represent the corporation he spent his life building. So on behalf of Grandpa Smacker, I'd like to present a check in the amount of five hundred thousand dollars to the culinary school that trained tonight's winner. We do this because we want to see the continuation of culinary excellence in New Orleans, and that means training from the world's finest chefs in the world's best kitchens with the highest quality equipment. The winning chef will receive a paid one-year lease at any location of their choosing within the city, where we will help them open a restaurant and continue to serve up meals that can only be called New Orleans's finest. Thank you."

He stepped away from the podium amidst a standing ovation and strode confidently to our table. He shook hands with Dad, Chase, and several other men before taking the seat directly across from me. His cool-blue gaze trained instantly on mine. "Lacy, you look lovely."

"Thank you," I whispered.

"I see you didn't have any trouble finding a new dress."

"I made it." The words jumped off my tongue, and I regretted them instantly.

Chase guffawed. "You made this? That's incredible."

Jack didn't look surprised. "It's very nice. When you said you had a schmancy dinner, I didn't realize you meant this one." He flicked his gaze to my parents.

Right. I didn't usually accept their invitations.

"I would've offered to drive you."

Heat bloomed in my chest as Jack and Chase stared at me. A familiar zing of tension electrified the space between us. "Dad sent a car. I didn't know you were the speaker, or I would've wished you luck. Not that you needed it. You were great."

He looked away.

I followed his gaze to a woman I recognized as his grandpa's girlfriend, Tabitha.

"Are we dating?" I asked Jack.

Chase leaned back. "What?"

I turned his way quickly. "Go with it."

Tabitha made her way to our table and slid onto the chair beside Jack.

He dipped his chin hard.

Chase continued to stare at the side of my face. "Is this for real?"

"Nope," Jack and I answered in unison, though he could've been a little less peppy about the answer.

Tabitha frowned. "What's wrong?"

Jack waved her off.

Chase fiddled with his phone, while I wondered what to say to Tabitha that would make me sound like Jack's girlfriend. I forced an awkward smile.

Chase put his phone away in a hurry, then shot me a wild look.

"What?" I asked.

He looked at Jack and groaned.

I rested my fingers on his shoulder. "Are you okay?"

Chase shook his head. "I think I might've overdone it with the predinner drinks."

He had predinner drinks? I hefted a pitcher of ice water from the table's center and filled a glass. "This will help. Can I get you something else?" I scanned the elaborately set table for something to settle Chase's stomach. Where were the bread baskets or appetizers? Wasn't this night supposed to be all about food?

Jack sucked his teeth and scrutinized Chase. "What's going on, Hawthorne?"

Tabitha moved her gaze slowly from Jack, to Chase, then me.

Chase tipped slightly forward. "Lacy?" he moaned. "I should probably go home."

"Okay." I dug for my phone. "I can call a cab and ride with you." I gave Jack an apologetic face. "I'll be back in less than an hour."

Chase pushed onto his feet. A set of car keys balanced on his palm. "I drove."

"All right." I excused myself, kissed Dad's cheek, and performed a small wave across the table to Jack. "I guess I'll be right back."

Chase went to the valet.

Jack followed me as far as the front door. "He's not sick," he whispered. "He's up to something."

Chase chatted with the valet outside the heavy glass door.

I wasn't convinced Jack was wrong. "Do you want me to stay?"

He gave Chase another long look. "Yes, but you should go. He can't drive if he's been drinking, and if I'm right, he may need someone to keep him out of trouble. Any idea what kind of trouble it might be?"

I pressed my lips and shook my head.

The valet brought Chase's shiny new sports car to the curb. Jack sighed. "Call me if you need me."

I walked outside, and Chase held the passenger door. "I thought you needed a driver."

He jogged around the hood and dropped behind the wheel without waiting for me to get in. "I'm feeling better." He motioned for me to hurry up.

Reluctantly I obliged.

He barked the tires as we sped away.

I buckled in and punched his arm. "You faked sick to get out of a delicious meal. Are you nuts? Where are we going?"

"That was improvisation and not my best work, but I had to think fast." He glanced my way. "Check Shannon Martin's Instagram."

I checked my phone. Shannon had put up three new photos in the last ten minutes.

Chase smiled into the night, accelerating smoothly toward the French Quarter. "He's at One Eyed Jacks right now."

I pulled dozens of pins from my hair and let the wind shake it loose. "My mother's going to be livid when I don't come back." I checked my face in the lighted visor mirror. Shockingly, the fear wasn't visible.

My phone buzzed. "Jack's texting me." I swiped the screen to life. "He says if I don't text him back to confirm this wasn't an abduction, he's coming after us."

Chase slid me an impish half smile.

I responded to Jack with emoticons. A smiley face, a tiny church, some drinks, and a river. "There, he should know that means we're heading to the Quarter."

Two hours later, we were in Jackson Square taking selfies with Andrew Jackson and his trusty steed. The great silver peaks of the St. Louis Cathedral rose proudly behind us, piercing a velvety sky. A smattering of people sat on the benches and in the grass, enjoying a stolen moment or taking in the beauty of my town. We'd followed Shannon's Instagram feed all around the Quarter, seeming to miss him at every turn. "This is like an elaborate scavenger hunt, and the only item on our list is mobile."

Chase took another picture of me. "Yes, but it's fun. If we catch him, we get a double win."

We crossed the street to the path along the Mississippi, toting coffees from Café Du Monde and a bag of warm beignets. Dark waters churned and glistened beside us in the moonlight. Chase swung the bag at me. "Do you want any more? There are two left."

I helped myself to a third delicious treat. "You're right, this has been fun. I haven't been this at ease in a long time.

Look at me." I stopped and struck a pose. "I'm dressed for a ball and eating sweets from a bag."

"Don't forget I bought you beads on Bourbon Street. The nice kind that light up."

The flashing necklace cast green-and-yellow light over my beignet. I giggled, and a puff of powdered sugar floated onto Chase's jacket. "All those people thought we just got married."

He dusted the material of his snazzy tux. "Those guys were so jealous. I filed their faces in my happy memory storage."

"Yeah? How about when the DJ at Bourbon Cowboy tried to bribe me with one lousy drink to ride the mechanical bull?"

Chase stopped moving and feigned seriousness. "You slid right off. Worst show ever."

I fell against his side in laughter. Puffs of powdered sugar lifted into the air. "I couldn't get my knees apart in this dress. I had to ride side saddle."

"That wasn't a ride. That was like a sliding board. Bull powered on. Lacy slid off." He tossed his cup in a trash bin. "Where should we go next?"

"Home. I have a ton of work to do, and I need to get out of this dress. Are you okay to drive?"

"Me? I'm fine. I nursed the same hurricane all over town. You're the one who fell off a bull," he snorted, "in a wedding gown."

I laughed too. Then I followed him in search of his car, wherever we'd left it.

Chapter Sixteen

Furry Godmother's tip for double-dating: Invite a friend.

I made a fresh pot of coffee when I got home and settled on the couch with Penelope. Chase walked me to the door like a gentleman, then headed home, wherever that was. A tinge of guilt pinched my chest. I hadn't even asked about his new place or offered to come by with a housewarming gift. If I didn't act soon, Mom and her crew would be around to revoke my southern woman card. "We have to think of the perfect gift," I told Penelope, stroking her soft fur. "Something that will make up for my delay." I held a small embellishments container in front of us. "I'm going to do something, and I don't want you to freak out." I opened the lid to my feather bin, and tiny bits of fluff floated out. Penelope rolled off me on high alert, ears perked, tail sweeping gracefully, watching for where the floater would land.

I adjusted my T-shirt and pulled the box onto my lap in her absence. My skin was still warm from a shower. "I'm going to make accessories for my peacock line," I explained.

"I want the pieces ready in time for Mardi Gras, so you can't eat my feathers."

I stitched a few plumes into a stretchy sequin headband and tugged the accessory onto Penelope's head.

She went rigid. Ears flat.

"It's beautiful."

She dove headfirst into the cushions and pawed it off.

I selected a handful of long, straight feathers from the bin and resealed the lid. I got busy attaching feathers to other headbands while Penelope kneaded hers to death on the cushion beside me.

Busy hands were good for the brain. I did some half-hearted Internet searches for Shannon and Annie, typing sporadically with one hand and scanning the results, most of which I'd already read. We hadn't managed to catch Shannon tonight, but I had plans to arrive on his doorstep in the morning. I skimmed though articles on Annie's nasty divorce and a few covering who-made-it-first disputes between her and other designers. Photos of Dylan Latherope were plentiful and deceiving. He looked downright poised on the screen. In reality, he seemed like a guy on the edge. I glanced at my drawn curtains. Where was he tonight?

"The memorial." I searched for coverage of the public memorial Bryce had mentioned was taking place today and found loads of coverage. Articles, photos, videos. I grabbed another set of feathers to sew while I watched some amateur footage taken at the event. Soft piano music tinkled in the background, nearly swallowed by the murmur of a thousand voices. A giant painting of Annie graced the rear wall of her Manhattan studio. A sea of people dressed in black carried champagne flutes and tiny plates with them through the space.

"You know who I don't see?" I asked Penelope.

She dove off the couch and pounced on a feather.

"Dylan Latherope. If he didn't fly home for the memorial, he could still be here playing cat-man." I tapped a finger on my cell phone, itching to call Jack and ask if he learned anything more from the man who'd seen someone dressed as a cat leaving the animal shelter, but it was almost two in the morning. I'd have to wait.

The video continued as I attached feather after feather to several headbands. Nothing much happened. The person behind the camera was more interested in the celebrities in attendance than Annie. "No one even gave a speech," the cameraman complained. "No one said anything about Annie Lane. That's messed up."

I agreed.

"I know," a woman's voice answered. I tuned in more closely. I'd assumed the cameraman was alone. "Where was her family?" the woman asked. "I wonder if she even knew any of those people."

The video ended. I watched it again, this time wondering along with the voice, where was Annie's family?

I opened a new search engine and looked for the most recent articles on Annie's family. Nothing. Stories of her death, but no press statements or personal interviews. Strange. I ditched the feathers to type with both hands and tried variations of the search. A few old articles surfaced with photos of Annie and her parents from my high school days. An article written in the late 1990s featured Annie at her college graduation, and another showed her at a national design competition in 2001. A young boy frowned at his feet in the photo. I squinted at the tiny script beneath. The Goodman Family. "Oh, my goodness." I'd completely forgotten that she'd changed her name when she started her label. "Annie Lane was born Annie Goodman." I switched gears and searched Annie Goodman.

There were an astounding number of people with that name, but perseverance won again. "Gotcha," I bragged to my laptop. Annie was featured in our local paper while still in high school. Her family was interviewed. Mom, Dad, Annie, *and her little brother, Ryan*. Once I had his name, I was able to find evidence of him in New Orleans, Nashville, and a number of other cities. I scrolled through his social media feeds, picking up momentum when the location tags changed recently from California to New Orleans. I enlarged his profile picture and slapped the couch. "Yes!" I grabbed my phone and flipped through the pictures I'd taken of Gideon's stalker wall. "It's him!" The unknown man carrying those boxes marked with *X*s was Annie's brother. So where the heck had he been hiding and why?

I snagged my phone and jumped off the couch to pace. My best thinking happened when I was in motion. I dialed Chase.

"Hello, gorgeous," he answered on the first ring.

I stopped pacing. "Did I wake you?"

"Do you need me?" he countered.

I chewed my lip, debating. "Actually I'm looking into Annie's life online. Are you still interested?"

An engine revved in the background. "You have no idea."

Chase pulled into my drive a few minutes later looking like he'd had a full night's sleep and a photo shoot before his arrival. I was in cotton shorts and a Salvador Dali T-shirt.

I opened the door and pulled him inside. Without thinking, I hugged him. "Thanks for coming." I reset the alarm. "This has been a really weird week, and I think I just found something interesting." I unloaded four and a half days of nightmares on him while he cuddled Penelope and teased her with feathers. Then I handed him my phone and laptop and explained my newest discovery.

"So you think her brother's in town and what? Hiding?"

"Why else wouldn't he have turned up by now if he's here?" Better yet, why had he been so pointedly absent during her rise to fame?

Chase turned to face me on the couch. "Why would he hide? That reeks of guilt." He cocked a knee on the cushion between us. "If you go see him, take me with you. This guy's huge." In case I hadn't realized, Chase gave my phone back to show me. Ryan's picture was on the screen. His massive biceps threatened his straining shirt sleeves. He wasn't tall or lean like Chase and Jack. Ryan was built like a brick, broad everywhere, and none of it was fat.

"Okay." I probably couldn't outrun him if he was a lunatic, and I certainly couldn't fight him. "Agreed."

Chase set my laptop aside and pointed a stretchy headband at me like a rubber band, ready to shoot. "What are these? Garters?"

I laughed. "No. They're headbands. Can you sew?"

"Not at all."

"Well, what good are you?"

He grabbed my feet and pulled them onto his lap. "Remember that time you rode a mechanical bull?"

I laughed. "Like it was tonight."

He curled warm hands around my bare calves. "You should probably get some sleep."

"No." I pulled my feet back. "You just got here. Don't leave so soon."

He tugged the throw from my couch over his shoulders. "I wasn't planning on it. I know better than to think you'd lead a madman to your parents' house, and I doubt I can talk you into coming home with me, so I'll just hang here with Penny." He stroked Penelope from her ears to the tip of her tail.

I rolled my eyes, unwilling to argue. "Thanks."

"You're welcome." His green eyes smoldered, inches from mine.

Conflict roared in my chest.

"Are you thinking about kissing me?" he asked cheerfully.

"Yes," I sighed. "You're well aware of the effect you have on women."

His gaze dropped to my mouth. "I only care about the effect I have on one."

Heat flooded my face, neck, and chest. My only serious boyfriend had quickly become an ex-fiancé who nearly ruined my life. It'd only been eight months since I learned that Pete the Cheat's plan to marry me was based on his secret knowledge of my parents' money and that he'd had a whole other life going with a woman from his hospital throughout our engagement. He'd betrayed me in every way possible just this year, and I wasn't over it. I was a mess who clearly couldn't be trusted to make romantic decisions without an intervention from the Dalai Lama or Magic 8 Ball or someone. Not to mention my parents adored Chase, and our families were tightly connected. He wasn't someone to play house with. "I can't kiss you."

His smile widened. "I can wait."

"Aren't you going to ask why or try to change my mind?"

He squeezed my hand. "I know why, and I could change your mind if I wanted."

"So confident." So right.

He curved a long arm around my shoulders and pulled me to his chest, stretching the knitted throw over our bodies on the couch. "Lie here with me. I'll be the big spoon."

I cracked up and bounced to my feet. "I am not spooning with you, Chase Hawthorne."

"I love when you use my full name."

"I know." I pulled the lamp string and left him in the dim light of my laptop. "Now get some sleep, and I'll thank you tomorrow by making breakfast." I scooted around the corner to my room, still smiling.

"What if I get scared during the night?" he called.

"Don't make me lock my bedroom door."

I climbed into bed feeling ten years younger.

* * *

I woke to the sounds of Motown. I puttered down the hall, half-dazed, hair frizzed, and leaned against the kitchen doorway.

Chase spun and sang off-key to the Jackson Five as he fried eggs and bacon on my stove, shirtless. I squinted at the delightful sight. His hair stood in every direction. His face pinched tight as he reached for notes that were impossible to most men postpuberty and pushed a spatula through a piping-hot skillet.

I rubbed sleep from my eyes and smiled. His jacket and dress shirt hung over a barstool at my island. His tie lay in a heap, like the cherry on top.

The song ended. Chase dialed down the volume and stared across the room at me. "Did I wake you?"

"No, but I'm glad I didn't miss the morning performance." I padded to the coffeepot and poured a cup. "I think the deal was that I would make you breakfast."

"I don't mind. Besides, bacon and eggs max out my skills in the kitchen. Might as well show off while I can. Hey." He pressed his palms to the countertop and leveled me with a curious stare. "Do you know most people don't buy bacon in five-pound packs?"

I laughed into my coffee. "It's for a new pupcake recipe."

He relaxed a little. "That's a relief. I thought I should probably take you directly to the coronary care unit after breakfast otherwise."

I ran a hand though my wild bed-head hair and groaned. "Men aren't supposed to see a lady in this condition. You're ruining my smoke and mirrors."

He shrugged. "I shouldn't make bacon without a shirt, but stuff happens. No one wants a grease stain on Armani."

The doorbell rang.

I set my coffee on the counter.

Chase wiped his hands on a dish towel. "I've got it."

Well, if it were the cat-man, Chase had better odds against him than I did. If it were anyone else, they could thank me later for the view. I grabbed my coffee and climbed onto a barstool to wake up.

"This is awkward," Chase said.

Jack entered my kitchen with Chase on his heels.

"Ah!" I jumped off the stool and ran for my room, splashing coffee everywhere. I pressed my back to the door and contemplated jumping out the window. I dove in front of my mirror and died a little when I saw my reflection. I raked a brush through ratty hair and wrangled the unaffected mass into a ponytail, then jerked a teal dress over my head and fastened a wide red belt around my middle. My reflection had improved minimally, but there were still sleep marks on my cheek and remnants of last night's mascara under one eye. I scrubbed a powder puff over my whole face, swiped my lips with gloss and my lashes with mascara, then groaned in frustration. There was nothing left to do without a shower and proper blowout.

I jerked my chin high and reentered the kitchen. The men stared at one another, then at me.

Chase had tossed his jacket onto a hook by the back door and threaded his arms into his shirt. His tie hung around his neck like a scarf, freeing the stool beside me. He dished breakfast onto three plates. "Detective Oliver brought you a café au lait from Café Du Monde."

I cracked the lid on the disposable cup and inhaled the sweet scent. "Thank you." Tendrils of steam climbed into the turbulent air. "You're out and about early." I smiled at Jack and pinched a piece of bacon between my fingers. "Everything okay?" I tried not to be distracted by the pulsing muscle in his jaw.

A bizarre electricity crackled around him.

Chase took the seat on my left and dug into his eggs, as if this wasn't the strangest situation he'd been in. "How was the competition last night?"

For a moment, I wondered if the question had double meaning.

Jack turned frosty eyes on Chase. "Is that the suit you had on at dinner? Where did the two of you go?"

I set my bacon down. "We went to the French Quarter. I texted you. You didn't get it? The emoticons were drinks, a river, and a church. The Mississippi. St. Louis Cathedral."

He dragged his cold gaze back to me. He didn't get it.

Chase leaned on the island, looking around me to Jack. "We were following Shannon Martin's Instagram. Lacy wanted to talk to him while his guard was down, but we never caught up with him, so we came back here."

Jack's chest rose and fell in steady breaths. His expressionless face gave nothing away, but he seemed a little peeved.

I fidgeted. "Shannon was Annie's protégé."

"I know who Shannon is."

I bristled. "Did you know Annie's brother, Ryan Goodman, is in town and that he's the one in the pictures from Gideon's office? He was the guy carrying those boxes."

Jack's eyes widened a fraction before returning to slits and refocusing on Chase. "How much has she told you about what's going on?"

Chase tipped his head left and right, weighing his response. "I don't know. Everything?" He looked at me for confirmation.

Jack expelled a huge amount of air and headed for the door.

I shoved another piece of bacon in my mouth.

Chapter Seventeen

Furry Godmother suggests: When in doubt, talk it out.

"Wait!" I chased Jack onto the porch. "Stop. I needed someone to talk to about all this, okay? It's a lot for me to deal with. Stalkers and killers might be your normal, but this is scary for me." I'd never dealt with the emotional aftermath of being mugged in Arlington before moving home to New Orleans, where I was promptly abducted by a lunatic who thought I'd stolen his diamonds. My anxiety levels were astronomical. I needed to know Jack understood. I'd been seeing a nice therapist since the summer, but it had only been four months, and frankly, I wasn't making great progress.

Jack slowed.

"Hey." I smacked his hand. "Stop."

He turned on me and gave the house a long look. "I came to make sure you're okay. You're obviously doing extremely well this morning, so I'm going to get to work. Enjoy your bacon."

"My bacon? What's that supposed to mean?"

He shook his stubborn head. "I've got to get to work. I'll leave you to it."

I snapped my hand out and caught his wrist. "Jack. Wait. Have I done something wrong?"

He faced off with me, jaw clenched.

"Are you angry that Chase stayed here last night or that I can't seem to stop looking into Annie's murder?"

He crossed his arms, blank cop expression firmly in place. "Both."

My heart thumped impossibly harder. *Both.* "Okay. I get that, but—"

"Do you?" he interrupted. "Do you get it?"

I stumbled mentally over the hurt in his tone. Jack was jealous. *Why?* Unless he was jealous *romantically*. Which made no sense. Jack had never given any indication he considered me as more than a friend and an occasional pain in his backside. I was mostly a citizen he'd sworn to protect, who got herself in a lot of hot water. Nothing I did should matter to him as long as it was legal. I lifted my gaze to Jack's ghostly blues. "No," I admitted, "but will you please come back inside and talk to me? You must have five minutes to spare. You're already here. At least finish your coffee."

He didn't move.

"Please?"

My front door creaked open. Chase stepped onto the porch in my apron. "Isn't anyone eating breakfast? It's getting cold."

I laughed.

Jack muttered something about breakfast and headed back to my house.

I retook my place at the island while Chase rinsed dishes and loaded my dishwasher. He whistled while he worked. I bobbed my head in time.

Jack watched me eat. "What do you need to talk about?"

I arranged the questions in my head by order of importance in case he tried to run off again. "How long have you known about Ryan Goodman?"

"We've been looking for Ryan since Thursday." Jack said, watching Chase as he answered.

"You've known about him since the day we found her?" I said, incredulous. "Why didn't you tell me? How did you know?"

He dragged his heated gaze to me and pulled the badge he wore on a chain around his neck out from beneath his shirt. "You may recall I'm an actual detective."

"All right then, Actual Detective, where is he? Have you questioned him? What did he say?"

Jack lifted his cup and blew over the steaming contents. "He's in the wind."

"Guilty," Chase announced, clicking my dishwasher shut. "Innocent people don't evade the police or hide after their sister is murdered. I called it."

"I agree," I said. "You know what else? That sneaky assistant, Josie, said she didn't know him. I asked her about the guy in basketball shorts carrying boxes into Annie's house, and she claimed to have no idea who he was. She's Annie's personal assistant. She was living there. She had to have met him. Why would she lie?"

"Guilty," Chase repeated. "Oh, or secret lovers."

I looked to Jack for an opinion, but his expression gave nothing away. "Maybe her lie had something to do with the boxes," I suggested. "Ryan was the only one who carried the boxes with *X*s, and Josie tried to take a box from Annie's office that night. That box also had an *X*. They could have been in cahoots for another reason. Maybe they were selling Annie's pieces on the underground." I hopped down and went to find the little pillow I'd brought home with her kittens. "If Josie lied about knowing Annie's brother, we need to talk to her again and see if she'll admit to the reason." I dropped to my knees and looked under my couch and coffee table.

"What are you doing here?" Jack's voice carried in from the next room.

"Hanging," Chase answered. "You?"

Uh-oh. The testosterone tsunami brewing in my kitchen was strong enough to flutter the curtains.

I jumped to my feet like a ninja, pillow in hand. "Found it!" I rushed the little satin treasure back to the kitchen and displayed it on the freshly cleaned chopping block Chase had left on my island. "It looks like a standard decorative number to me. These are really cute in gift baskets with chocolates or perfume." The little rectangle was made of soft navy satin with plenty of stuffing, ruffled edges, and embroidery on top. White threads formed two letters: AL. The famous Annie Lane logo.

Chase poked the pillow with his finger as if it were the Pillsbury Doughboy. "I suppose these will be worth money now that Annie's dead. Do you know if her logo has been trademarked? If these are the last ones ever made, they could sell for a mint in the right circles."

I stabbed a knife through the pillow.

Chase jumped back with a less-than-manly squeal.

I rolled my eyes.

Jack was on his feet, one hand extended toward me. "Lacy?"

Chase moved to Jack's side.

"I'm just seeing what it's made of." I worked my knife through the stitches along one side. "I'm tired and frustrated, and nothing has been what it seemed all week. Why should this be any different?" Someone had hidden jewels in my store last summer, and it occurred to me that this could be another situation like that one. "What if Josie or Annie's brother were stealing from her and walking her stuff right out the front door without her knowing?" I set the knife aside and looked at Jack. "Did Annie make any insurance claims recently before her death? Did she file any reports for missing or stolen items?" I worked my fingers into the stuffing and piled it on the island, then turned the satin inside out. "This is really ugly stitchwork. Obviously outsourced." A pill of disappointment soured in my stomach. Was my hero a fraud? Had she sold the pillows as her own when they weren't? Had she stolen her protégé's designs? What other nuggets of dishonesty would I find if I kept looking?

Jack separated the wad of fiberfill with his fingers. "Nice work, Lacy." He raised a small baggie for inspection. He made a call with his free hand. "We need to pick up Josie Fresca again. Put out a BOLO on Ryan Goodman." He hung up and stared at the little baggie caught between his fingertips. Several brightly colored pills lay inside. "I guess we know what Josie was hiding."

Chase locked his fingers behind his head. "Whoa. How many of those pillows were at her place?"

I reached for the baggie, but Jack pulled it away. "There was a box of them in Annie's office," I told Chase. "And there were a bunch of pictures of her brother carrying similar boxes."

He tucked his shirt into his pants and buttoned it high. "All those boxes with *X*s."

"Yeah."

Chase tied his tie and slid his jacket on. "Okay, so this is good news. If Annie's death was about drug money, then her kittens are safe and so are you. Unless they know you took that." He pointed to the shredded pillow. "In that case, you're a loose end."

"Fantastic."

He smiled. "At least we know why the boxes were all marked with an *X*."

I raised my brows. "We do?"

"That's Molly. X. Ecstasy. It's really popular on the club scene."

"Molly?" I asked. I'd heard about it on the news but had no real firsthand information.

"MDMA," Jack said.

I pursed my lips and made a mental note to research the drug later. "If Josie and Ryan had a Molly business going under Annie's nose, they probably weren't the ones to kill her. They needed her to move their merchandise." I lifted my phone and took a picture of the pills. "Unless she found out and confronted them."

"What are you doing?" Jack asked.

"Keeping a photo log." My cell phone rang, and I froze. "Unknown caller."

Chase extended his hand. "Do you want me to answer it?"

Jack narrowed his eyes. "You think that's the guy with the song?"

I lifted my shoulders to my ears. "It can go to voice mail."

Chase took the phone and hit the speaker button. "Answer," he whispered. "You've got a cop here."

Jack nodded stiffly.

Right. Besides, it was only a call. No matter how many times I heard the music, it couldn't hurt me. I exhaled slowly and answered as normally as possible. "Hello?"

The dreary, ominous music began.

I covered my mouth with one hand and pointed frantically at the phone with my other.

"You follow me. I follow you. You follow me. I follow you." The creepy voice promised all my worst nightmares.

I considered covering my ears, but it was too late. I knew the words. They echoed in my head most of the day. I was never alone, not at work and not at home. I rubbed the chill from my arms.

Jack took the phone from Chase. "This is Detective Jack Oliver."

The line went dead.

Jack made another call on his cell phone. "Yeah. I need a trace on the last number to call five-oh-four, five-two-two . . ." He repeated my phone number to whomever he'd called.

Chase stepped around Jack and into my personal space. "Why don't you stay with me until Jack figures that out?" Worry tugged the corners of his eyes and mouth. "I have plenty of room. I'll be a perfect gentleman."

"No. It's okay," I said at the same time Jack said, "No."

Something that looked a lot like hurt flashed in Chase's eyes. He turned his back to Jack. "Then stay with your folks. Please."

"You know I can't." I hated the grim expression on his normally jovial face. "Maybe I'll buy a whistle."

He laughed. "Don't you have a license to carry a concealed weapon?"

Memories of my mugging rushed back, yanking my already wild heartbeat to a sprinter's pace. "Yes, but I don't want to shoot anyone!"

Chase pulled me into a hug and chuckled as he stroked my back. "I don't think a whistle is the answer. Why'd you bother getting the permit if you won't carry?"

It wasn't the first time I'd been asked. "I like having rights and knowing the laws, and I happen to believe strongly in education and options." My chin jutted forward. "And also in whistles."

He released me and pulled keys from his pocket. "Fine. I'll stay here again tonight." He planted a kiss on my cheek and let himself out.

Jack stared at the closed door until Chase's car revved to life out front. "He's not staying here again, and for the record, I don't approve of whatever you two were up to last night."

My head spun. "What are you talking about?"

"Chase Hawthorne should not know so much about this investigation. Neither should you, for that matter."

I crossed my arms. "Now that I know Ryan's in town, and he had a possible reason to attack his sister, I want to go back to the French Market and see the artist making those big animal heads." He didn't keep records or pay taxes, but maybe he'd remember Ryan's face if he'd bought a mask from him.

"Which artist?"

"Come on. You drive." I snapped the lid back onto my coffee. "Where do you do the most Molly busts in the Quarter? I'll show Ryan's and Josie's pictures around. See if anyone knows them."

Jack swung a thickly muscled forearm in front of me like a guard gate. "Slow down. First of all, I'm homicide, not narcotics. I don't handle drug busts. Neither do you. I need to make some calls before I'll know where Molly's most popular in the Quarter. Second, once I have that information, I'll let the narcotics division handle the investigation from there." He pointed to himself. "Homicide." He pointed to me. "Shop owner." He wagged the finger between us. "Not narcotics."

I loaded Penelope into her carrier. "Can we drop Penelope off at Furry Godmother? She likes to play with Spot, and Imogene's opening for me today. She'll be glad for the company since I'm going to be late."

Jack took Penelope's carrier from me and motioned me into the day.

I set my alarm and locked up. "Chase can stay with me if he wants to, by the way. Don't think you're the boss of me because I'm letting you drive me to work."

He wrenched the passenger door of his truck open and waited for me to climb inside, then passed Penelope to me in her carrier. "You *let* me drive you? The way I recall, you demanded I drive you. Big difference. Huge." He shut the door and rounded the hood to the driver's side.

I scrolled the Internet on my phone. "I'm going to show that artist making papier-mâché animal heads at the Market a picture of Dylan Latherope, too. I don't know why I didn't think of showing pictures before. Maybe he'll recognize one of my suspects. I've been thinking it was Dylan in the cat costume, but maybe it's Ryan. I'm going to ask about Josie, too. She could've bought the mask and given it to Ryan. She's definitely not the one wearing it. Whoever's in those black coveralls is broad. Josie's a bean pole." I held up my pinky finger for visual reference. "I haven't heard from Dylan Latherope since you threatened him with your personal restraining order, but he wasn't in the footage I found online of Annie's Manhattan memorial. I bet he's up to something. I should call my dad and tell him to batten down the hatches. It doesn't take a genius to connect me to the local veterinarian. Once Latherope realizes that, he's sure to go badger Dad."

Jack listened as I talked through the gobs of information flooding my head. We made it to Furry Godmother in record time. Imogene was just turning the sign from Closed to Open when Jack pulled half onto the curb out front.

I hauled Penelope's carrier out with me. "Good morning, Imogene. Would you mind keeping Penelope here for a while? I've got a new lead on the guy who's stalking me, and Jack said he'll take me to check it out."

She looked at the open truck door behind me. "Good morning, Detective Oliver," she drawled. "How are you doing this fine morning?"

"Very well, Miss Imogene. You look pretty as ever. How're the grandkids?"

I let my head fall forward. I was in too big of a hurry to wait while they exchanged southern niceties. I rolled my head up and made big puppy dog eyes at her. "I won't be long, and I really appreciate it."

She took Penelope and waved me off. "Go on. You two kids have fun. Hope you put that dime in your shoe. Don't try to hold me responsible if you didn't."

I climbed back inside Jack's truck and shut the door. I couldn't remember where her weird dime was.

Jack powered my window down. "What was that?" he asked Imogene, who was saying something.

I curled my fingers on my lap, itching to run to the market if we didn't start driving soon.

Imogene stepped closer to the truck. "I just wondered if you two were getting breakfast somewhere nice. There won't be many folks to talk to in the Quarter just yet."

I looked at the clock on Jack's dashboard. Eight fifty.

Jack leaned across me and spoke through the open window at my side. "I'm sure she'll find something for me to get into."

Imogene laughed and headed into Furry Godmother with my cat.

The weight of defeat pressed my shoulders forward. "I guess I can go in and work for a while. The market won't be busy for a few hours." Why was it so early? It felt as if I'd been up for hours.

Jack gave me a side glance. "Can I trust you to stay here if I let you out of my truck?"

"Let me out?" I twisted on the seat to gape at him. "I'm not a prisoner." *Am I?* I gave him my business face. "I'm a grown woman. I can go anywhere I want."

"No."

"What do you mean, no? Yes."

"No. You can't do anything you want because you want to come up with cockamamie ways to twist yourself into my homicide investigation. That's called obstruction." He broke the final word into syllables.

"That's ridiculous. My ideas are fantastic."

He stared.

I tapped my foot against the floorboard, begging my brain for another fantastic idea. It was a little too early to look for artists at the market and way too early to question night clubbers about drugs. "How about we visit Shannon Martin until the market opens? Chase and I never found him last night, so I'd planned to go see him this morning anyway. Wherever he is now, he's probably hungover and willing to answer my questions if I promise to go away. Take me there. Let's talk to him."

Jack eased his truck into traffic. "This is why I can't leave you alone."

"You're having fun," I teased. "Admit it."

He didn't admit it, but something new blinked through his blank cop stare. "Am not."

Chapter Eighteen

Furry Godmother's words of warning:
Be prepared. Life can change on a dime.

I scrolled through Shannon's Instagram feed as we drove toward his apartment. Two new pictures emerged. "He's at Café Du Monde."

Jack changed direction quickly. "Which one?"

"At the market." Yes, Café Du Monde had more than one location, but the one that counted was at the French Market, steps from Jackson Square, nestled in the heart of the French Quarter. I'd grown up eating beignets there, and so had my mother. In fact, so had my grandparents. Any other location was subpar at best, though I was admittedly biased.

"I thought this guy was supposed to be hungover and ready to answer all your questions?"

"Me, too." I unfastened my seat belt. "I'll be right back."

I hurried across the street toward the oldest café in the city. The beloved green-and-white-striped awning ruffled gently in the wind. A line of customers wrapped the perimeter of tables and stretched onto the sidewalk. Scents of chicory and powdered sugar floated to my nose.

I scanned the scene, praying I hadn't missed him again.

A dramatic-looking man with gel-spiked hair and a dancer's figure leaned against the counter near a napkin dispenser, chatting up a café worker who was busy filling orders. I gave his latest selfie one more look. "Gotcha."

I cut through the line and stopped close enough to shake his hand. "Shannon Martin?"

"Yeah?" He swung his head my way with a wide, toothy smile. His whiskey-laced breath nearly knocked me over.

I covered my nose discreetly. If anyone lit a match while he was talking, the whole place would go up in flames. His outfit hadn't changed since Chase and I had started tracking him last night. Shannon wasn't at home nursing a hangover—because he was still going strong in the Quarter.

"Hi. I'm Lacy Crocker. I follow you online." I took a big step back and attempted to seem starstruck. "I'm so excited to see you're in my city. Though I'm also really sorry to hear about your mentor, Annie Lane. That must be really hard for you."

The smile melted off his face. "Yeah. I'm heartbroken." He collected his cup and a napkin from the counter. "I've got to go."

I followed. "Can you believe someone walked into her house and whacked her on the head like that? I'll bet there aren't many people she would've let inside." I sidestepped spilled drinks and fallen napkins as we weaved through the labyrinth of occupied tables. "She would've let you in, though, right?"

Shannon stopped fleeing and turned on me. "Who are you?"

"Lacy Crocker." I stretched a hand in his direction. "I run a pet boutique on Magazine Street."

He scoffed. "I meant, how are you important? Why are you here? Are you a reporter or something?"

"I told you. I run a pet boutique. Do I look like a reporter?"

He examined my outfit, unimpressed. "You look like a church lady," he slurred.

I huffed and adjusted my big red belt. "I was in a hurry." He approached the corner at a pace I could match. "Can we talk about you and Annie?"

The light changed at the corner, and Shannon hustled into the crosswalk. His black skinny jeans hung from his svelte figure. The fitted rock star T-shirt barely reached his waistband. "No. I'm leaving. I need a drink, and I want you to go away." He looked up and down the street as if he was expecting someone. Sunlight glinted off the diamond stud in his nose.

I'd finally caught him, and he was getting away. "Wait. Please don't go yet. When was the last time you saw Annie? Where were you Thursday afternoon?"

Shannon flung an arm overhead and lingered in the middle of the street, apparently trying to gain the attention of any driver willing to stop. "I was at an exhibition on Royale Street. Check my Instagram, and stop following me, or I'll call the police, Lacy Crocker from Magazine Street." A motorcycle pulled over, and he climbed aboard. Shannon whispered something to the driver and wrapped his arms around a man who looked like he'd just hit the jackpot.

"Who would want to hurt Annie?" I asked the puff of black exhaust as they motored away.

Jack pushed off the crumbling brick building on the corner and headed my way. "I'm guessing that wasn't his Uber."

"More like his getaway car. He wasn't helpful, but he didn't do it. He said he was at an exhibition on Royale Thursday." I scrolled backward through his photo account, looking for proof to support the alibi. "It's true." I turned my phone screen in Jack's direction. "He took a ton of pictures that put him in the Quarter all afternoon."

"I'll still need to talk to him," Jack said. "Might as well check the market while we're here. It's early, but I'd hate to waste the trip. If we miss the guy making papier-mâché animal heads, I'll come back later."

We were too early. The market was a bust.

Jack drove me back to work. He got a text several blocks from Furry Godmother and practically peeled away before I had both feet on the sidewalk.

I opened the shop door with a sigh. Chasing clues was exhausting. It was good to be back where I belonged. A handful of customers perused the shelves, unaffected by my entrance.

Imogene took notice. "How was breakfast?"

I stuffed my purse under the counter behind the register. "I didn't get any breakfast, but I did get blown off by one suspect and eluded by another. Shannon wanted nothing to do with me, and the artist wasn't at the market. No one knew who he was or how to reach him."

She frowned. "Today's off to a rough start. How was your night? Was the dinner good?"

I rolled my head over my shoulders. "I missed the actual dinner portion of dinner. How about you? How was your night?"

"Good. Veda finally got that nasty spirit. Maybe we can go back to playing cards now."

I smiled. "That's great. So what did she do with him?"

Imogene made a face, as if my question was absurd. "She put him back in the basement where he belongs."

"Of course." I nodded. "Well I'm glad that's taken care of so the two of you can relax."

"Excellent advice. You should try to do the same."

"I'm working on it." I finger-combed my windblown hair. "Jack's putting the narcotics unit on alert about a possible link we made to drugs and Annie's death. It's starting to look like none of this is about her kittens."

Imogene furrowed her brows. "You don't sound convinced."

"I am. My head's a little fuzzy. Tired I think." Something niggled at the back of my mind. I swiped my phone to life and flipped through the pictures on Shannon's Instagram feed from Thursday afternoon. There were plenty of photos, but if I were being picky, I'd say that Shannon was conveniently missing for a two-hour window near Annie's time of death. Maybe he'd decided that he didn't need his face in every photo, or maybe he'd left his phone with a friend as an alibi.

I texted the new idea to Jack. If I was on the right trail, and Shannon had intentionally left his phone to create an alibi for murder, then I'd solved the case.

The murder would've been premeditated. I pinched my bottom lip between my thumb and first finger. The crime scene suggested an act of passion and a weapon of convenience.

"Are you sure you're okay?" Imogene asked.

"No." I set my phone aside and took some cleansing breaths. "I'm not. Everything about this case is disjointed. I don't know which way is up, or if there is an up."

I grabbed a pencil and sketched some very ugly chickens. "I might as well get started on making Mom's pins." Though, no one would ever wear them, and I couldn't tell her what I knew. There was no way the Jazzy Chicks would raise more money than the Llama Mamas if the Llama Mamas were in a parade. "What do you think?" I turned a sketch toward Imogene.

Her eyes widened. "I think nice people doing bad things makes for bad juju, and you don't need any more of that." She turned on her black orthopedic heels and went to check on the customers.

I started over. She was right. On the off chance Mom won, the pins should be glamorous and eye-catching so that folks who saw the Llamas wearing them would want to know more about the Chicks. Making ugly pins would do more harm to the Chicks than the Llamas.

My phone rang, and I broke the lead on my pencil.

Jack's face appeared on the little screen. I heaved a sigh of relief and cradled the phone between my ear and shoulder. "Hey. Any luck finding Shannon or Ryan or Josie or the cat-head maker?"

"Nope, but I learned a few things you need to know."

"Like?" I stepped away from the sketchpad.

"According to his file. Ryan Goodman has some anger issues. He's had a few arrests for bar brawls and several tickets for road rage behaviors. He's even checked himself in and out of rehab several times. Do your best to steer clear of this kid."

"Anger issues." I repeated his words back to him. "Did he have enough issues to kill his sister?" It would explain why he went to ground when she died instead of coming out to speak for her or the family. The stints in rehab said everything else. "I'd bet my best recipe that Annie intentionally kept his existence a secret. Either so Ryan's problems couldn't sully her brand or in the hopes that avoiding undo stress from the spotlight would give him a fighting chance at true rehabilitation." I almost couldn't blame her. *Almost*. Being her brother's advocate would have done far more for everyone involved than treating him like the family wart.

"I'll know more once I talk to him. I also found rave busts in three cities last year that occurred within fifteen miles of a hotel where Annie and Josie were staying on business, but it'll take time to match the pills in your pillow with pills taken from the busts. All the information I have is circumstantial," Jack said. "Just stay away from Ryan, and while you're at it, stay away from Dylan Latherope, too. That guy's squirrelly. I ran into him after I dropped you off, and we had a little chat. I'm not convinced he's a killer, but he's definitely off his nut. Speaking of your best recipe," he said.

I walked mentally backward. What had I said about my recipes? "If you want one of my recipes, just ask."

"Can I have one of your recipes?" His voice was borderline playful, a sound I rather enjoyed.

"Which one? I'll text it to you."

"Don't do that," he said. "No texting. Your recipes are proprietary."

I waited several beats, but he didn't continue. "And?"

"Are you still willing to talk to strangers about Tabitha?"

I straightened my posture. "Yes, please."

"I spoke to the Grandpa Smacker production manager about you. I delivered one of your pupcakes to his office and pitched a pet line for local stores this fall."

My jaw dropped. "You stole a pupcake, and I had no idea. You're good."

"You offered to help. I'm taking you up on it."

"Wow." I rocked back on my heels, baffled. "Corruption is real."

"Not funny."

"Wait. Did you say you want to add a pet line at Grandpa Smacker? With my stuff?"

"If you have a legitimate reason to be at my grandfather's company a few hours a week, you might have time to overhear something useful to my investigation. Everyone clams up when I'm around. Apparently I'm intimidating."

I steepled my fingers and smiled against the phone.

"What do you think?"

"Oh," I dragged the word into several syllables. "That's clever."

"And the company pays well for this kind of contract. I wouldn't ask you to do something like this for free. It's business. An official Grandpa Smacker contract, if we can convince the board that they need it."

I chewed my thumbnail.

"I know you want to upgrade your kitchen. This would easily do all that and more."

Images of granite countertops and stainless steel appliances paraded through my brain alongside six-burner ranges and double ovens. Side-by-side refrigerators with large-capacity freezers fanned their doors at me. I didn't like the idea of taking money from him, but I also couldn't give up my recipes. One maybe, but a line worth? How many was that?

"This could be the deal that gets me answers and my grandpa some justice."

"Okay." How could I say no?

"Great. Pick the recipe you want to test run, and I'll set the appointment with marketing and management."

I clapped silently. I wasn't sure which news was more exciting—an opportunity to make Furry Godmother pupcakes a national brand or the fact Jack had asked me to get intimately involved in his personal investigation. "You trust me," I teased.

"Yeah. I do."

"Thank you," I said. I wouldn't let Jack down.

I smiled absently at a car parked outside my shop window where my little VW normally sat. "I almost forgot you drove me here, and I'm stuck."

"No. You're not. What time do you want me to pick you up tonight?"

"Six?"

"See you then." He disconnected.

I stewed. I didn't plan on going anywhere, but I missed having the option.

I sketched another chicken button. Maybe the key was to make the buttons ridiculously large. Large buttons were embarrassing and easy to read. Like tiny billboards of free advertising.

Imogene moseyed back to my side when the last few customers filtered out. "I like that button."

"Thanks."

She nudged me with an elbow. "Did you say there are drugs involved in this mess?"

"Yeah."

"Maybe you'd better listen to that handsome detective. Drugs are bad. Drug users? Worse. Dealers? Awful. Nothing good can come from bothering those kinds of folks."

I didn't disagree. "The drugs." I snapped upright. I'd told Josie about Gideon's stalker wall. There were pictures of Ryan carrying the drug pillows on there. A cat-man was seen fleeing the animal shelter. Ryan probably went there to steal the photos and ran into Gideon, so he knocked him out. Latherope wasn't the cat-man. Ryan was.

I texted my theory to Jack.

He didn't respond.

I grabbed my purse and dug through a mess of tangled receipts, open packets of catnip, and loose chewing gum for one small rectangular piece of information. Annie's lawyer's number. I dialed and crossed my fingers I got him and not a voice mail. My mind whirled too fast to leave a message.

"Bryce Kenney," he answered.

"Hello, this is Lacy Crocker. Is this a bad time?"

"Not at all—how can I help, Miss Crocker?" His voice was accompanied by the click-clack of a keyboard.

"Did you know Annie's brother, Ryan, is in town?"

The typing stopped. "No," he answered hesitantly, "but Ryan tends to come and go on his own schedule. Has he been in contact with you?"

"No. I'm just chasing a hunch. Have you met him?"

"Once or twice over the years, but very informally. Why do you ask?"

I gnawed the sensitive skin of my lower lip, already raw from the past five days of nervous nibbling. "How was his relationship with Annie?"

"Miss Crocker," Bryce whispered. "Has something happened?"

"No. I thought you might have some insight into him or his relationship with Annie."

He cleared his throat. "Perhaps speak with Josie. I'm afraid I can't help."

"Talking to that woman is like riding the Tilt-a-Whirl. The last time I finished, my head was spinning, but I hadn't gotten anywhere."

He chuckled. "That sounds right on par with my experiences as well."

"Does the name Shannon Martin sound familiar?"

"No. Should it?"

"Probably not." I slumped. "Thank you for your time." I disconnected and went back to sketching victory pins.

"Look out," Imogene warned.

A heartbeat later, my mom blew through the door like a Louisiana hurricane. Her sleek bob was mussed, and her eyes were wild.

I lowered my pencil slowly. "Hi, Mom. Everything okay?"

She dropped her oversized designer bag on the counter and clapped her hands. "I'm here for a look at the ugly chicken pins. The ones those Llama Mamas will be wearing all month long."

"I'm working on them now."

"Great. Can I see one?"

I slid the newest drawing in her direction. "I'm still in the drafting phase. What do you think of these?"

Confusion lined her brow. "They're pretty. They're not supposed to be pretty. That's the point."

I curled my toes inside my sandals. A little voice warned me to tread carefully. Land mines ahead. "I think you should have pins that represent your chicks. Something snazzy and adorable. Something you'd be proud to wear."

She scoffed. "Honey, please. This is a competition for a reason. The losers have to be punished."

"What if you're the loser?"

"Can't happen. I've just confirmed another generous donation from my old sorority sisters. I should've thought of them sooner. They've never ceased to provide for me in my times of need."

I kept a lid on my thoughts about this situation qualifying as a time of need. To her, I supposed it was. If she didn't get money fast, she might have to wear an ugly pin. Gasp.

She hiked her bag back onto one shoulder. "The bond between sorority sisters is powerful. You'd know that if you'd stayed the course."

I tapped my toe silently. "That was your course. Not mine. I never wanted to be a sorority girl."

"Or a Crocker," she said, suddenly sullen, "but I supposed you're stuck with that. I want to see a mock-up of my pin by the weekend. An ugly one." She blew Imogene air kisses and walked out.

I tipped forward and rolled my head against the counter.

Imogene's perfume arrived before she did. She patted my back. "Your mama didn't mean that. She's under a lot of pressure."

I wrenched myself upright. "This day is made of yuck."

"Mm-hmm," she hummed. "You better go home and get my dime back in your shoe, because it's about to get a whole lot worse."

I followed her gaze through the front window. Dylan Latherope stood outside the café across the street, staring at my shop.

"I'll be right back." I marched outside, phone in hand.

He moved immediately in my direction. "Do you have them? My babies? Cotton and Cashmere?" His voice was weak and sniveling.

I squared my shoulders and tipped my chin. "No. I don't. I'm no longer the caretaker of Annie's kittens, so you can stop following me."

His red-rimmed eyes widened in desperation. "Where are they? What have you done?"

"The kittens are safe. They just aren't with me. I didn't like being stalked, so they were placed in a safer location until Annie's estate can go through probate."

"Who?" he demanded. "Who stalked them?" He whipped his hand forward and snagged hold of my arm.

I wiggled, unsuccessful at loosening his grasp. "You! Now let me go, or I'm calling Detective Oliver." I lifted the phone with my free arm. Jack's face was on the screen, ready to save the day. My thumb hovered over the green call button.

"Those are my cats," Latherope wailed. "Not yours. Not hers. I found them. I brought them home and nursed them to health after some idiot tossed them out on the roadside. I named them, fed them, cared for them. They're mine, and Annie took them just to hurt me." He yanked my arm and tightened his grip until I felt my pulse beating beneath his meaty fingers.

Panic whooshed through me like water through a broken dam. I lifted my right foot and slammed my heel into his toes. Unsatisfied I yanked my knee upward until it connected with his crotch, and he yelped. He released my arm in favor of cradling his injury.

I ran for Furry Godmother, calling Jack as I ran. He didn't answer.

9-1-1 seemed like overkill.

From the safety of my shop window, I watched Mr. Latherope climb awkwardly into his SUV and inch away.

Imogene clucked her tongue. "Like I said. You'd better fetch that dime."

Chapter Nineteen

Furry Godmother supports the right to privacy. She's sadly alone.

Jack went to find Mr. Latherope, but I hadn't heard back by closing time. I locked up shop and got a ride home from Imogene. I couldn't help wondering about the implications of Latherope's behavior. If he'd grabbed me, a virtual stranger, on a public sidewalk, what was he capable of doing in private to someone he knew well and had fought with many times?

I fed Penelope and Buttercup their dinners, then settled in to make some headway on the llama hats and scarves. If my designs were headed down a parade route, I had more riding on this order than keeping Mrs. Hams happy. If the right person saw them, they could be featured in a local article or a national magazine. I'd gladly accept any and all coverage of my work. My partnership with Annie Lane was out the window, but I hadn't lost hope.

The scarves went quickly, and the finished products were spectacular. Definitely a fit for any New Orleans parade. Unfortunately, the repetitive process of stitching sequins had left too much time for idle thoughts, and I'd concocted a lengthy and heartbreaking list of the people in Annie's orbit with a motive to kill. Her brother and assistant were at the top of my list—drug dealers in the wind. Closely behind them was Shannon Martin. Annie had put the famous AL label on his designs. Was that agreed upon? Or had she stolen them outright? Could she also have stolen her crazy ex-husband's kittens, as he claimed? Animal activists, as a whole, were at the bottom of my list. No solid reason to hurt her, but they seemed collectively off-balance when it came to her.

I'd almost forgotten about Gideon, the Heart to Heart shelter owner. I took a break and texted Scarlet:

Need to brainstorm. Can you talk?

I hated to call when there was a new baby in the house. I'd seen what Scarlet could do to people who woke the baby, and I didn't need that kind of wrath.

While I waited for her to respond, I called the hospital where Gideon was in recovery and posed as his sister. The nurse who answered refused to tell me anything about him but slipped by saying I should stop by in person after dinner. I reasoned that meant he was awake but not taking calls. An unconscious man wouldn't have dinner. If I wanted to talk to Gideon, I'd have to go to the hospital and convince him to talk.

My phone buzzed with a response from Scarlet.

Chase is here. Should I sneak away?

I answered,

Bring him.

The more input the better.

On our way.

I smiled. A phone call would've worked, but alone time with Scarlet was better.

I grabbed a string cheese and an apple for dinner and got back to work.

Forty minutes later, headlights flashed across my front window. Penelope jumped onto the sill for a closer look. Her long tail swished over the ledge behind her.

I shifted the llama scarves onto the coffee table and went to open the door.

Scarlet jogged onto the porch and pulled me into a hug. "Hey, you. I'm so glad you called. I want to hear everything about your life and eat dinner with someone who won't poop or puke on me."

"No promises," I laughed.

She took my hand and beamed. "I brought a surprise."

Chase climbed out of the shiny red sports car at the curb. He smiled over two pizza boxes and a pile of chip bags. "I hope you're hungry."

"You have no idea." I locked the door behind him and followed the tangy scents of tomato sauce and hot, salty cheese to the kitchen. Chase unloaded his arms and spread the bounty on my cheery white countertop.

I grabbed three glasses from the drying rack and filled them with ice. "You guys didn't have to bring dinner. This is too much."

Chase cracked open a two liter of soda and filled the glasses. "I'm terrible at making decisions, so I overorder. It's my thing."

"In that case, I accept." I helped myself to a big slice of veggie lovers and subdued a moan.

"Okay." Scarlet rubbed her palms together. "What's up?"

"I need help with a plan."

Chase crossed his arms and leaned back against my counter. "Is this about what happened earlier with that designer's ex-husband?"

I gave Scarlet the stink eye. "You told him about that?"

She shrugged. "I was upset for you. This mess with Annie Lane is scary, and you're right in the middle of it. Your house was broken into. You were attacked in broad daylight. You're being stalked by a guy in a cat costume." She paled as she spoke. "Actually, Carter and I were discussing this earlier, and he suggested I take you and Poppet to my family's home in Martha's Vineyard until this blows over."

"That's a fantastic idea," Chase said. "I vote for that one."

I bit into my pizza and wrapped the stringy cheese around one finger until it broke. I chewed methodically before responding. "First of all, thank you, and Carter, for a really wonderful offer."

She arched a brow. "But?"

"But," I continued as graciously as possible, "I don't want to."

"Of course not," she deadpanned. "You're clearly in danger here, so where else would you want to be?"

"I need to be here to keep my store alive." I wiped my mouth on a paper towel. "Plus I think I know how to wrap this investigation up."

Chase barked a laugh, then reached for a second slice of pizza without further comment.

I returned my attention to Scarlet. "I have a plan."

She gave me her business face. "Let's hear it."

I filled Scarlet in about the pills hidden inside the little pillows. Shockingly, Chase didn't contribute to my explanation, despite the fact that he'd been there when I'd discovered them. "So." I pulled a tiny pillow from my sewing bag on the counter. "I made this at work."

Chase took the pillow from my hands. "It looks just like the one you tore up." He raised confused eyes to mine. "Jack took it as evidence."

"Correct. So I made another. It wasn't hard. The pillows were clearly mass-produced. No craftsmanship at all." It seemed everything I thought I knew about Annie had been skewed and filtered for the press. Smoke and mirrors. In truth, she had an ugly divorce from Latherope, an addict brother she hid from the spotlight, and she sent her pillows to be sewn by laborers, when it's clearly stated on her website that any item bearing he famous AL logo was handcrafted by her. I pushed irrational feelings of personal betrayal from my mind. "What's important is that Josie doesn't know Jack took the pillow from me. What if I invite her over for tea and pretend this is the pillow I took from her house?"

"But she's on the lam," Scarlet said. "Why would she come here for tea?"

"She doesn't know *I* know she's on the lam." I took the pillow back from Chase and tossed it to Scarlet. "So I'm going to open an Instagram account and put up a picture of my pillow, then tag Josie in it. I'll caption it with something like, 'Mourning the loss of my personal hero. Thankful for this token I kept after my last visit.' Josie will see it and think I have some of her drugs. She'll have to come."

Scarlet nodded slowly. "That's a solid way to reach her if she's hiding. She's probably ditched her phone by now. And you're right. She'll want the pillow back."

"When she reaches out to me, I'll invite her for tea."

Chase was statue still and slightly pale. "You're talking about a criminal. A drug dealer at best. A murderer at worst. You can't invite her over and provoke her. That's a terrible plan—possibly the worst I've ever heard."

I raised both palms in frustration. "This is why we're brainstorming. I need to talk through things."

He relaxed by a fraction. "So you're just making plans. You don't seriously intend to confront her?"

I dragged my gaze back to Scarlet. Chase was starting to sound like Jack. "What if I meet her somewhere in public instead, like a café for lunch or coffee? I can download an app on my phone and record our conversation, so whatever she says will be documented."

Scarlet frowned. "I don't think you can use a recording against a person that doesn't know they're being taped."

Chase rubbed the back of his neck. "Actually, she can in the state of Louisiana, but just because it's admissible as evidence doesn't mean it'll be accepted without predicate."

I smiled. "You're a lawyer."

He raised his eyebrows. "Yeah."

It hadn't sunk in before that moment. Chase was back to stay. He'd set down roots and had taken up the law. I shook off the weird smile creeping on my face. "What's predicate?"

"Well, you'd have to prove it's Josie's voice on the tape. You'd also have to prove you didn't doctor the recording in any way. You can't present parts of a conversation that sound incriminating. It has to be admitted as a whole."

"Okay. Easy. No tampering." I shot Scarlet a face. He made it sound like I was angling to do something sketchy.

"Right," Chase continued, "but even then, a recording created by a cell phone app might not be determined as capable of making the kind of recording that guarantees all that, plus clarity and accuracy. Wind, background noises, anything that can muddle or distort her voice or words will be a problem."

I deflated. "I could still try."

"You can try, but I think there are too many what-ifs to risk meeting with this woman anywhere."

Scarlet hopped off her stool and retrieved a bottle of water from the fridge. "I can't have any more soda. The caffeine keeps Poppet up." She cracked the lid and sipped gingerly. "If you get to talk to Josie, what do you plan to ask? What would you gain? It's not like she'd admit to committing a crime."

A new idea emerged. "What if I put a tracking chip in the pillow?" I dropped my chin and widened my eyes. "How about that? Then Jack could find her."

Chase tapped his phone, fully ignoring me.

Scarlet looked mad. "Where do you buy a tracking chip?"

"I'm not sure. eBay?" I said.

She looked to Chase.

He shrugged. "eBay has everything."

I stuffed a chip into my mouth and crunched. "Once she has the pillow, Jack can track her. Then she won't be in the wind. No. Wait." I shook my head and helped myself to another chip. "She might rip the pillow open as soon as she leaves, find the tracker, and bring her crazy boyfriend to get me." I stomped one foot. "Darn it."

Scarlet tapped her nails on the counter. "I like where this is going, but you need a better plan."

Maybe Jack didn't need to track her with a chip. "Maybe Jack could just be at the café when she arrives and cuff her."

"Better." Scarlet nodded.

I finished my slice of pizza, lost in thought. "You know the worst part? Even if I somehow flushed Josie out and Jack got his hands on her, I don't think it would get us any closer to finding Annie's killer. Josie and Ryan are wanted for drugs, not murder. Ryan was Annie's brother. I can't imagine him killing his own sister. Can you?"

Scarlet gasped. "Heavens, no."

"Spoken like a couple of only children," Chase said. "Siblings fight. Accidents happen. Also, some people are certifiable. And if Ryan was using drugs at the time, he's capable of all sorts of things. In case you're keeping track, that's one more reason to stay away from both of them."

"All right, but there has to be something I can do," I said. "I'm going bananas sitting around wondering when the next awful thing will happen."

Chase refilled our cups with soda. "You could take Imogene up on her offer to contact Annie. Get the facts straight from the ghost's mouth."

I groaned. "I need a serious suggestion, please."

"That *was* a serious suggestion."

"Chase," I scolded. "You're an attorney at the state's leading law firm. You're bright and educated. How can you buy into that junk?"

"How could you grow up in the country's most haunted city and not? You know what else I bought the minute I joined the family firm? A whole case of Imogene's other-lawyer-be-stupid spells."

"Oh my word."

Scarlet laughed. "I think we should spend some more time working on the plan. Let's sleep on it and regroup tomorrow."

I rested my elbows on the island beside the pizza boxes. "I should probably get Jack involved somehow." Not that he'd bother hearing me out. "Maybe I could call him at the last minute, once it's too late for him to interfere and stop me."

Someone pounded on my door.

Scarlet shot me a puzzled look. "Expecting anyone else?"

"No." I looked to Chase, hoping he'd accompany me to the door in case the cat-man was feeling frisky tonight.

Chase sealed the pizza box lids and stacked our leftovers in a tidy pile, utterly ignoring me.

The pounding continued, but Chase didn't look up.

"I guess I'll get that." I moved slowly through my home, angling for a look through the front window. A big black truck sat at the curb.

I opened the door. "Jack? We were just talking about you."

He brushed past me to the kitchen.

"Sure. Come on in." I locked up and putted behind him. "Are all the men in my life acting strangely tonight, or is it just me?" I asked Scarlet.

Jack stopped in the kitchen doorway and shook Chase's hand.

Scarlet leaned around the wall of testosterone. "Men always act strangely. That's why God created women. To help them."

Jack glared.

"What?" she said. "It's in the Bible."

He braced broad hands over narrow hips and nodded at Chase. "Thanks for the heads-up."

"No problem, man." Chase hefted the leftovers off my counter and stepped into my personal space. He formed an impish grin. "Sorry, Lacy, but I don't want you to get hurt, and I'd rather you argue with him than me. I'm the good guy. I saved your cat." He dropped a kiss on my cheek and headed for the door.

Scarlet hugged me good-bye. "I'm his ride. Guess it's time to go. Nice to see you again, Jack. Call me later, Lacy."

The door sucked shut behind them. And I was alone with a very angry detective.

"What do you think you're doing?" Jack grouched. "You know whatever you're up to is disastrous when Chase sells you out. He's usually your biggest enabler."

"I'm not up to anything. We were brainstorming," I grumbled. Didn't anyone know the rules of brainstorming? No tattling. "I can't believe he ratted me out."

"Believe it."

"Is this a scold-and-run or are you staying for a visit?"

He looked me over. The flat cop expression gave nothing away.

I sighed. "Can I get you anything? Water? Coffee? String cheese?"

"No."

"Fine." I padded to the couch in my living room and pulled a llama scarf onto my lap. "At least sit while you yell."

He lowered his lean frame onto the cushion beside me. His dark jeans and black boots were a strong contrast against my cream upholstery and muted-gray throw rug. The sleeves of his navy button-down were rolled to his elbows, and the white T-shirt underneath was fully exposed. He'd unbuttoned the entire shirt at some point.

"Bad day?" I asked.

"Long day. I was on my way home when Hawthorne put up the bat signal."

I tucked a foot underneath me and looked as serious as possible. "You're Batman in this scenario?"

"I'm always Batman."

I threaded a needle with a giggle. "Thank you for not yelling."

"I'm not a yeller."

No. He was a brooder, and something was definitely wrong tonight. "Did you ever catch up to Mr. Latherope?"

"Nope." Jack dropped his head back and stared at my ceiling. "He's gone. Ryan's gone. Josie's gone."

"This case is getting to you?" I guessed.

"It's chaos. I don't like chaos."

I stopped stitching. "I'm making it that way, aren't I?"

"You aren't helping." He didn't look my way. "I like control, but when you get involved, I'm torn down the middle. I can't be all-in on my job if half my head's worried about whether you're going to do something stupid."

"Then don't worry about me. Focus on your job." If he liked control, he'd never like me any better than he did now. A thorn of disappointment pricked my chest, and I mentally flicked it away.

Jack shifted on the cushion. He dug into his shirt pocket. "I protect and serve. That makes you my job, especially since you seem to need more protection than everyone else combined." He held a closed fist out. "Here."

"What is it?"

"Open your hand, and I'll give it to you."

I set my work aside and uncurled my fingers. I searched his face for some clue about the gift, unable to imagine what he might have for me that fit into one hand.

He placed a small pink whistle on my palm. "I assume you haven't gotten your own yet."

A strange emotion tugged in my chest. "Thank you."

"Yep." He turned his face back to the ceiling and kicked off his boots.

I relaxed beside him. The little whistle had a tiny daisy on each side with white petals and bright-yellow centers. "I really don't have a plan, and right before you knocked, I said I wanted to include you in whatever I came up with."

He turned his face my way. "Well, let's hear what you've got so far."

"Yeah?"

"Why not." He sighed and dragged himself into an upright position. "I've done all I can do for today on the Annie Lane case, which wasn't much. I had some unrelated news I'd planned to share with you over coffee tomorrow morning." He lifted an eyebrow, possibly waiting to see how long I could stand it before he finished that story.

"You go first."

"You're in at Grandpa Smacker. The board's excited about a potential new product line, and they're available to hear your pitch next week." Pride lifted his words.

"Next week? That's great." Was he proud of himself? Of *me*? "Thank you for letting me help you." The words were out before I'd considered them. He'd finally let me in.

Jack waved me off. His warm expression loosened the tension in my shoulders. "Your turn. What are you up to that caused Chase Hawthorne to phone me?"

I toiled over the best way to begin. I was enjoying the look in his eyes too much to ruin it by delivering bad news, which was what he considered all my plans to be.

"Lacy?" He spoke my name slowly, using his luscious southern drawl to its full advantage. If that wasn't enough, he locked me in the most sincere and powerful look I'd ever seen him wear.

The transparent color of his eyes pulled me closer. "Yeah?"

"Let me protect you."

Every fiber in my body longed to agree, to let Jack make sense of the nightmare. I wanted to unload my fears and every detail of my half-cocked plan.

So I did.

Chapter Twenty

I waited anxiously by my shop window the next night, fiddling with my Faux Real display and wondering why Jack had agreed to this stupid plan. I darted my gaze over the busy street outside, watching every face that passed, searching the shadows for a giant black cat head or any sign that Josie was really coming.

One of the turtles dove off a rock, and I nearly collapsed.

"I think I changed my mind," I announced to my bosoms—or more specifically to the tiny recording device I'd attached to my bra.

"Too late." Jack's confident tenor drifted from the darkened hallway to my ears. "Everyone's in place. Let's see if she takes the bait. Remember, try to get her to admit to knowing something. She won't really announce her guilt, but maybe we can get a loose thread to pull her down by."

I tracked shadows over the floor with each set of passing headlights. "This isn't a scene from a scary movie," I told myself. "This is a scene from an action film where the intelligent, creative female character saves the day."

"What about the strapping young detective with a keen wit and striking blue eyes?"

I huffed in the direction of my dark stock room. "This is my movie."

"No argument then?" he said. "You do think I'm all those things."

"Maybe I didn't want to be rude by arguing."

He chuckled. "Yes. It would be so unlike you to argue."

"I can hear you laughing."

"Well, try hearing this. We've got plain-clothed officers watching the store from every conceivable entry point. I'm ten feet away, and you're safe."

I toyed with a thin silk head wrap, twisting the material around my fingers until they turned white. "I can't believe you let me talk you into this. You're supposed to be the voice of reason and stop me from doing dumb stuff like this," I grouched. Memories of my abduction washed through my anxious mind. I rubbed my chest where it began to ache. "This is 'The Good Ship Lollipop' all over again." When I'd tried to ferret out a killer on my own this summer, I wound up tied to a stage prop at gunpoint while Shirley Temple pumped from hidden speakers. I'd never hear that song again without crying.

"It's not," he said. "This is nothing like that."

"I hate that song."

"Me too." His voice drew nearer, but he was invisible in the dark hallway. "You went behind my back then. This time you've brought me in on your plan, and NOPD has everything we need to make it work, so breathe."

I inhaled deeply and blew the air out.

Security lighting illuminated the space in eerie, unfamiliar ways. The silence seemed to nip at my heels and crawl over my skin. The moment was frozen. Even Spot the vacuum rested in his recharge cradle. Outside, life went on as usual, as if nothing was amiss, as if I weren't moments away from puffing into a brown paper bag.

The fuzzy white noise of Jack's radio stung the air. "We've got eyes on the suspect," a strange voice announced. "She's approaching from the west. One minute to impact."

I didn't like the sound of that.

"Operation Kitten is a go," Jack said.

"Kitten?" I glared down the dark hallway. I hated when Jack called me that. "I thought we'd gotten past that."

"Copy," Jack responded to his team in the all-business voice I'd come to respect. "Radio silence from here."

We'd have to revisit this operation's stupid title later.

The little bell over my door jingled lightly as Josie crept inside. "Hello?" She was dressed in black from head to toe. Even her long, fine hair had been stuffed into a dark hoodie. My A-line dress and pearls seemed suddenly, comically inappropriate.

"I'm here." I pulled my shoulders back and lifted my chin, forcing a lifetime of pageantry and debutante lessons into practice. "I'm so glad you came." I rushed to her side and reached for her wrists. "Are you okay?"

"Yeah." She looked me over, distrust in her eyes. "You invited me, remember?"

I nodded emphatically. "I wasn't sure you'd come, and I don't know how to tell you this, but I think you're in danger."

Her eyes went wide. "What do you mean? I thought this was about the pillow. You wanted to return it."

"No." I feigned shock. "No. I just needed to talk with you. Alone. Do you remember the man in the pictures I showed you? The guy carrying those boxes?"

"Yeah," she spoke slowly, scanning the darkened shop. "What about him?"

"When you couldn't identify him, I did some digging. He's Annie Lane's brother, and he's been arrested before. He's a drug dealer. I think Annie found out, and he killed her." I lowered my voice further. "I think he's been following me."

She lifted her brows. "Really?"

"Yes." I used my most breathless voice. "After I met with Gideon, the man from the animal shelter, someone broke in and attacked him! He's in the hospital. It's really bad." I looked over my shoulders and scanned the street beyond my window. "I spoke with you right after I spoke with him. I'm afraid you'll be next."

Josie produced a cell phone from her pocket and tapped her thumbs against the screen. "What about the pillow? Is it here?"

"Sure, but I'm keeping it. Annie was my hero." I couldn't make out her expression. A long shadow had fallen over her mouth as she moved deeper into the shop. "Josie? Did you hear what I said? You're in danger."

She glanced up from her phone. "What were you saying about drugs?"

Nerves bundled in my gut, tightening until I thought I'd be sick. I refused to think about who she'd probably contacted and forced myself to concentrate on the task at hand. "I think Annie's brother was dealing drugs in the cities where she visited. I think she caught him and confronted him. I think he killed her to shut her up. I don't have all the details," I hedged, "but I've seen him in town this week, and the timing of Gideon's attack is worrisome at best. If I'm right, and he's been following me like I suspect, then he saw me talking to you. You could be next. You need to go somewhere safe until the police can find him."

She made a duck face. "Where's the pillow?"

"What?" I made a show of looking directly at it on my counter, then snapping my attention back to her. "I don't have it with me."

She sauntered to the counter and lifted it. "You don't say?"

I faked my disapproval. "Did you ever see or hear anything that could support my theory about Ryan? Maybe you can help me build a case for the police to arrest him. We'll be safe once he's in jail."

"That's not going to happen," she said. She slid her phone into her back pocket and stared at me.

"Why? Aren't you worried? Everything I told you is true. He's a drug dealer. He had access to Annie and motive to lash out."

She didn't answer.

Operation Kitten wasn't going as planned. I'd assumed she'd cheerfully throw Ryan under the bus to deflect suspicions from herself. Desperation clawed at my chest. She needed to give me something to pull on.

The door swung open, and my ears rang as the little bell banged and rattled against the glass, much like my heart against my ribs.

I struggled for breath. "I knew it."

The cat-man released the door behind him. It echoed in my head as it sucked shut, sealing me in and the world out. He moved toward me in slow motion, tilting his weird head over one shoulder and herding me back from the windows. Out of view from my plain-clothed backup. I could only pray that Jack was still listening.

I opened my arms like an airplane and positioned myself between the intruder and Josie, continuing the ruse and praying I'd survive my stupid plan. "It's him, Josie. Call nine-one-one."

She swept around me to the cat-man's side and curled her body against his.

Ryan Goodman twisted the big head off his shoulders. A younger, more masculine version of Annie glared at me. His sandy, cropped hair dripped with perspiration from time spent under the cat head. "Did you get the pillow, babe?" He devoted rapt attention to me, even as he spoke to Josie.

"Yep." She presented the little pillow to him on her palms, an offering to her god. "Just like I promised."

"I don't understand," I balked, probably overacting. "You knew?"

Ryan's smarmy smile was the definition of creepy. His ruddy cheeks and sheer size made him appear significantly more dangerous than he had in the pictures from Annie's moving day. "Good job." He kissed her nose. "Now let's take her for a ride. She's seen my face."

I scooted back, suddenly preferring the demented cat head. "You know what? I'm actually fine here. No ride needed. You can take the pillow and go." I worked my fear into a smile. "Enjoy the city. Take a carriage ride. I can see you two crazy cats are in love." I cringed at the unfortunate word choice and scurried deeper into the room, prepared to make a run for it if needed. "I'm going to go home and rethink my theory. Clearly Josie's not in any danger."

"I'm not," she said, "but you are." She beamed. "You shouldn't have taken this pillow, or stuck your nose in our business, or invited me here tonight, but you did all those things, and now you get punished."

"No, thank you." My mouth dried, and my palms began to sweat. I looked beyond the criminal couple to the window and listened intently to the silence of my shop. Where was Jack? Where was my backup? Everything was going wrong.

Josie snapped her thin arm out and captured my wrist. "Come on. Let's go."

"No." I yanked free. I sidestepped the register and came face-to-face with Ryan. "You might have Josie fooled, but not me." My voice warbled with terror, betraying the faux-confident expression I struggled to keep in place. "I'm not going anywhere with someone like you."

He tucked the big cat head under one arm. "I didn't fool Josie. We're in love. And you *are* coming with me."

"In love? I think it's pronounced *brainwashed*," I said.

His frown turned dark and malicious. "You're awfully mouthy for someone about to get hurt."

Josie made another grab for my arm and missed. "We're in love," she demanded. "Who wouldn't fall in love with a rich, handsome entrepreneur like Ryan? I knew I had to have him the minute I saw him."

"And she did," he bragged. Josie landed her next attempt on my capture and jerked my arm hard enough to form tears in my eyes. I batted the tears and tried to pry her bony fingers from my arm. Where the heck was my backup? Why wouldn't these two admit to anything? "Is that what you call drug dealers these days? Entrepreneurs?"

"Hey," he protested. "I have my own business, just like you. I DJ at parties all over the country."

I cleared panic from my quickly closing throat. "Raves," I said. "Not parties. Don't try to make what you do sound classy. You sell your pills from the DJ booth? Is that how it works?"

He didn't flinch or confess.

These two were tough. I pulled in another deep breath and tried again. "No. You probably have a system. You're too smart to just walk in with a pocketful of pills. How does that work, exactly?"

He turned his beady eyes on the little pillow. "Did you check it?" he asked Josie.

She released me and tore into my handiwork, digging desperately through its contents, covering the floor and my feet in shreds of fiberfill. Desperation seized her face. "There's nothing in here." She turned pleading eyes to her beau. "It's empty."

Josie dropped to her knees, pulling bunches of white fluff into bits. "Where are the pills?" she seethed. She rose to her feet in defiance. "You stole them." She closed in on me until our chests nearly touched. Her statuesque frame loomed over my acceptably average one. "What'd you do with the pills that were in the pillow?"

I dropped my head back for a better view of her livid face. "You had drugs in that pillow?"

"Yes! We want them back. Now!"

"Or what?" I squeaked. "Or you'll kill me like you killed Annie?"

Josie fell away, and Ryan's hands were around my throat in an instant. The cat head rolled onto my clean shop room floor, stopping where Josie had landed with a soft thud. A slew of profanity and spittle hit my face with his every rancid breath. "I'd never hurt my sister! Ever! Do you hear me? She was my sister!"

My windpipe ached beneath his grasp. My body swayed in his control as I gasped for air. Finally, my flailing fingertips hooked on a nearby display and pulled it over with a crash.

Spotlights poured through the darkened windows instantly. The overhead lights snapped on, and Jack materialized from the hallway like a vampire from the rafters. "NOPD," he shouted. "Release her!" Before my attacker could obey, Jack clubbed him with the butt of his gun. Ryan landed in a heap beside his nutso girlfriend.

I stumbled against the wall and slid down until my backside hit the ground. I rubbed my throat and swallowed deep lungfuls of air as my shop burst into a flurry of activity. The attack had lasted only seconds, but it had felt like eternity. Hot tears blurred my vision and poured over my fiery cheeks. Fresh out of dignity and decorum, I tipped over onto the cool floorboards and cried.

Jack's face swam into view seconds later. He tugged my eyelids open and hollered for a paramedic.

I was floating, flying in his arms, through my shop and into the night. Carousels of red-and-blue lights swept through the sky, punctuated by the occasional yellow-and-white flasher on an ambulance or fire truck.

Jack settled me onto the warm wooden slats of a bench and placed a handkerchief in my hands. "I am so sorry." His voice was low and tender as he peeled hair off my tear-streaked cheeks. "This is all my fault. I didn't know he had his hands on you. I heard him yelling, but I didn't know. I couldn't see." He stopped to clutch the back of his neck and swear. "I shouldn't have let him get near you. I should've interrupted the minute he walked in. I should've never agreed to use you as bait."

"It wasn't your fault," I croaked. "This was my idea." I pressed the soft cotton handkerchief against my eyes.

Jack moved back a few inches. "I could have said no to you. I should have." He dug angry fingers into his hair and pulled until it stood in every direction, then turned away mumbling.

A pair of paramedics climbed down from a newly arriving ambulance and headed our way.

Jack motioned them to stop. "We need someone over here. This woman was assaulted by the man inside."

One paramedic opened my shop door, looked in, then back at me. "What happened to the guy?"

"He fell," I croaked.

Jack rubbed his stubble-covered cheek. "Take a look at her first. He'll keep."

The second paramedic nodded.

I waved him away. "I'm fine."

He crouched before me and pulled a penlight from his pocket. EMT was written in big white letters on his navy-blue shirt. "Hey. I'm Tucker." His bright smile and deep-brown eyes were engaging. Under better circumstances, I might have said so.

"Can you follow this light without moving your head?" he asked.

I obeyed.

"That's great. Is it okay if I touch your neck? I see some bruising there."

"Okay."

"My hands are cold." He smiled. "My grandmama always said, 'Cold hands. Warm heart.'"

I was instantly thankful for the coolness of his skin on the tender flesh of my throat. He worked his fingers down the slope of my neck and gently prodded behind my ears. "Any pain when I do this?"

I knotted the handkerchief in my hands. "A little." Emotion clogged my throat, garbling the words.

"It's okay." He dropped his hands from my neck, placing them on the bench instead, one on either side of my thighs. "There's bruising. It'll look worse before it looks better, but that's okay because it will mean you're healing physically. It's okay to do whatever you need to recuperate emotionally. Lots of rest. Hot tea. Bourbon." He winked. "I recommend a good talk when you're feeling up to it."

"Talk?" Jack asked.

Good to know he was eavesdropping. Then again, he'd told me once that *nosy* was part of his job description.

Tucker nodded, eyes focused on me. "I find that victims of trauma gain a lot by saying what's on their minds. Releasing the fearful thoughts into the universe is often cathartic. Trust me."

"All right." Jack postured behind him, arms crossed, face grouchy. "I'll take it from here, buddy."

"Tucker." He stood and extended a hand to Jack, who reluctantly shook it. Tucker gave me a parting smile. "If you ever need to talk."

"Thanks."

He wandered inside, leaving me with a cranky Jack.

"Well," I prodded, "did you get enough to arrest them for the drugs?"

He grunted.

"Jack. What's that mean? I don't speak Neanderthal." I gave him a gentle shove.

He twisted at the waist and cast me a fleeting glance. An almost smile tugged his mouth. "Maybe enough for a warrant. I don't know. My thoughts are . . ." he waved his hands over his head in big circles.

"You look silly doing that."

He dropped his hands to his sides. "This shouldn't have happened."

I forced myself onto shaky legs and moved into his personal space, careful to keep my voice low. "Well, we couldn't have known Ryan would show up. I was supposed to bait her with the pillow, then get her to flip on Ryan, either for the drugs or for Annie's murder. I was certain she'd say something to direct suspicion away from herself."

Policemen escorted Josie and Ryan onto the sidewalk.

I rested my palm over the throbbing skin of my neck. "She's loyal. I'll give her that."

Ryan held an ice pack to his head where Jack had whacked him. I longed to snatch it away and slap him with it.

Jack followed their sad little parade to a pair of cruisers parked on the corner. He fixed Ryan with a death stare.

"You're going down on two counts of attempted murder. My friend here," he nodded to me, "and Gideon at Heart to Heart animal shelter. Before I'm finished, I'll have enough evidence to add first-degree murder."

"Murder." Ryan growled. "You sonofa . . ." Ryan lurched toward Jack, thwarted by the officer holding cuffed hands behind his back.

"I don't think he likes people mentioning that," I told Jack.

The officer pulled him away, but the foul language continued.

Jack smiled at Ryan. "Kidding." He held his palms up. "I know you didn't do it. The angle of impact was all wrong. Forensics show Annie's killer was at least four to six inches shorter than you, but accomplice to murder is still on the table." He turned to Josie. "The killer was someone around five foot eight. Someone Annie would have willingly allowed into her home. Someone she'd easily have turned her back on during a visit." He looked back at Ryan. "Any ideas?"

The profanities spouted anew. Ryan dove at Josie, once again stopped by his restraints.

Josie squealed and tripped over the feet of her arresting officer. Fear left splotches on her ivory skin. She was busted, and she knew it.

The officers worked to separate the lovebirds while Ryan continued his hands-free attack.

I turned to Jack, dumbfounded and struggling to process the downward spiral my night had taken. "I still can't believe this wasn't about the kittens. Ten grand a month for their entire lifespan is a potential gold mine."

"What?" Josie gasped.

Ryan stopped fighting to gawk at me. "What?" he echoed.

The officers took advantage and stuffed the handcuffed pair into the waiting cruisers.

The crowd snapped photos and lost interest.

Jack watched until the taillights disappeared into a sea of traffic, making them indistinguishable from every other car and cab on the street. "Let me take you home and make you some hot tea."

"Fine, but I'm going to listen to the EMT's orders and add a little bourbon. Whatever happens after that can't be helped."

Jack's cheek twitched. "What do you think might happen?"

I rolled my eyes. "Knowing me? I'll tell you anything you want to know and be asleep in an hour."

"Bourbon it is."

Chapter
Twenty-One

Furry Godmother supports the right to
bare arms but encourages a wrap.

Jack had talked me into staying at my parents' house, and Mom had plied me with hot toddies until I fell asleep on the sofa. I woke ten hours later, covered in grandma's quilt. My tongue was stuck to the roof of my mouth, and my head felt like I'd fallen on it. A bottle of water and two aspirins greeted me on the coffee table.

I took the pills and groaned upright.

The bitter scent of Mom's chicory coffee filtered through the house. I shuffled toward the kitchen, quilt over my shoulders like a superhero cape.

"There you are." Mom kneaded wet hands into her apron. "For a while I thought you were sixteen again and planned to sleep all day."

I squinted at the time on the stove. "It's eight o'clock."

She stripped off her chevron-patterned apron and hung it on the wall hook. "Imogene's running the store today. You'll work from home. I had her bring your things."

I poured a mug of coffee and processed her words. "What things?"

She shoved the door open to the dining room. "There. She said this was everything you'd been working on lately. We left it on the dining room table so you'd have a nice flat workspace. I'm making a run to the store soon for whatever else you need. I thought I could help you with your baking."

"Thanks," I whispered. My throat was rough and gravelly from the previous evening's trauma and generous nightcaps.

"You're welcome."

I cupped my palms around the steaming mug of coffee and inhaled the moment. Toddies aside, there was something about being home that took the edge off. I'd done my best to avoid sleeping over all week, but with my stalker in custody, it seemed safe enough to be there. I didn't have to worry about leading danger to their doorstep. No one seemed to care about Annie's kittens—except Latherope, who was in the wind—and I wasn't in a hurry to be alone, possibly ever again. "Where's Penelope?"

"With your father. He took Cotton and Cashmere to work with him this morning. Penny seemed interested, so he took her too. Voodoo's skulking around here somewhere, probably plotting my demise. She's a terrible hostess, and she blames me for those Siamese interlopers."

I snorted.

Mom dusted her palms and let the dining room door swing shut. "Well, make me that list so I can get going."

I scratched the ingredients to all my greatest hits on a pad of paper Mom kept on her counter.

She kissed my cheeks and vanished. Nothing stood between my mother and shopping. The sooner she left, the longer she could browse before they kicked her out at closing. My grocery list was likely the last stop on a full itinerary that included lunch with the ladies and a trip to her favorite boutique.

I started sewing and didn't stop, willfully losing myself in the creative process as I struggled to make sense of all the nasty things that had happened to me. I replayed the night's events on a loop, wondering what I could've done differently and how soon I'd stop feeling Ryan's hands on my neck.

"Knock knock." A familiar voice tore through my angst.

I sprang upright from my hunched position at the table. "Holy!" I pricked my finger with a needle and scattered sequins all over creation.

Imogene padded softly into the dining room. Her puffy salt-and-pepper hair stretched toward the ceiling. "How are you doing, sweetie? A little antsy, I see."

I scooped my materials back into sensible piles. "You scared the bejeezus out of me. What are you? A ninja?"

"Your mama's on her way home. She invited me for dinner."

"Dinner?" I checked my watch. It was after five. "Yeesh. I missed the whole day."

"You didn't miss anything at the shop. Lots of lookie lous and nosy nellies asking all sorts of things that fall under the none-of-their-business heading. I missed you and Penelope, but it looks like you had a productive day all on your own."

It was true. My to-do list was done, and I'd moved on to mocking up pieces for my Mardi Gras line.

"How's your neck?"

I forced a tight smile. "Fine. A little tender. The skin and muscles are tight, maybe swollen. I hope Mom's not going to any trouble for dinner. Honestly I'd be happy with some tomato soup and grilled cheese."

"Aw." Imogene took the seat beside mine. "That's what I used to make you when you were a little girl." She motioned to my neck. "Let me see."

After my morning coffee, I'd taken a short break to shower and dress. I'd arranged a vintage Pucci scarf under the collar of my blouse and fastened it with a brooch. "Really I'm fine." Ryan's meaty fingers had left eight dark, discernable lines on my skin. I rested my hands over the scarf for protection. When I let myself think about the attack too long, my windpipe narrowed.

Imogene pushed my bag of feathers aside and unloaded a little stone jar from her enormous handbag. She wiggled the lid free, and the scent of death flew up my nose.

"Yikes." I pressed my hand to my face. "What is that?"

She tugged my hand away. "A poultice. This will heal those bruises you're hiding under that scarf."

I replaced the hand she moved with my other one. "It stinks. I don't want it."

"It doesn't stink." She released my first hand and reached for the other. "It smells like healing magic."

I swapped hands and covered my face again. "Uh-uh."

"Stop that."

"No."

The sound of Mom's heels snapping over hardwood floors sent a flood of relief through my body. Winning a fight with Imogene was impossible without an intervention.

Mom marched into the room, hands on hips. "What in heaven's name is going on in here?"

I'd arched my back against the table's edge, attempting to politely elude the stinky poultice. Imogene, determined to heal me, had pinned my arms across my chest and was loading up her fingertips with whatever had rotted in that jar.

"Help," I said.

"Imogene, really," Mom scolded. "Let her up."

Imogene relented with a sour look. "I can fix those marks so they don't hurt anymore, but she's too stubborn to let me."

I adjusted my scarf and smoothed my blouse. I wasn't the quick-fix type. I preferred to stew in times like these and plot revenge I'd never exact.

Mom came closer. Her upper lip curled in distaste. "Good grief." She cupped delicate fingers over her nose and mouth. "What is that putrid smell?"

Imogene recorked the bottle. "A poultice."

Mom uncovered a droll expression. "Imogene, please. You know Crockers don't believe in that gobbledygook."

Imogene paled. "You might get away with saying those things in here, but you'd be wise to keep it to yourself outside these walls. Dismissing magic in this city is like saying New Orleans ain't hot." She looked at the ceiling like it might fall on her.

Mom glanced at the chandelier. "I'll take my chances. Now put that stink away so we can get last night behind us." She looked at me with appraising eyes. "How do you feel?"

"Fine."

"Excellent." She clapped her hands. "Then let's move on. The Chicks loved the sashes. I delivered them yesterday, and we had a photo session for the 4-H brochures. Now how are our buttons coming along?"

I twisted at the waist to retrieve one from her table. "I finished them this morning. The glue should be dry if you want to try one on." I passed the oversized medallion to her with care.

"New Orleans Jazzy Chicks rule the roost," she read.

I'd used the Jazzy Chicks logo as my central image, doused the empty space in yellow glitter, and circled the logo in text. The pin was striking but understated and large enough to be read from several yards away. Something she and the Chicks could be proud of in the event they won their bet with the Llama Mamas, which was admittedly unlikely.

"They're lovely."

"Thank you. I know they weren't what you asked for."

She pinned the button onto her creamy cashmere cardigan. "Nonsense. You were right. It's important to take the high ground any time we can."

"Exactly."

She fluffed her hair. "It makes your enemy seem petty and stupid."

I should have anticipated that.

Imogene chuckled long and deep. "Hear, hear!"

Voodoo slunk into the room like a mirage, sticking to the perimeter and observing silently. I lowered my hand to entice her.

Imogene braced wrinkled hands over her knees and rocked onto her feet. "If you won't let me use my poultice, then I'm going to put the kettle on. Who wants a hot toddy?"

"Me," Mom and I spoke in unison.

Imogene shuffled out of the room, and Mom fell onto Imogene's empty seat. "I'm sorry I rushed off this morning. The last week has been a lot to take in."

She wasn't joking.

"I'm glad you decided to stay with us last night. If I'd known a few nightcaps could get the job done, I'd have tried that sooner."

I turned on my seat, accidentally bumping her knees. "Are you okay?"

She blinked glossy eyes. "Yes. I worry too much, I suppose. It's in my nature. To rub salt in my wound, the good Lord saw fit to deliver me a daredevil daughter who runs headlong into danger at every opportunity." She swiped tears from the corners of her eyes and groaned. "It's who you are. I know." She exhaled a shaky breath and turned stern eyes on me. "You can't imagine the fear a mother has for her child. There simply aren't words."

"I'm sorry." I wouldn't have said I "ran headlong into trouble," exactly, but it must've seemed that way to her, so I kept the opinion to myself.

She nodded and sniffed. "I know." She pressed a palm to my cheek. "Well, at least it's over. Jack got the bad guys. Yes?"

"I guess. He took Ryan and Josie in last night, but I haven't heard from him since he dropped me off here." I'd hoped he'd at least call to check on me, but he hadn't. "He said Annie's assistant fit the height requirement of the killer, but Annie's brother seemed sincerely shocked at the idea she could've done it. If she did, I don't think he had a clue." Which was funny because they were supposed to be in love. I'd never been in true, honest love, but *I just killed your sister* seemed like the sort of important information couples should share. "Neither of them seemed to have known about the kittens' trust either. It's as if there's no communication between these people. Annie and her brother. Annie and her PA. The PA and the brother." Maybe I was too transparent. I told Penelope and Buttercup everything.

Mom stood. "You're overthinking it. You solved the crime. Relax. Be happy."

"I know you're right, but I still have so many unanswered questions."

"It's only been a week since you found that poor woman's body. Look at all that's happened. It's no wonder your mind is reeling. It's a lot to process, but it's over."

I slumped. "You're probably right."

"Of course I'm right. Now, have you chosen a gown for Saturday night's event?"

"I've been kind of busy."

She wrenched me off the chair. "It's lucky for you I'm such a planner. I had my stylist deliver a rack of gowns this morning. We took them to your room before you woke. She's incredible. Let's see what she brought."

I followed Mom up the rear staircase to my room. The space hadn't changed in the more than ten years since I'd moved out. Soft shades of blue and silver still covered every inch of space. Gentle white accents and endless throw pillows gave the illusion of standing on a cloud. Books spilled from overcrowded shelves, and glass beads dripped from the chandelier in the ceiling's center.

I inventoried the dress rack. All dresses I couldn't afford but would give my blood to own. "Wow."

"Didn't I say so?" Mom asked, filling the space beside me.

I dared a look into her eyes. "This feels like I won the lottery. Aren't you angry with me for everything that's happened this week?"

"I'm not happy, but complaining rarely changes your behavior. I'm glad you're home, and I don't want to cause a big rift that makes you leave again." She grabbed the hem of her waist-length sweater and tugged it hard. "You're doing well, fitting in nicely, and seem to be happy. That's all I've ever wanted." She lifted her chin and turned toward the rack. "What are you waiting for? Try something on."

I wrapped my arms around her.

She stiffened for a moment before squeezing me back. "What's this for?"

"Because I love you. I love this town. I love our family. Even our differences. You're not going to chase me away. I left last time because I was young and wanted to see what I could accomplish on my own. Now I know. I can do anything I want, and I can do it with you and Dad at my side. Having you with me doesn't diminish my work." I released her and smiled. "Just keep your money in your pockets. I'll get the finances figured out too, eventually."

She nodded. "Fair enough."

I released her. "Well, step outside—this isn't a locker room."

She stymied a smile and marched away.

I slipped into a teal mermaid dress and inhaled to zip. "You never told me what kind of event I'm judging."

Mom reopened the door and peeked in. "It's called 'Somewhere and Nowhere.' It's some sort of interpretive dance competition." She returned to my side and twirled a finger, indicating I should spin.

I wobbled in a circle. "I don't know anything about interpretive dance."

"So?"

"I also don't know how I'm supposed to walk in this thing with my knees strapped together."

"Like a lady," she suggested. Her eyes twinkled with mischief.

"I can walk like a penguin. Is that close enough?"

She laughed. "Take it off." She turned her back on me, clearly not intending to leave again.

"What about the competition? How can I judge something I know nothing about?"

"You don't have to know anything about interpretive dance. You smile, nod appropriately, and look stunning. Then copy whatever score the judge beside you gives the contestants."

I shimmied free of the teal torture device and tossed it onto my bed. I slipped into a stretchy, nude-colored sheath with a black lace cover. "This is nice." The straps were wide over my shoulders, and the neckline was modest, leaving the form-fitting shape to speak for itself.

Mom turned. "It looks like you're naked under the lace."

"I think that's the idea, but it's well designed. The length is right, and the neckline is striking."

"I don't like it. Try another one."

I gave my reflection a reluctant good-bye and tossed dress number two beside the first. I fingered the hangers, flipping past colors I loathed to ones that could work. "How about this one?" I held a white high-low gown against my chest and hooked the hanger over my head.

Mom groaned. "Take that off your head. I don't like this one either. White for an evening event in the fall is tacky. I thought my stylist was better than this. I'm going to have to talk with her about her selections for you. Choose better this time, or I get the next pick."

I rehung the white gown and went back to searching. "What's this?" I worked the tangle of dresses apart, honing in on something red smashed between a royal-blue Versace and a petal-pink Calvin Klein. "This is an Annie Lane original." Scarlet. Strapless. Belted. Tea length with a flared skirt and tiny rosettes along the hem. I zipped it over my hips and stared at my reflection.

"Oh, my." Mom moved into view beside me. We wore matching expressions of awe. "This is the one. It's marvelous. As if it was made just for you."

I lifted a hand to my neck.

"Don't worry about that. I'll call my makeup girl. She can cover anything. Stretch marks, dark circles, war wounds. She's fantastic. Wear your hair down and borrow one of my diamond necklaces. Everyone will be too busy gawking at your beauty to notice a little added neck makeup, not that anyone would once she's done with you."

I lifted my arms and examined the slight droop beneath my wimpy bicep. If I was stronger, I might have been able to defend myself against Ryan last night.

Mom pointed at my arm's reflection in the mirror. "Imogene calls those nana flaps. Wear a nice shrug. No one will notice."

I gasped. "I do not have nana flaps."

"Of course not, darling."

I wrapped my arms around my middle and pushed the ugly thought aside. *Nana flaps.* Maybe I'd look into local yoga classes. Fitness and Zen in one tidy package would save a fortune on therapy.

I paused to luxuriate in the feel of couture I could never dream of affording. "Is it horrible that I don't want to take it off?"

"That's how you know this is the one. Just look at your face." She made a peace sign and pointed it at her eyes. "It's all right here. Since we're having a nice mother-daughter tête-à-tête, I should tell you I saw this look on you Monday night at the dinner where Jack spoke."

My cheeks heated stupidly. "I don't know what you mean."

"Sure you do. There's no sense in denying it. A mother knows."

Did she? Was there something to know? Panic fluttered in my chest. "Do you think he knows?"

She made a sad face. "Honey, men are daft, clueless creatures, bless their hearts. They aren't intuitive. They need things explained, and even then they confuse easily."

"Mom," I sighed. "That's not true, and it's not fair to slander an entire gender."

"What? It is true. Do you know I once set the table for dinner when you were young, and the phone rang? I went to answer it, and two minutes later, your father hunted me down to ask if that was dinner on the table. I mean, what else would it have been? Props for a play? Trust me. Men need more guidance than you'll ever understand."

"Apparently." I turned my back to her. "Unzip me?"

She obliged. "Anyway. You definitely have something worth exploring with Chase Hawthorne. I saw it, and you know it."

I let my eyes slide shut as I smiled. I opened them before turning around. *Chase.* "We'll see."

She beamed. "Clean up and come down for dinner. Nothing fancy tonight. Salads and cornbread. Fresh fruit for dessert." She let herself out and closed my bedroom door behind her.

I changed back into my clothes and adjusted my scarf over the bruises. Mom was certain that the truth was in our eyes. If that was true, what did it mean for finding Annie's killer? Ryan seemed genuinely shocked to learn Josie was a suspect. In fact, so did she. And he was too tall, which counted out Dylan Latherope as well, but not Shannon Martin.

Was there a chance I wasn't as safe as I thought? Could the killer still be out there? Did he also see me as a problem?

"Lacy," Mom called up the steps. "There's been a change in dinner plans. Imogene made grilled cheese and tomato soup."

"And hot toddies," Imogene hollered.

Maybe I could stay one more night. "Coming!"

Chapter
Twenty-Two

Furry Godmother's tip for the perfect look: Wear it with a smile.

I woke early the next morning and contacted Mrs. Hams. A lifetime of setbacks had taught me that perseverance was the key to success. No one was going to chase my dreams for me. So I lovingly packed the Llama Mamas' scarves and hats in tissue paper and layered them in a series of logoed garment boxes.

Mrs. Hams was available for delivery in an hour. She'd welcomed the visit but warned she wouldn't be alone. The Llama Mamas were meeting for brunch.

It was a beautiful day for an autumn drive. I left the windows down and let my hair fly. I'd loved the freedom and purpose of driving since my very first lesson. Some days, car keys in my hand still felt like a ticket to see the world.

The Hams Plantation was a fantastic destination: historical, beautiful, and approaching its bicentennial birthday.

Her home, like many of the properties in the area, had begun as a small farming venture and grown into something else entirely. The Hams family had protected their wealth and land through war and peace, feast and famine, and for more generations than most families had been in America. To Margaret Hams, River Road was more than a seventy-mile strip of land—it was her home and her legacy. Loyalty to her family's lifestyle was at the root of her beef with my mother. The Conti family had also lived on River Road once, but my great-great-grandfather had sold the plantation and moved to the city during the late nineteenth century. Mrs. Hams called Mom out on it during a charity event several years ago, and the fundraising feud was on.

I eased onto her bumpy gravel drive with care. Rows of ancient oaks stood sentinel on either side of the lane, weaving long, bearded arms into a canopy overhead. I imagined myself in a ball gown and carriage instead of houndstooth and a Volkswagen. I slowed further to absorb the moment. Visiting Mrs. Hams was as close as I'd ever get to being in a Jane Austen novel.

The grand estate came into view with majestic white columns and tall black shutters. A knot of women gathered around a large patio table covered in pitchers and glasses. I parked and waved.

Margaret Hams met me with open arms. "Welcome." She ushered me to the table and poured me a glass of sweet tea. "Ladies," she announced, "this is Lacy Crocker. The one I've been telling you about."

A round of nods and knowing smiles spread over the little crowd. Each face was mildly familiar but not identifiable.

"Thank you for having me. I'm truly sorry for the intrusion, and I won't keep you long." I took the last empty seat and balanced the Llamas' garment boxes on my knees. "I finished your parade ensembles last night and couldn't wait to see what y'all thought." I stuttered on the *y'all*. I'd worked hard to cut that out of my vocabulary when I left home, but the little devil had been sneaking into mind more and more often since my return. I'd been able to keep it off my tongue until now. I blamed the plantation.

I loosened the bow on the top box and lifted the lid, hoping to seem more confident than I felt. I'd failed miserably at covering the marks on my neck with makeup and resorted to a jaunty length of silk. A scarf wasn't easy to pull off without looking like an airline stewardess or one member of an acapella team.

Mrs. Hams lifted the first scarf/hat combo from the top of the pile and held it up for all to see. She stuck her fingers in the slots I'd allowed for pointy llama ears. "Darling." She passed the items around the table. The women chatted happily, petting the soft material and inspecting the stitches. Mrs. Hams smiled at me. "You're every bit as talented as that unfortunate woman you found last week."

"Annie Lane," I said. "Her name was Annie Lane." I could only dream of cultivating half her skills in my lifetime. I'd imitated her for as long as I could remember, hoping to develop a career like she had. In all those years, I never dreamed she'd meet such a sad end with so much left to do in this world. And the longer I thought about it, the more certain I was that her killer wasn't in jail.

Images of Annie's kitchen crime scene flamed into mind. Yes, Jack said Josie was the right height to be Annie's killer, but why would Josie cut off the hand that fed her? Annie might've discovered what the strange couple was up to, but I couldn't imagine her turning her brother in for his crime. I'd followed Annie online for years. I'd read her autobiography, her blog, every article she'd written in her rise to fame. Family was important to her. Even if she had kept Ryan a secret, it was likely meant for his protection. The spotlight can be hot, and for an addict, it might've been deadly. I paused at the unfortunate choice of words. If it was in Annie's nature to see everyone as redeemable, it would explain why she'd kept Josie on as the world's worst personal assistant.

I chewed the inside of my bottom lip. Annie deserved better than the tragic way her life had ended. She deserved justice. Everyone did.

"Lacy?" Mrs. Hams's voice pulled me back to the moment. "Can you finish them in time?"

I blinked. "What?"

She wiggled a hunk of beige felt before my eyes. "The pins. We've finalized our ideas, and this is what we want. Can you finish them before the parade?"

I gave the material a closer look. She'd cut a llama shape from tan felt and sewed a black bead on its head, presumably as an eye. Faux brown fur ran down the figure's neck and back, ending as a puffy makeshift tail. A big red heart was drawn in marker on the animal's side. The words "Chick magnet" were written across the heart in black.

"Get it?" she asked. "It's a play on words because the Jazzy Chicks will wear the pins. The llamas will be Chick magnets."

"Hmm," I said, certain my mom would cheerfully go to jail for my murder after this.

"It's a loose translation. None of it is literal, of course."

"Of course." Except for the fact that her felt llama was literally the ugliest thing I'd ever seen.

Mrs. Hams took the pin away and flipped it over in her hands. "We'd like you to make them with two layers of felt so they can be stuffed with a little something. We want them to be 3-D."

Dear Lord. I performed a mental sign of the cross.

"Can you have them ready before the parade?"

I stared. "When is the parade?" I'd been tracking time lately in terms of the number of days since Annie's murder. Eight. I'd stopped thinking of Thanksgiving or any other future event.

She furrowed her brow. "A week from yesterday."

Yikes. "Oh, yes, of course. It's no problem."

My phone rang, and Jack's blank cop-face lit the screen.

Margaret and the women seated nearby craned their necks to see the caller.

"I'm sorry. I need to take this. Hello?"

"Lacy. Where are you?" Jack's voice was low and tight. Something was wrong.

"I'm visiting Mrs. Hams. Why?"

"We found Dylan Latherope." Sounds of rushing water poured through the phone with his voice.

I braced myself for something awful. A bolt of panic shot through me. "Are my parents safe?"

Silence overcame the table before me. The Llama Mamas leaned in closer.

Jack sighed into the speaker. "Your folks are fine, but you might want to head home soon."

"Why? What happened?"

"Why don't you meet me at the station? I'd assumed you were in town when I called. I don't want you making the trek from River Road all worked up."

"I'm not worked up," I screeched.

A rush of whispers flooded the table.

Okay. I was a little worked up.

I composed myself and tried again. "You can't call me and imply something horrible has happened, then refuse to say what it was. Whatever you've got is no worse than the forty-seven bloody scenarios my mind has already concocted." I cast an apologetic smile at the Llama Mamas.

"Meet me at the station," he repeated.

"Talk." The word erupted from my mouth with more force than I'd intended, startling several Mamas.

Jack didn't speak.

A car door shut on his end of the line, silencing the rushing water. "He's dead," Jack said.

"What? Who?" I imagined Mr. Latherope sneaking into Gideon's hospital room and pressing a pillow over his face. "Why?"

"Uniforms pulled Dylan Latherope from the river this morning."

I pushed hastily onto my feet and dropped both hands to my side. My phone bounced off one thigh, caught in my white-knuckle grip. "I'm sorry," I told the ladies. "I have to go. I'll have the pins ready for you on the morning of the parade. Thank you for the tea and hospitality."

Margaret and the Mamas stood in unison. Their expressions ran the emotional gamut from confusion to dread.

"Are you okay to drive?" Mrs. Hams asked. "One of us can take you back. Another can follow in your car."

"Oh, no." I waved her off and forced an awkward smile. "I'm okay. It's okay." I backed up.

"Your cheeks are flushed."

"It's very warm." I fanned my face in support of the words. "Thank you again." I nodded my good-byes to the other women and made a controlled run to my car.

"It's barely seventy-five." Margaret's voice was loud and clear as she kept pace with me. "Well, don't forget the sample pin."

"Thank you. See you next week." I fell behind my wheel with the ugly felt llama and poked as slowly as possible through the unfathomably long tunnel of trees. I set my phone in one cup holder and piped the call through my speakers for hands-free driving. "Jack? Are you still there?"

"Yeah."

"Was it a suicide? An accident? Latherope was definitely unstable, but was he suicidal? He was desperate for those kittens and probably grieving. Do you think he was grieving? He and Annie hadn't been divorced that long, and they'd been together for years. Do people really get over things like that?"

"I wouldn't know. How fast are you driving?"

I turned onto the main road at the end of Mrs. Hams's lane and crammed my foot against the gas. "Forty." Give or take twenty-five. "Was it suicide?"

"We won't know the cause or time of death for certain until the medical examiner gets him on the table, but he's got a lot of bruising and several bumps on the head. The injuries could be from an attack like Annie and Gideon's, or they could be from the rocks along the river's edge. We've had a lot of rain. The river's engorged, angry, and tumultuous. Any amount of time in the water this week would beat a person up pretty bad."

Something in his voice didn't sit right. He didn't think it was an accident or suicide. Ice pooled in my gut. "You think Annie's killer did this." My tongue swelled. A blow to the head fit Annie's killer's MO. He'd said Josie was the right height for that job. "Do you think Ryan or Josie killed him?" What had he said about an indeterminate time of death? "Was he dead before you arrested them?"

"Like I said. We won't know until the ME can take a closer look."

"Is there anything you do know?"

"Well, for starters, there's one fewer person in New Orleans with plans to hassle you."

"Not funny." I slowed to the posted speed limit, having lost my motivation to rush. I needed to think. "Have you gotten anything useful from Ryan or Josie?"

Jack grunted a humorless laugh. "Ryan turned on Josie the minute I got him alone. He went nearly insane at the thought she could've killed his sister. We had to call the nurse to sedate him. I've never seen anything like it."

"Drugs?" I asked. What else would make someone behave like he had at my shop?

"Maybe. We didn't do blood work. Just read him his rights and locked him up. He copped to the drug charges but fingered Josie as the brains behind the operation. He was the doting, clueless boyfriend. His words. Not mine.

I have better ones for a man who'd lay his hands on you like that."

I nodded at my windshield. A measure of peace settled over me. I stretched and flexed my aching fingers. My shoulders relented their positions beside my ears. Jack had my back. However this ended, I would be okay. "So," I asked, hoping a change of subject would puncture the tension, "any new information on your personal investigation?"

"Not yet."

"That's okay," I said. "Soon you'll have an inside woman."

"I wish you didn't have to get involved. You've got enough going on right now without getting involved in my mess."

"I don't mind."

"Are you sure working with me won't cut into your time for making feline footwear and guinea pig gowns?"

I smiled. "You're trying to taunt me, but I make incredible feline footwear." Not that any cat on earth would tolerate the cute booties. "Seriously. I know how important this is to you, and I'm glad to help. I'm also a great listener if you need one."

"I know."

"I'd also like to offer my excellent brainstorming services."

He snorted. "I thought what you said about Tabitha potentially blackmailing Grandpa's friends was worth exploring."

I perked. "And?"

"I revisited the guys I'd spoken to before and posed the possibility."

I merged into traffic and took the next right with renewed vigor. "Go on."

"The men were clearly startled by the question. Some oozed guilt and anxiety. All were evasive. My gut says you're right. Tabitha had something on them, and they don't want it getting out."

"So she *was* blackmailing them." I slapped my steering wheel. "Knew it."

"You didn't know it. I don't know it. It's just a vibe I got from them. No one has given me anything substantial enough to bring her in, and she's moving out, so I'm losing proximity, too. Maybe I'm wrong," he rushed on. "Maybe I'm seeing trouble where there isn't any because I want to blame someone for my loss. You were right. Grief does things to us."

"Um, no." I squinted into the sky, waiting for a stoplight to change. "I didn't say that. That sounds like a self-help book. There was GHB in your grandpa's system. That's real, and it's not normal. Maybe we're coming at the problem wrong and it's time you switched gears."

"What do you mean?"

The green light snapped on, and I motored through the intersection. "Maybe instead of trying to figure out the big picture before she leaves, we should focus on nailing her for the GHB. We know she did that, and if we can prove she was dosing him and it led to his death, you could charge her with murder. Then, if you still want answers about her big plan, she might swap information for a reduced sentence."

Jack laughed. "You've got it all planned out. How much thought have you given this?"

"The whole scenario came to me as I was talking. It's the curse of a creative mind. I'm only twenty minutes away from the city now. Do you still want to meet at the station?"

"Rain check?" he asked. "Not to meet at the station. We could meet for dinner sometime or coffee."

I wrinkled my nose at the immediate downgrade from dinner to coffee, but I liked the invitation.

"No?" Jack asked.

"Yes," I said. "Yes to the invitation." I rubbed a hand over one eye in frustration. My mother would send me back to polishing school if she could hear me rambling like this.

"Okay. We'll talk about this more then. For the record, I don't want you getting involved in this thing with Tabitha, but you're right, I could use a sounding board, and maybe together we can figure out what I'm missing."

"What do you mean?" I asked.

"I'm not sure. There's something about the reactions of Grandpa's friends that keeps niggling at the back of my mind, but when I try to hone in on it, it evaporates. It's like I know the answer but can't think of it."

I knew the feeling. I faced the same frustration when I thought of poor Annie. The pieces of my puzzle weren't lining up yet, but they would. A surge of camaraderie overcame me. "Maybe I can visit those guys with you sometime. Be a second set of eyes and ears."

"I'd like that. If you're comfortable."

"I am." My smile widened. "What are you doing tonight?"

I flipped my blinker on and merged with traffic headed for the city. Squat homes and shabby roadside lots slowly gave way to the urban sprawl. My heart fluttered the way it did every time I was so close to home.

"Latherope's death is going to keep me busy a while, but I doubt I'll have it sorted by nightfall. Why?"

"I'm judging an interpretive dance event at seven. It's called 'Somewhere and Nowhere.' Mom put me up to it, but I'm not hating the idea. You should stop by."

"Interpretive dance." He spoke the words as if they had no meaning. "Where?"

"The Orpheum Theater."

He whistled. "Fancy."

"You don't have to dress up. If you're coming from work, I'm sure your badge will get you in."

"I'll see what I can do."

I took the next exit with a wider smile. "Fair enough. Good luck with your work."

"Back at ya," he said.

Chapter Twenty-Three

Furry Godmother supports the arts,
mostly through generous candy purchases.

Theatrical black-and-white flags billowed gently outside the historical Orpheum Theater in the Central Business District, where concrete, hotels, and the Superdome ruled the landscape. Hundreds of patrons cluttered the sidewalk, dressed to kill. Others streamed in and out of the theater's doors like ants at a picnic. Limos and Town Cars taxied slowly toward the venue, delivering couples clad in couture and diamonds.

I slid from the cab, wondering why no one had offered me a limo, and tipped the patient driver before beetling into the mix. I gave my name at the door and hurried toward the stage, where I assumed the other judges were waiting. The front-center aisle had a sign as anticipated: "Reserved for Judges." The seats were empty.

I hadn't been to the Orpheum since high school, before Hurricane Katrina had left it in need of a miracle. Before that, I'd fumbled through countless pageants and dance recitals on the Orpheum stage, discovering that having two left feet is in fact a disability and not the charming quirk it's portrayed to be on television.

I sank into a soft blue chair and awaited further instructions. According to my watch, I was only thirty minutes early. The audience would be seated soon. I turned at the waist, seeking my fellow volunteers. The room was empty, but the view was amazing. The impeccable renovation transported me back nearly a century to opening night. Everything from the regal blue-and-gold scheme to the elaborate plasterwork overhead had been returned to its original glory. I closed my eyes and imagined sitting between my mom and dad at one of our dozens of trips to this place. The theater had smelled like popcorn and perfume with a hint of cigar smoke.

Heavy footfalls patted down the aisle behind me. I opened my eyes and prepared a smile for whoever was headed in my direction.

Chase fell into the seat beside mine. "You beat me here. I tried to pick you up, but you were already gone."

"Nice to see you, too." I smiled wider, enjoying the way he seemed to pop up all over town. "What are you doing here?"

"Judging this contest." He gazed at the stage. "What sort of contest is it again?"

I swiveled, adjusting the short length of material on my thighs. "Did my mother put you up to this?"

He nodded his head yes. "No."

"I see. And did she tell you not to tell me she put you up to it?"

More affirmative nodding. "No."

I turned back to face the stage, free of his dazzling green eyes. "This place takes me back." The Orpheum was home to the Louisiana Philharmonic Orchestra.

"I played bass until high school," he said. "I wasn't bad."

"Really? Dad insisted I try the cello. I was terrible." I gave the cavernous room another look. "I haven't seen any other judges. Do you think we're the first ones or the only ones?"

"I don't know. The lobby's full of people." He stretched his legs out in front of him.

As if on cue, the auditorium's rear doors opened. People bustled inside, chatting and laughing and pointing at the magnificent theater before them. Scents of popcorn and perfume followed them down the aisles, whisking me into a state of nostalgia.

Chase leaned forward in his seat. "Maybe we were supposed to meet backstage?"

"Maybe."

He stood and frowned at the stage. "I'm going to see if I can find out."

"Good luck." I waved.

Chase disappeared stage left.

A line of fancy-dressed women and one portly, balding man manifested moments later, stage right. The little parade headed my way. "Lacy Crocker?" the man asked, peering over the top of his rimless round spectacles.

"Yes." I stood to shake his hand. "I'm sorry. I didn't get instructions on what to do once I'd arrived."

He handed me a clipboard and pen. "Watch the show. Make notes. Give each act a score. Sign the bottom. There's one sheet for each act."

I flipped through the stack of papers on my clipboard. "How many acts are there?"

"Twenty-four. Each act is limited to five minutes, and we allow a one-minute break between performances, so we'll get through eight or nine acts an hour. There'll be a ten-minute intermission at the one-and-a-half-hour point. I'll collect score sheets from the first half at that time. We'll begin again immediately after intermission and finish in three to four hours."

My jaw dropped.

Chase bopped back into view center stage and jumped down. "There you are."

Chase shook the little man's hand. "Chase Hawthorne."

"Nice to meet you, Mr. Hawthorne. I was just giving instructions to Miss Crocker."

I raised my eyebrows at Chase. "Yes, it sounds as if we'll have the honor of watching interpretive dance for three or four hours."

Chase's congenial smile fell. "Really?"

I fanned the stack of score sheets on my clipboard. "Yep. One sheet for each performance. Isn't that great?"

The man produced another clipboard for Chase.

He frowned. "Terrific. Do you sell Sno-Caps?" Chase asked, a hint of humor in his voice. "Raisinets?"

"No." The man snipped, his tone suddenly pretentious.

I no longer liked him.

"What about gummy bears?"

The man folded his hands in front of himself. "Perhaps there's time for you to run to a gas station before we begin."

"There's plenty of alcohol," I offered. "There are six different bars in here."

Chase gave me a cocky smile, then slid his eyes to the man. "Can I get a beer?"

The man sighed. "The Orpheum stocks several craft and local options, yes."

"What about beef jerky?"

The man walked away.

I grabbed Chase's sleeve and laughed against it. "You're awful. Why did you provoke him like that?"

"What?" He smoothed a palm down the length of my arm. "I like gummy bears. Besides I'm a lawyer. Rattling people is my job."

"I don't think that's your job."

"No, it is. Can I get you some jerky?"

I tucked my skirt against the backs of my thighs and lowered onto my seat. "No, thank you. Maybe a white wine."

"On it." Chase headed upstream through the thickening crowd, in search of sustenance and alcohol.

I tried not to think about four hours of pretending I understood interpretive dance. At least I had Chase to keep me company.

I fiddled with my shoddy manicure and ran through a mental list of work obligations. Sleepless nights and a productive day off had me caught up on orders. I could bake ahead for this week when I got home. There was always plenty of baking to do. And I needed to write a proposal for the new Grandpa Smacker line that the company couldn't say no to.

My phone rang inside my beaded clutch. I snapped the little purse open. Mom's face lit the screen.

"Hello?" I angled away from the judge on my right, hoping for a little privacy.

"Lacy? This is your mother."

I waited.

"Did you know the Llama Mamas are in the Thanksgiving Parade?"

Uh-oh. "What?"

"Can you believe it?" she gushed. "I called the mayor's wife today to see about getting the Jazzy Chicks onto the king's float. Obviously, the chicks can't walk in the parade, but they can ride. And those little sashes you made are so perfect. When the photographer sent me pictures from our photo session with the 4-H'ers, I knew the Jazzy Chicks belonged on television. Then I thought, why not the parade? That's televised locally, and it's a huge event."

"What did she say?" I bounced my knee. "Are you in?"

"Yes! I e-mailed the promotional shots, and she loved them. She agreed to get the Jazzy Chicks onto a float where they can be seen, maybe not the king's float, but somewhere. She does all the finalizing for the parade, so I know it's going to be great."

My other knee bobbed wildly beside the first. I sensed there was more she wasn't saying. "And?"

"And I'd like to see those stupid llamas raise more money than us now."

"Ah." There was the ever-competitive woman I knew and loved.

"I made a sandwich board with a number to call for donations to the children's hospital. Once everyone sees our little chicks with their snazzy sashes and a plea to help the children, we're going to raise enough to build a better family area for the parents and siblings to wait during surgeries and treatments—or maybe a new children's library. Those Llama Mamas are going to wear our pins right through Christmas after this. I bet Margaret Hams and her plantation ladies thought they had this bet all wrapped up. Ha!"

The woman beside me jumped.

I pulled the phone from my head to protect my eardrum.

"Congratulations, Mom. This is a fantastic turn of events, but I should probably get off the phone. I'm at the Orpheum right now, judging the Somewhere Nowhere thing."

"Fine. I'm going to call an emergency meeting with the Jazzy Chicks." She disconnected.

That had gone better than expected. Mom was too busy gushing to force me to confess I'd known about the llamas in the parade. As silly as competing with another organization to raise money seemed, her heart was in the right place, and it helped her deal with her hostility. Anytime I could avoid being on the receiving end of Mom's hostility, I was happy.

Chase returned with a bottle of wine and two glasses.

"No jerky?"

He settled the bottle on his lap. "No. This place is dead to me."

I laughed. "Well, at least you brought plenty of wine. If I'm watching an entire night of interpretive dance, I could use a drink."

The woman beside me heaved a sigh.

Chase made a droll face at her and then turned back to me. "Did I see you on the phone?" he asked, turning the bottle to my empty glass. "Everything okay?"

"Yeah. It was my mom." I waved him off.

Chase snapped his fingers. "I keep forgetting to return her dishes."

I froze, freshly filled glass pressed to my lips. "Why do you have my mother's dishes?"

He rolled his head over one shoulder and looked up at me through thick black lashes. "She and Imogene delivered casseroles to my door every night at seven o'clock for a week after I moved in." He lifted his head, shamefaced. "I ate seven casseroles. I couldn't say no. Domesticity is hard."

"When you moved in where?"

"Next door."

I lowered my glass, baffled. "Next door to what?"

"Next door to your parents." He spoke the words slowly.

My thoughts scrambled. Mom had invited me to a party last week for the new neighbor. I stared at Chase. "You bought the house next door to my parents?"

"You still owe me a drink for blowing off my welcoming party."

"That had to cost a fortune." My little fixer-upper had taken my entire savings to procure. Suddenly I felt like a kid who'd decorated a big box and hung a welcome sign.

He shrugged. "I'd wanted a place across the river in Algiers, but Dad insisted I stay in the Garden District. He said the law firm was selling a certain impression to clients, and no one wanted an attorney who rode a ferry."

"You could've taken the bridge."

He laughed.

"Sorry. That was dumb. I'm just . . ."

"Flummoxed?"

I shook my head. "Yeah. Something."

Chase leaned on our shared armrest. "I don't suppose you have any boy-next-door fantasies you want to explore?"

I brushed hair off my shoulders, thankful for the magic of Mom's makeup girl and the distraction of a diamond necklace. "You wish." The fact I still owed him a kiss for saving Penelope heated my cheeks.

Why hadn't my mom told me Chase moved in next door? She lived to share juicy information like that. "What?" I squirmed. "You're still looking at me."

"You look"—he hesitated—"Give me a minute; I'm trying to articulate my thoughts about you in that dress without swearing."

I laughed. "Take your time."

His expression softened. "How about exquisite?"

"Accepted. Thank you."

The lights dimmed, and the crowd quieted.

Chase helped himself to another long look before turning to face the stage.

We watched knots and clusters of dancers, mostly in black, moving in overly dramatic bursts for the next ninety minutes. I applauded and whistled when the curtain dropped and the lights rose again. Thank heavens.

I scribbled frantically across several blank pages on my clipboard. My mind had wandered during the second half of the performances, and I'd forgotten to score those acts.

Chase stretched an arm over the back of my seat and yawned. "What are you writing?"

I didn't look up. The pretentious clipboard distributor was moving in our direction, collecting score sheets. "I forgot to fill some of these out." I leaned toward the woman on my right and peeked onto her paper.

She stiffened and flipped the sheets over.

"Jeez, it's not like we get credit or anything," I mumbled. *Nice flow. Well executed. Explosive and dynamic.* I jotted generic comments I'd seen on the backs of my favorite books.

"Here. I'm going for popcorn." Chase handed me his clipboard. "We only have ten minutes for intermission, and the lines are probably outrageous. Can I get you something?"

"No thanks." I scribbled eights for everyone's score.

"Miss Crocker?" The little man stopped behind me, breathing onto the top of my head.

"Sorry. I'm just finishing. These are Chase's." I stopped writing and freed the completed score sheets from Chase's clipboard. "Ohmygosh." I swallowed a laugh. The sound bordered an ugly snort. "No. Wait." Chase had drawn three stars on each paper. No comments. No numbers. Just three stars. "One more minute. I'm sorry." I finished my comments and tucked Chase's papers beneath mine, then handed the stack overhead.

"Thank you," the man said. He didn't sound like he meant it.

My phone blinked to life in my lap. I swiped my finger over the screen to read my message. Chase had sent a selfie with someone dressed as a giant popcorn.

I giggled softly, then texted my mom:

Why didn't you tell me Chase lives next door?
Do not say because I didn't ask.

Mom thought she saw something of interest between Chase and me. Was she right or just hopeful? I gave the photo another look. Chase was basically a man-child, but to hear Mom tell it, they all were in one way or another. Chase was a loyal friend, and he made me laugh. I trusted him. That was big. After Pete I'd made solid plans to never trust another man again. Being home had changed most of my plans. Everything was clearer to me in New Orleans. From here, I could see Pete was the exception, not the rule. Still I was never a gambler, and I didn't see any reason to put my heart in harm's way again. Why muck things up?

Something else Mom had said circled through my mind. My thoughts shifted to Ryan and Josie. I'd seen genuine shock in both Ryan and Josie's eyes the night Jack accused her of killing Annie. Maybe she'd faked the surprise, or maybe she was guilty and genuinely shocked that the cops were able to connect her to the murder. I wasn't convinced of either. I wanted more time with Shannon Martin. If I was disappointed at losing a potential partnership with Annie, how upset was Shannon that she'd stolen his designs? Did she steal them? Maybe she'd bought them or had made some other arrangement with him. I needed to ask Jack if they'd brought him in for questioning yet.

Annie's ex-husband had made a solid murder suspect before he died. Why was he dead? Was it a suicide? Did he feel guilty for killing Annie? Was it grief?

Or was he murdered?

I let the thought spin. Dylan Latherope was too tall to have been Annie's killer, but he was obsessive. What if he'd skulked around long enough to figure out who killed Annie and then confronted them?

I flipped to my phone's photo gallery and swiped through the pictures I'd taken this week. I was missing something.

I texted Jack.

> Do we know what killed Dylan
> Latherope yet? Was he murdered?

The phone vibrated back instantly. Unfortunately, the response was my mom's, not Jack's.

> I didn't tell you he was my new neighbor
> because Chase wanted to tell you himself.

That was probably something I should think about, but not right now. I tapped the top of my phone, urging Jack's reply to appear. When that didn't work, I shook it a little.

With Latherope dead and Ryan and Josie in jail, there was no one left in Annie's circle to gain from her loss. What would happen once her estate settled? I stared at a picture of Josie. It was Bryce, Annie's attorney, who'd pointed me in her direction. He was also the one who'd warned me about Dylan Latherope wanting the kittens. Bryce had offered to take Cotton and Cashmere off my hands more than once. He was the executor of Annie's will. He knew about the kittens' trust. He knew about Ryan and the drugs. Bryce knew everything.

Including how to frame a pair of not-too-smart drug dealers for murder.

Chapter Twenty-Four

A Furry Godmother reality check:
Honesty is the best policy. But insanity is a better defense.

Bryce killed Annie!

Sudden heart-pounding realization set in. Perspiration broke along my forehead. I'd thought two things the moment I met Bryce. He was good-looking, and he was short. Given recent findings, I was willing to bet he was roughly five foot eight.

The phone vibrated in my sweat-slicked palm. Jack.

Let's talk in a minute. I'm parking now.

I'd nearly forgotten I'd invited Jack to join me tonight. That was perfect!

I stood and set the clipboards aside.

"Where are you going?" the woman beside me hissed. "The lights are going down."

"Bathroom," I blurted. I dashed into the aisle and jogged toward the closing double doors to the lobby.

Chase moseyed through, heavy-laden with snacks. "What's up? Did I take too long?"

"No," I huffed, out of breath and on the verge of a panic attack. "It was Annie's lawyer. Bryce killed her for the kittens and the trust. I need to get to my parents' house. Jack's outside. I'm taking him with me. I'll call you as soon as I can and fill you in."

Chase stepped in front of me, effectively blocking my path. His hands were too full to grab me. "Jack's outside the theater?"

"Yes. He just parked." I wiggled my phone between us as proof. "He texted me a minute ago."

Chase gave the doors a skeptical look. "Let the cop deal with Bryce. Tell Jack what you know, then come back inside. I'll drive you home. Don't get involved confronting a killer."

"I won't. Promise." I lifted onto my tiptoes and kissed his cheek. "Cover for me with the other judges." I tipped my head in the direction of our seats. "I won't be long. If I am, I'll text you so you know I'm okay."

He took a big side step, allowing me to pass.

I ran easily through the empty lobby, thankful for impeccable timing. Everyone had taken their seats, effectively clearing a path for me. I pushed the front door open and bounded into the night with a thrill in my heart.

I didn't see Jack, so I responded to his text.

Bryce killed Annie.

My car slid swiftly against the curb.

I froze. I'd arrived in a cab.

My driver's-side window powered down, but the driver didn't get out. Notes of an eerily familiar song drifted from my speaker system. *You follow me. I follow you. You follow me. I follow you.*

Bryce glared at me from behind the wheel. "Get in. Don't make a scene, or your cat's dead."

Behind him, my cat carrier was strapped to the back seat. Penelope peered through the window, clearly annoyed.

"How'd you get my car?" I gasped.

"Spare keys in the kitchen."

My head and tummy coiled with fresh panic and nausea. "I set the alarm." The sting of tears bit my eyes. Conspiracy theories rattled around my head. Did the alarm company sell my information? Did Bryce use his attorney status to illegally request my code?

"I watched you type your password the day we met."

"No." I shook my head, disbelieving. "I didn't."

"Yes. First, you let someone break in and steal Cotton and Cashmere. Then I told you about their microchips."

The memory overcame me. He'd seemed so kind and sincere, like a decent human being.

"You locked up on our way out. I watched."

"Lacy?" Jack hollered from the corner, cupping his hands around his mouth.

"Get in now," Bryce growled, "or Penelope's going for a swim with Latherope in the mighty Mississippi, carrier and all."

I reached for the passenger door and opened it slowly, hoping to simultaneously pacify Bryce while giving Jack enough time to be a hero. Jack went rigid. I gave him a long, desperate look, unable to put off the inevitable. My car began to creep forward. "Sorry," I mouthed before climbing into a moving car with a murderer.

Jack scowled and broke into a run.

Bryce jammed the gas, and we peeled away from the curb, nearly hitting a construction dumpster. The passenger door swung shut, bouncing off my right leg before I could get it fully inside. "Ah!" I yanked my knee up and pressed my palms against the roof, praying I wouldn't fall out.

Bryce swerved around a woman in Dior, flinging me into the center console and successfully slamming my door. The power locks clamped down a moment later, sealing me inside.

The sound reverberated in my head and pounded through my throbbing leg.

He honked and swore. "Why are there so many people?"

"Slow down!" I screamed, terrified for the pedestrians pressed against buildings as we tore past.

Bryce looked right, and his mouth fell open.

I followed his gaze.

Thanks to the human obstacle course, Jack had passed us, running parallel on the sidewalk. He slid across the hood of a taxi cab at the corner and landed feet wide, gun pointed at Bryce's head. The lapels of his high-end suit jacket ruffled in the wind. His crisp white shirt screamed Bond. James Bond.

He made time to change before coming. My heart softened, stupidly.

Bryce stood on the brake, throwing my body forward like a rag doll and smacking my forehead into the dashboard until I saw stars.

I might've sworn while fumbling to lift my aching head and fasten my seat belt before the inevitable impact. I sent up a more fervent prayer that we'd all survive.

Bryce released the brake, changing plans and mashing the gas pedal to the floor.

"No!"

Jack launched himself out of the way, tumbling over the gravelly road.

I swiveled at the waist, hoping he wasn't badly hurt. I flipped my visor down and checked the mirror.

Jack rolled to a stop against the tire of a large SUV.

Bryce jerked the steering wheel, and I faced forward, praying again for the public at large. We bounced onto a rare bare section of sidewalk and roared around the corner before landing back on the street inches from a gray sedan on my side.

I screamed and braced for a hit that didn't come.

The sedan's driver honked and gave me the finger.

"What the hell is with this guy?" Bryce marveled into the rearview mirror.

I angled for a better look.

Jack ran full speed down the middle of the street behind us. He'd stripped off his jacket, and his tie flew crazily over one shoulder. His black dress shoes weren't made for a footrace or parkour or whatever he had in mind next, but his arms and legs pumped hard. Determination worked his face into a series of harsh lines and angles. Despite the unthinkable effort, we were in a car, and unbeknownst to Jack, apparently, he was only human. The distance between us grew until my hope faded with his features.

A familiar black Camaro plunged into my periphery, tearing down a pitted brick alleyway and heading straight for us. Police lights flashed beneath the custom grill.

I turned and winced. Pain shot through my head and down my spine. "Oh." I pressed a hot palm to the back of my neck. "I think you gave me whiplash." My vision blurred. I touched the window with my fingers. "Henri," I whispered. Tears of hope blurred my eyes. Could he catch us? Force Bryce to pull over? Help me?

"What the—?" Bryce spotted the police lights and groaned. "Man, the cops down here are insanely dedicated. What are you? Like a local princess or something?"

"Something," I sniffled. "To a few people, anyway."

Bryce yanked the wheel again. "Well, where I'm from, a person can take a few minutes to reflect on their wrongdoings and formulate a plan without being hounded. This is borderline harassment." He jammed the gas again, cutting through the crush of stalled traffic and entering a side street from the wrong direction, leaving Henri in the alley across the way.

I pressed my nose to the glass as we barreled around the corner, avoiding miles of taillights.

Behind me, Penelope meowed.

A small sob escaped my lips. Penelope rarely said anything. Clearly, she understood this was not going to end well. For me, anyway. "Please don't hurt my cat."

Bryce pulled my car into a parking deck and wound his way to the top at an uncomfortable speed. "Shut up. I need to think." He shifted hard into park between the last empty pair of white lines. "Excuse me." He pointed to the glove box at my knees.

I moved out of his way.

"Thanks." He opened the compartment and retrieved a gun.

"Holy smokes!" I yelped. "Why do you have a gun?" An even better question was why I'd move my legs aside so he could get it so easily? Damn southern manners. I hadn't even considered what he might've put inside. All I kept in the glove box were some unpaid parking tickets and a half-eaten granola bar.

Bryce gripped the gun in one shaky hand and covered his eyes with the other. "This is not what was supposed to happen." He pounded my steering wheel with his free hand. "You were supposed to get Annie's kittens for me. I was going to tie you up and leave you behind while I made my escape. Now I need a new plan." He gave up on the steering wheel and pounded his forehead instead. "Think. Think. Think."

"Maybe you can still let us go," I suggested. "I'll grab Penelope and get out. You can go wherever you want. I'll tell the local authorities you didn't hurt me, and everything will be okay." The throbbing in my head and leg said I was far from okay, but I wasn't dead, and I planned to stay that way.

Bryce slowly turned his face toward mine. Panic danced over his pale features. "Everything will be okay?" he whispered. "Everything will be okay? That's what you think?" His voice boomed with the final question, sending pain flares through my brain.

I nodded carefully. "Absolutely."

He pointed the gun at me. "I need you to get Cotton and Cashmere from your dad. Oh, don't look so surprised. They have trackers, and hiding them at your next of kin's house is a little obvious. Your dad is a vet."

"Why do you want them? Why not just leave us here and go? You know the police are on to you." Why worry about her kittens at a time like this? "Oh. For the money. Sorry. I knew the answer to that." I pressed my lips shut before I said anything else stupid and got myself shot. I pretended to lock up my mouth and toss away the key.

He grimaced. "Well, you don't have to make me sound like some callous monster. I need the money, and I care about those kittens." His erratic gaze jumped and darted through the quiet parking deck. "Annie always left them behind. She put them in Camp Bow Wow and Meow while she traveled the world. It was awful, so I offered to keep them instead. I wanted to show her they mattered to me. I thought one day, maybe we'd make the situation permanent." He made a little smile. "I could've made them happy."

I wasn't sure who he meant anymore. "Annie and her kittens?" I peeked into the back seat to check on Penelope. She'd flopped onto her side, having given up the hopes of escaping anytime soon. Not me. I felt along the seat's edge for my fallen clutch.

Bryce rested his head against the seat back and looked at my roof. He bounced the hand with the gun against his bobbing knee. "This is all her fault, you know?"

I tried to wiggle the toes on my aching leg. Searing pain put a stop to that experiment. "Whose? Annie's?" I croaked.

"Who else? I'm in debt up to my jockey shorts, and she pays me a retainer I could cash with the office vending machine. It's ridiculous. I'm a valuable asset to her team."

I did my best to look as if I cared. "*You're* the one who tried to break into my house that night after Charlie took the kittens."

He tapped the gun on my steering wheel. "Tried. I'm not exactly a professional lock-picker, and a nosy neighbor interrupted me. I just wanted the kittens, and I needed that ten grand back. I still do. How did you get your door fixed so quickly?"

"Detective Oliver knows a guy."

"Oh." He rolled his head in my direction. "This time I had to bust the door. Your insurance plan should cover that."

"Great."

"I grabbed your car and cat but couldn't find the money. Where'd you put it?"

"I don't know." I scraped my mind to recall where I'd last seen it. It was hard to concentrate with mind-numbing pain and a far-too-calm killer pointing his gun at me. *Jack*. "Detective Oliver has the money. You know the kittens weren't at my house that night either, right? I'd already moved them. In fact, I was with my parents while you were trying to break in."

"Of course I found that out later, but they were supposed to be with you." He made a choking sound. "They were supposed to be at the pound, but you got involved and decided to keep them. Did you even have them twenty-four hours?"

"They were stolen," I snapped. "You didn't have to tell us about their trackers. Why didn't you go get them yourself and be done?"

"What if the abductor refused to hand them over? What could I do then? You were the one with the cop."

Right. I kept forgetting Bryce was a weasel. "Why not insist on taking them from me as soon as I got them back?"

"I don't know," he growled. "Why is hindsight twenty-twenty? I never dreamed I'd even have to ask for the cats. I thought you'd beg me to take them after that dumb blogger broke into your house. Besides, the cops had already deigned you as the caregiver. I could've picked them up from the pound and been long gone if you'd let them go there as planned. And after all that, you didn't even keep them! You gave them to your dad who lives and works at the southern Fort Knox."

"I was trying to protect them." I pressed a palm to my throbbing head. "What about the money? Why tell me about it, leave it with me, then come back for it a few hours later?"

"I wanted you to assume the trust was her killer's motive."

"*Your* motive."

He made a sour face. "I wanted to point you at Ryan or Dylan. Ryan's a drug dealer. He should be in jail. And Dylan is a jerk."

"Was." My tummy churned. Penelope and I were at the mercy of the world's worst criminal, and he'd threatened to pitch her into the river.

He shot me a feral expression. "I don't want to talk about him."

"You killed him, right? They found his body." I softened my voice and dropped my hand to my lap. "He's huge and a little crazy. How'd you manage it?"

His lip curled back, either in a sinister grin or distaste—it was hard to tell with the double vision beginning. "I met him at the river to talk with him about ways he could regain possession of the kittens."

"But you weren't going to give them to him."

"And he was never going to stop coming for them." Bryce's voice cracked. Tears pooled in his eyes. "They're all that's left of her." He sniffled and ran a sleeve under his nose for good measure. "I wasn't letting them go."

"Because you want to collect the trust," I said.

"No! Not everything is about money! Don't you know that?" He grabbed his hair in both hands and pulled until his scalp reddened from the pressure. "Everything's gotten completely out of hand." He tipped his head back and screamed.

I needed my phone before he turned his crazy on me. My clutch had slid onto the carpet between my seat and the door when he'd wheeled away from the curb like a lunatic. I winced at the reminder of my aching shin. Thanks to the head injury, I'd almost forgotten I had legs. My calf was swollen and turning black and blue where it had been smashed in the slamming door. Forget wiggling my toes. I could barely stand to move the whole leg.

I stretched my fingertips deeper until they brushed the rough edges of my beaded purse. Adrenaline surged. My phone was in that purse. I leaned slightly toward the door, hoping not to draw my captor's attention. My fingernail caught on a bead and inched the purse up, only to drop it again.

". . . so you see," Bryce continued his pointless monologue, "I had to buy all those things for appearances' sake. Annie Lane wouldn't have been seen with an attorney driving a Chevy and dressed by Kohl's. I had to play the part of a high-powered professional so she'd keep me on hand. The ruse was fun at first, but I couldn't keep it up. She wanted me at her beck and call, flying around the world to meet her every time she had an emergency. I've borrowed money from my credit cards and bank so many times that they stopped lending. I asked Annie for a larger retainer because I couldn't pay my bills." He laughed humorlessly. "She told me I should hire a financial advisor. She was so caught up in herself, she didn't see anyone else. The entire human population was a prop in her world. The kittens' trust was the only answer I had left. That money would've fixed my life. It would've fixed everything."

Got it. I pinched the clutch open with my thumb and first finger and felt around the contents. "Did you come to New Orleans to talk to her, or was there another emergency?"

"Both. Another former protégé is suing her. The usual."

"Shannon Martin? What do you mean by 'the usual'? Do you mean she stole designs more than once?"

He looked exasperated. "What have I been saying?"

Beats me. I powered my phone on and swiped the screen. How could I call for help without looking?

"What are you doing?" Bryce went on alert. He pointed the gun at my searching arm.

"Nothing." I needed that arm. I imitated a statue. "Have you given any more thought to letting me go? I won't tell anyone you abducted us."

"No." He turned away again.

I went back to poking blindly at my phone.

"It's sad." He laughed softly. "They really were Latherope's kittens. He brought them home one day when he found them in a bag on the street. They were banged up and nearly starved. So small. I never thought they'd live, but he nursed them to health. He spent all his time with them, treating them as if they were the human children he wanted and Annie didn't. She only took them in the divorce out of spite."

"That's awful." My heroine had really turned out to be a bust. Were all people awful?

"That's life," he said. "The kittens were his based on the law of finders keepers, but that's not a solid legal argument. Plus, Annie had the money and better legal representation." He waggled his eyebrows.

"Didn't you say Latherope represented himself?"

His proud smile fell.

Don't insult the man with the gun, dummy. I looked away. "Sorry. Head injury." I needed a subject change. "So why did he and Annie break up? The tabloids never said." He didn't want to answer me before, but I figured attorney-client privilege went out the window once he'd confessed to her murder. He had no reason to pretend he hadn't at this point.

"Dylan cheated on her."

"Jeez."

"He said she was never around. He was bored and lonely. Felt unwanted and deprived of her affections. Blah blah blah. Standard housewife syndrome."

I made an ugly face at him.

"It's true. I hear it all the time."

"Isn't anyone faithful anymore?" I asked, more to myself than the whackadoodle seated beside me with a gun. Maybe if we sat there long enough, Jack or Henri would find us. I doubted I could make a run for it with a bum leg and whiplash, not to mention hauling a cat in a carrier.

My phone vibrated against my fingertips. I swiped the screen in every direction, hoping to take the call and not accidentally reject it.

"No one's faithful anymore," Bryce said sadly. He pressed the heel of his hand against his eye. "Besides me."

The weight of his words landed on me like a sack of bricks. He really didn't care about the kittens' trust. He wanted them because they were so important to her. "You loved her."

He turned wide eyes on me. "She didn't love anyone. She wasn't capable."

"But you loved *her*. That's why it hurt so much that she didn't appreciate everything you did for her. She didn't even notice your efforts. That's why you hated her ex-husband. He'd hurt her. I'll bet you and Annie fought that day in her kitchen, and you reacted out of passion, not realizing how much damage one moment could cause."

A tear fell over his cheek. "Her idiot brother caused her endless grief, and she covered for him. She fussed over him. I think she might've loved him, as much as she was capable. Though, more than anything, she worried about what might happen to her reputation if he was caught with those drugs. We'd discussed it a hundred times."

"She knew." I wasn't sure if that surprised me or what it would take to surprise me anymore.

"He grew more reckless by the day. A public arrest was inevitable. When I pressed her to turn him in and put some space between her brand and his crimes, she fired me."

I held my breath. Oh, that was bad.

"She fired me!" he screamed. "I did everything for her. I saved her legally on a continuous basis. I kept her kittens when she traveled. I dropped everything to run to her, all around the world, whenever she called. I loved her, and she couldn't be bothered to notice."

"I'm sorry."

He gave me a sad smile. "When she didn't wake up, I realized I'd made the whole thing worse. Ryan was the beneficiary of her entire estate. I'd helped her make it that way when she and her family had a rift over him two years ago. They wanted to put him in rehab then, but he begged her, and she took his side. She always took Ryan's side."

"Her parents were cut from her will?" That's why they weren't at her televised memorial; they were estranged from her. That was probably why they'd had it in the first place. Someone paid them for the rights to air it. *Reality television.* I scoffed, recalling the giant painting of Annie propped in the corner.

"Yep."

"That's why you put me onto Josie's trail. You wanted her to get thrown in jail so Ryan would follow. He can still inherit her estate from jail, you know."

His face turned red.

"You know that. Sorry." I pretended to lock my mouth again.

"Stop doing that," he yapped. "It didn't work last time." Bryce powered our windows down. "Why is it so freaking hot down here? It's November. No wonder you people are so wound up. This heat is unbearable."

I tried to roll my eyes, but it hurt. Scents of dirt and oil leaking from beater cars filtered up my nose and ratcheted my head pain by ten thousand.

He popped the driver's side door open. "Do you hear that?"

"I hear my ears ringing from when you smashed my head on the dashboard."

"You should've been wearing your seat belt. It's the law." He climbed out and stood poker straight, listening.

I jerked my phone onto my lap and flipped it around. I swiped the sleeping screen back to life. The headache had done a number on my vision, but I recognized Jack's blurry face beneath my fingers.

"Clear." An unfamiliar voice sounded softly through my phone. The word simultaneously echoed off the parking deck walls.

Bryce ducked inside and released my seat belt. "Get out. They're here. How the hell did they find us?" His gaze landed on my phone, then swept upward to meet my eyes. A devastating look of betrayal changed his features from panic to anger. "You!"

I swung my door open and jumped out the passenger side, ready to run toward whoever was clearing the deck floor by floor. Whoever they were, Jack wasn't far from them. My foot hit the cement, and I crumbled. Pain shot through my busted leg, sending me tail over teakettles onto the filthy garage floor. I wailed. Could a slamming car door have broken my leg? I wrapped both hands around my calf. The bruising was worse. Black-and-purple waves had crept over my skin until I barely recognized the appendage as my own. I couldn't run. I couldn't even stand, and now that I'd tried, the pain was all I could think of.

Bryce skulked around the car and slammed my door. He winced at his mistake and stilled to listen for the cavalry. "Get up," he hissed.

"I can't." My gorgeous, scarlet Annie Lane original was streaked in dirt, motor oil, and I didn't want to think about what else. The rosette-lined hem was frayed and torn where I'd landed on it. My knees were raw and bleeding.

He kicked my phone away from me and crushed it under his foot. "Get up!"

"I can't." The tears came hard and fast. "I think you broke my leg."

Bryce's narrow eyes widened as he stared at my injured calf. I could nearly hear the wheels turning in his bat-filled head. I was dead weight for him. Immobile. The worst kind of hostage.

"Clear." The word echoed up the curving ramp, setting my heart rate to hyperdrive. A steady cadence of footfalls moved toward us.

Bryce crouched beside me, hidden partially by my car. He scanned the scene, looked at me, then took off running toward the elevator.

I swung my legs around with a whimper and grabbed my clutch, still wedged inside the car. I freed the most important gift I'd ever been given and pressed it to my lips.

I blew into Jack's little daisy-covered whistle until I thought my lungs would explode, and then I blew some more.

Who would care for Penelope if I didn't make it? She didn't have a trust. Did I need a will? A lawyer? My heart pounded, and blood rushed in my ears. Sweat gathered on my brow. Hot tears scorched jagged paths over both cheeks. Poor Penelope. I refilled my lungs and blew again.

Booted feet appeared everywhere, on the ramp, around my car.

I kept blowing until Jack stopped me. His strong hand cupped the whistle and moved it away. He pulled my head to his chest and muttered something unintelligible beneath my ugly sobs. "Are you okay?" His gaze found my wrecked leg before I could answer. "We need a medic on level five," he informed someone on the other end of his walkie-talkie. He tugged my eyelids open. "Extensive bruising on the head and right lower leg. Possible broken tibia. Possible concussion."

"The elevator." I pointed in the direction where Bryce had taken his exit. "He was headed to the elevator."

Jack hooked an arm under my knees and wrapped the other around my back. In a moment, we were moving in large rocking strides back down the parking deck's narrow ramp. I buried my face in the curve of his neck and cried. A burst of fresh horror struck at my heart. "Penelope!"

"We've got her," he whispered. "She's okay. You need a medic."

I settled my head against his chest and concentrated on the steady rhythm of his breathing. The sweet, predictable cadence of his footballs lowered my heart rate to something near normal.

A man's cry opened my eyes. *When had I closed them?* Sunlight sent bullets of pain through my head. We were on the ground floor, moving quickly onto the sidewalk.

Bryce lay outside the elevator, cheek pinned to the ground, screaming about his rights. His arms were twisted to the spot behind him where Henri's knee was wedged.

"You have the right to remain silent . . ." Henri's thick southern-Louisiana accent loosened the pain in my chest.

I was safe.

A sob broke from my lips, and I wept openly for about a million reasons and also for just one.

I'd survived.

Chapter
Twenty-Five

Furry Godmother and all of New Orleans agrees:
Everyone loves a parade.

Thanksgiving morning was pure chaos. Two weeks had passed since my abduction, and I was working on a sunnier disposition. Penelope and I were resilient. We'd spent a few days licking wounds, and I'd eaten my weight in Ben & Jerry's, but we came out on top. Chins up. Shoulders back. Tails high.

The local support system was as vast and dedicated as it was loopy. Mom's friends had dropped by to check on me often during the days when I was housebound with pain-killers and a terrible attitude. They'd brought casseroles and cakes, then pretended to use the restroom or get me water from the kitchen, only to clean those rooms before leaving. Some asked how serious things were between Chase and me, then left a business card or photograph of their most eligible son, grandson, nephew, neighbor, etc.

Imogene had chauffeured me around all week, including a ride to the shop this morning. I wanted to gather last-minute supplies before the parade. Furry Godmother was closed for the holiday, but I had new designs on my mind, and Imogene was good company. She didn't ask a lot of questions.

My phone buzzed on the counter. Mom's number lit the screen. Again. She and the Jazzy Chicks were in position at the start of the parade route, riding the last float. "Mom wants to know if we're outside yet," I told Imogene. I sent a quick response to let her know I'd be there in a second. That was only a partial fib.

Scarlet's family had claimed their spots along the route after breakfast and invited Imogene and me to join them. So my spot was saved, but it took me more than a second to get anywhere these days. I wrapped a soft pink scarf around my neck and buttoned my vanilla wool swing coat to my collarbone. The temperatures had dropped into the fifties this week, but my winter wardrobe was on point, thanks to the time I'd spent in Arlington.

"Ready?" Imogene asked. Her black poncho hung to her knees. She hefted my purse over one shoulder, lifted two flattened pop-up chairs under her arms, and gripped a snack bag with her left palm. "Come on." She hooked my elbow with her free hand. "Let's go, Hop-a-long."

I stuffed crutches under my arms and imitated a penguin all the way to the shop door. I leaned my weight against the glass, pushing it wide and holding it for Imogene to pass.

"Thank you, Miss," she said.

I locked up and followed Imogene into the crowd, swinging a giant cast-covered leg.

People of every age group and demographic had lined Magazine Street, fizzing excitedly in anticipation of the parade. They snacked and chatted as cool autumn air pinked their cheeks and nipped their red noses. Scents of coffee and beignets hovered overhead. I bounced my chin to the sounds of a lively marching band pumping several blocks away.

"Finally!" Scarlet ran to meet us. Her skinny jeans belied the fact she'd had a baby a few short months ago. Her hunter-green sweater and matching headband made her look ten years younger. The freckles helped. "We're over here."

We squeezed between bodies to a large section of concrete that the Hawthorne children had claimed with sidewalk chalk. Two lines of pop-up chairs faced the road. Pint-sized versions in front of large ones. A red wagon filled with canvas totes stood between the last big chair and a lamppost. Blankets, toys, bubbles, chalk, and snacks spilled from the pillaged bags. Three small Hawthornes drew excitedly on the ground at our feet.

Imogene set up our chairs and motioned me into one.

"Where's Poppet?" I asked Scarlet.

"Fussing." She took her seat and smiled. "Carter and Chase took her for a walk to settle her down. I'm hoping she'll fall asleep."

"Poppet can sleep through a parade?"

Scarlet pointed to her boys, squealing and rubbing chalk sticks in one another's hair.

"Right."

"You're adjusting well." She ogled my cast. "Nice crutches, huh?"

"Do you like it?" I'd covered the light-pink cast with butterflies in every shade of sharpie I owned. I'd started the project out of boredom. Too much time on my backside with too many painkillers in my system. Eventually I fell into a rhythm and looked forward to seeing the final result. "I'm thinking of marketing a pet line to local vets."

"Cute."

Imogene dropped a ball of yarn onto her lap and put the business ends of two red knitting needles to work. "She's supposed to keep it raised, but she's stubborn."

"I'm fine."

"You've got a broken leg," she argued.

"It's only fractured. And it's a clean fracture. Barely significant." I gave Scarlet a pleading expression. "Really."

Scarlet looked skeptical. "How long do you have to wear the cast?"

"Another couple weeks. Thank you for everything you've done, by the way. I've deeply appreciated it, but I think it's time you set your minions free."

Thanks to Scarlet's social connections, my doorbell had rung at precisely seven every evening, when a woman with a casserole dish appeared on the porch. It was crazy but also endlessly delicious and unexpectedly moving to see so many people rally for my recovery.

I had a stack of thank-you notes to write.

She narrowed her eyes. "Let them feed you for another couple weeks."

"No, thank you. It's only a fracture. I don't need all the fussing."

Imogene performed a stage sigh. She fed fresh yellow yarn to her needles. "Stubborn."

"I'm fine."

Even Chase had fallen into the circus. Stopping at my place on his way home from the office every night. He'd strip off his jacket and tie, unbutton his dress shirt, and tell me animated stories from his days at the office. He helped me with anything I needed—just last weekend, he had stuffed a dozen incredibly ugly felt pins for Mrs. Hams. He administered my pain meds, refilled my water glass, and made me laugh until my sides ached. He also told me that he'd changed his mind and come after me the night Bryce kidnapped Penelope and me. He saw us wheeling away and called 9-1-1. He saw Jack chase our car down the street. He said it was the most frightening moment of his life. I knew what he meant.

The first float rolled into view. People clapped and swayed to the music of a peppy swing band.

I bent over to drag my snack bag close enough to rest my cast on.

A pair of dark-blue jeans wedged their way into view. Jack's face appeared a moment later when he crouched in front of me. "Hey."

"Hi." I cursed the tangle of emotions weaving their way to the surface. "Long time no see."

"Yeah." He lowered his head and raised his eyes. "I was chasing a lead on that thing we talked about. I hope you're not mad."

"Why would I be mad?" I brushed off the pang of disappointment. I might've spent a few nights hoping Jack would check on me after my run-in with a psycho, but he hadn't. He had things to do. Leads to chase. "How'd it go?"

"Dead end."

"I'm sorry."

"That's how it goes." He made a small smile. "How's the leg?"

"Healing. My head's okay, too." The bruising and goose egg had lingered for days, only truly disappearing last night.

The parade stopped in front of us. A marching band danced and played something I couldn't identify. Maybe a school fight song. Skipping girls in small skirts shook shiny pom-poms and shouted into the air.

I focused on Jack's steely blue eyes. "No concussion. In case you were worried."

"I never worry." His mouth curved into the lazy half smile I loved. "Your head's too hard to crack."

I lifted my little fist. "Want to test yours?"

He snorted. "Put that away before you hurt yourself."

A tidal wave of beads landed on the sidewalk and skittered against Jack's boot.

Scarlet's kids dove over them in a pile of pant legs and coat sleeves.

I dropped my fist onto my lap. "You can schedule the meeting at Grandpa Smacker anytime. I'm well enough to make the pitch now, and I have a presentation on my laptop."

"There's no rush." His gaze drifted to my cast.

"I'm fine. Set the appointment. It'll be a great opportunity for my business." All the time I'd spent on my backside lately had illuminated some obvious things I'd missed about the opportunity. For example, having a Grandpa Smacker label on my treats meant an increase in business at the shop. If people knew the recipes originated at Furry Godmother, they'd stop by for something fresh and discover my handmade couture as well.

Jack didn't look convinced. "If you say so."

"I do."

"Have you seen the paper?" he asked, smoothly changing the subject.

"Yes," I picked invisible lint from my jacket. "Bryce was charged with two counts of murder. He's a lawyer. Any chance he'll get off?"

"None." Jack didn't look happy. "Don't forget car theft, the unlawful entry of your home, and two counts of abduction."

"Thanks for including Penelope in that. She was afraid of her crate for days." I exhaled long and slow. "So it's a done deal for him? He won't be back on some misguided vengeance mission?"

Jack flinched. "No. He's working on a plea deal, but he's spending the rest of his life inside regardless. If he gets the deal, he'll waste his years in a white-collar facility instead of federal prison where he belongs. He might've been white-collar, but his crimes weren't."

"What's his leverage?" What ammunition did Bryce have at his disposal?

"He offered full cooperation. Anything we wanted to know, including the details of how he killed Annie and Dylan Latherope."

"How did he get Dylan?" I knew he got Annie with an unplanned sneak attack, but I'd spent more time than I'd ever admit wondering how a little guy like Bryce had gotten the jump on a hulk like Latherope.

"He invited Mr. Latherope to a private meeting at the river, where they were supposed to discuss the return of Latherope's kittens. Bryce put a rock in his briefcase for the occasion. He gave Latherope some bogus papers about the kittens' custody. When he bent over to sign, Bryce cracked his melon and rolled him into the river. Then he tossed the rock in."

"Premeditated." My tummy lurched. "Poor Mr. Latherope thought he was finally getting his kittens back, but instead he was lured to the scene of his own murder." Nausea and fear rippled through me, leaving goose bumps on my skin. Bryce had seemed unstable in the car that day, but the more I learned about him, the more he seemed like a burgeoning serial killer.

"I'd been following him from day one," Jack said.

"What?" I deflated against my seat back. "Why?"

He pressed a hand to his chest and retrieved the shiny detective badge hanging from a chain beneath his shirt. "Cop."

I smacked his hand. The badge swung. "You even wear that thing on Thanksgiving? Do you ever take it off?" My cheeks flared instantly. An obvious and unfortunate side effect of my medications.

"I'm a cop every day."

"Fine." I pressed cold hands to my cheeks, hoping to lower the temperature. "What about Bryce tipped you off? He looked harmless to me."

"Everyone's a suspect. I've told you that. When I checked into his financials, they were a mess."

I scoffed. "He said Annie didn't pay him enough. Though, he admitted to overspending as a means to impress her."

"No amount would've been enough. I suspected gambling debts at first, but I think he's got a drug problem. Ryan admitted to selling him prescription painkillers once when they were on the road with Annie. Bryce wasn't one of Ryan's regulars, which tells me Bryce was desperate when he asked. You don't go to your boss's brother for casual drug use."

I wrapped bone-chilled arms around my middle.

"Did you ever catch up with Shannon Martin? He was probably the only person on my list that had a good reason to be mad at Annie."

Jack watched Scarlet's kids tossing beads at one another. "Yeah. He was mad, but he was proud she'd want her name on something of his. He's suing for rights to the designs and hoping to get some leverage in the fashion community from her obvious endorsement."

"And Gideon?" Had the animal shelter owner-slash-stalker ever been released from the hospital?

"He's fine. Annoying, but he'll live."

The parade marched on until the Llama Mamas came into view. I whistled. They were sparkly and snazzy in their candy-corn-colored hats and scarves. I waved and hooted at Mrs. Hams.

Scarlet reappeared from the street, herding her kids back onto the sidewalk after they'd collected beads and trinkets from the ground. She set them in a row and hoisted a bag from her red wagon. She fell into her seat. "Hey, Jack."

"Hi, Scarlet."

She wiggled a pair of juice boxes in our direction. We declined.

Imogene chose apple cranberry and poked a little bendy straw into the top. "Mm. Mm. Mm."

My restless mind circled back to the mysterious lead that had kept Jack away all week. "So tell me about your dead

end. It must've started out as something good. I haven't
seen or heard from you in a while."

"Yeah." He scrubbed a hand over the back of his neck,
shifting the material of his open leather bomber and revealing his department-issued sidearm safely at his side. "I'm
working on it."

I leaned forward, locking our gazes and capturing him
in my BS detector. "I thought the lead didn't work out.
What do you mean you're working on it?"

He glanced away.

The parade slowed again, and the final float came into
position. A jazz band bringing up the rear burst into dance.
Cameras clicked and snapped around us. A line of professional mascot-sized turkeys danced the Macarena. Mom
and a group of waving women smiled from their perch
upon the float. They wore matching Jazzy Chicks shirts
and smiled wider than the mighty Mississippi. Their hens
wore felt sashes and pecked cluelessly around a miniature
barnyard. A space heater puffed against their feathers.

I gave Jack a questioning look. His attention was locked
on the hoopla before us.

"Woo-hoo!" Scarlet bounced to her feet, swinging
beads overhead like a propeller.

In the street, Chase and Carter danced with the turkeys beside Mom's float. They wore plastic golden crowns
and wild, goofy smiles. Scarlet's husband, Carter, sprang
up and down on his toes with Poppet strapped to his chest.
Chase performed the moonwalk and the snake, nowhere
near the beat of the jazz band bringing up the rear.

Scarlet grabbed her kids' hands and led them into the
street, shaking their behinds and swinging their arms.

Maybe it wasn't only Chase who was cuckoo. Maybe it was in the Hawthorne genes.

People filed into the street behind the jazz band, abandoning their chairs and forming a second line parade. Electricity sizzled in the air. My heart lifted, and my shoulders shimmied.

Chase locked his gaze on me and pulled his jacket open dramatically. He wore a Jazzy Chicks shirt underneath, exactly like my mom's.

Jack laughed. "Once the dust settled, I realized I still had the ten thousand dollars for Cotton and Cashmere, and I didn't know what I was supposed to do with it, so I called a lawyer. Chase said the monies were part of Annie's estate, intended for the cats' keeping."

"Her estate goes to brother," I said. "He's still in jail. How can he care for them?"

Jack smiled. "He's not. Cotton and Cashmere are about to become New Yorkers."

"Her parents."

"Yeah. They're devastated at losing Annie, but having her kittens will be a bit of a comfort to them."

I thought of the televised memorial service. "I'm sure the trust won't hurt either."

Imogene pushed onto her feet. "Well I can't sit here and watch something like that going on in front of me." She left her knitting on the chair and shook her moneymaker into the mix of folks still trailing in the second line.

I hooted and clapped.

Jack took Imogene's seat. He dropped her yarn into one of the bags she'd left behind. "Sorry you can't join along."

I shrugged. "It's New Orleans. Another parade will be along any minute."

He laughed. "That's true."

"So tell me about the lead," I pressed.

He rubbed giant palms over his thighs and braced his elbows on the chair's arms. "I might've found a link between Tabitha and a man at Grandpa's company."

"What kind of link?"

"I'm not sure. Romantic, perhaps? Maybe something else."

I waited for him to elaborate.

He watched me with cautious eyes.

I lifted my hands. "If there's something to over-hear, I will hear it." I drew an *X* over my heart. "Set the appointment."

He gave me a sidelong glance. His incredible blue eyes crinkled at the sides.

"How about you and I discuss the potential pet line and espionage over lunch?"

"It's Thanksgiving. Why don't you come to my parents' house and eat with us tonight? We can talk shop afterward."

Jack hesitated. "I don't know."

"Come on. Without you, it's just the three of us." And without us, he'd be alone. "My parents would love to have you, and your presence will shift some of Mom's attention off me."

He didn't seem sold.

"Jack?"

"I'll come if you confirm with your mom first. I don't want to impose."

"Done." I flipped my phone over and sent the text. "Anything else?"

"I won't go empty-handed," he said. "What can I contribute? Do you like bread pudding?"

"Sure. As long as Tabitha didn't make it."

He checked his phone. "No roofies. Got it."

My smile grew impossibly wider. "We're starting to make a pretty good team, you and I. Remember when you thought I was a murderess? Now you're letting me in on your secret investigations. We've come a long way, Detective Oliver."

He blanched. "It frightens me that that's your interpretation of what's happened in the past four months."

"Because I'm scary-good?" I teased.

"No."

"Because you didn't know how good it felt to have a partner?"

"I had a partner. You're not my partner. You're a civilian. More of nuisance, really."

I nudged him with my elbow. "Don't pretend."

His cheeks twitched.

"It's okay to smile," I said seriously. "People won't think you went soft. You won't lose any street cred or anything."

His icy eyes sparkled in the midmorning sun. "You're too happy. What's wrong with you?"

"I've got a good partner," I said.

"We aren't partners." He got comfortable in Imogene's chair. "I hope your friends come back soon."

"Why? Do you have somewhere to be?"

"Well, yeah. I've got to go home and bake bread pudding."

I stared down Magazine Street at the nearly invisible members of the second line parade. "You're right. Let's go." I hobbled onto my feet. "We can take their things to my house, and they can swing by later." We had brainstorming to do.

Furry Godmother's Autumn Apple Pupcakes

Makes 12 full-size pupcakes.

Celebrate the season with these healthy and delicious treats for your pup. You probably already have the ingredients in your pantry!

Ingredients

4 tbsp. honey
½ tsp. vanilla extract
2¾ cups water
¼ cup unsweetened applesauce
1 egg
1 cup fresh diced apple
1 tbsp. baking powder
4 cups flour
Ground cinnamon

Directions

1. Preheat oven to 350 degrees.

2. Line a muffin pan with paper cups or prep your tin.

3. In a large bowl, mix honey, vanilla, water, applesauce, and egg.

4. Mix baking powder and flour in a separate bowl.

5. Slowly stir the flour mixture into the large bowl and blend well.

6. Sample your diced apples.

7. Sample one more. Maybe let your doggy check your work.

8. Fold remaining diced apples into the mixture.

9. Spoon mixture into muffin tins.

10. Sprinkle lightly with cinnamon.

11. Bake for 60–75 minutes or until a toothpick inserted into the center comes out dry.

12. Remove tins from oven and cool completely on a wire rack.

Furry Godmother's Cat's Meow Shredded Chicken Biscuits

Makes 15–20 biscuits.

Taking holiday cookies to friends and neighbors? How about treating their fur babies, and yours, with these easy-as-Christmas holiday biscuits?

Ingredients

1½ cups cooked and shredded chicken
½ cup chicken broth
¾ cup white flour
¼ cup whole wheat flour
⅓ cup cornmeal
1 tablespoon melted butter

Directions

1. Combine shredded chicken, broth, and butter in a large bowl.

2. Add cornmeal to wheat and white flour.

3. Pour dry ingredients over the chicken mixture and knead.

4. Roll dough to ¼ inch thickness.

5. Pinch dough into quarter-sized balls and flatten them to ¼ inch thickness with your thumb.

6. Place on an ungreased cookie sheet.

7. Bake at 350 degrees for 20 minutes.

Furry Godmother's Cheesy Kitty Yum Yums

Makes 2 dozen Yum Yums.

Bake up a batch of warm kitty lovin' with these cheesy Yum Yums! Simple, healthy, and so delicious—even your cat will approve.

Ingredients

½ cup white flour
¼ cup whole wheat flour
¾ cup shredded cheddar cheese
5 tablespoons grated Parmesan cheese
¼ cup plain yogurt
¼ cup fine white cornmeal

Directions

1. Combine cheeses and yogurt in a large bowl.

2. Stir in flour and cornmeal.

3. Knead dough, adding water as needed.

4. Roll dough to ¼ inch thickness and cut into your favorite holiday shapes.

5. Place cutout Yum Yums on greased cookie sheet.

6. Bake at 350 degrees for 25 minutes.

Acknowledgments

I have so many people to thank for this book, this series, and the fact I'm not hiding under my bed. Thank you, Jennifer Anderson and Keri Ford, for reading all my ugly, jumbled first-draft words. There wouldn't be a finished product without you. Thank you, Kathryn Long and Janie Browning, for the hours you spent scrutinizing my completed manuscripts for plot holes, plot bunnies, and other avoidable tragedies. You make my work better. Thank you, Jill Marsal, my brilliant and dedicated agent. Jill is the cheerleader and advocate every author needs, and I am eternally grateful for her. Thank you, everyone at Crooked Lane Books, for taking a chance on me, for bringing my characters into the world, and for letting me tell more of their stories. I still can't believe you picked me. A deep, humbling curtsy to the friends who support my weird ways and pretend I'm not completely bananas. I'm sure our lively discussions have worried more than one couple seated near us at a restaurant. Thank you, Darlene Lindsey, for your unwavering and near pathological belief in me—not to mention your untold hours of babysitting while I write and travel. Thank you, precious children, for putting up with your awkward, quirky, harebrained mother and loving me anyway. Finally, thank you, Mom and Dad, for making me believe I could change the world, and thank you, sweet Husband, for supporting me every day while I try.

Read an excerpt from

CAT GOT YOUR SECRETS

the next

KITTY COUTURE MYSTERY

by *JULIE CHASE*

available soon in hardcover from
Crooked Lane Books

CROOKED
LANE

NEW YORK

Chapter One

Furry Godmother's advice for business:
Get a PFA. Personal Feline Assistant.

"Hold still, please," I whispered to Penelope, the adorable black-and-gray tabby on my lap. Her striped paws kneaded my thighs in anticipation of freedom.

A pair of pint-sized silver wings bobbed against her back as she tried to bite my fingers.

"There." I snipped the thread and poked my needle into a stuffed tomato on my parents' dining room table. "You're officially the cutest little Cupid I've ever seen." I fluffed the length of her dress and tugged the sleeves. "Do you feel pretty?"

She leapt from my lap and skulked into the kitchen.

"Good idea. Test it for comfort."

I scrutinized the fit as she went. "How does it feel around the collar?" I asked her retreating figure. "Are the cuffs too snug? Why can't you talk?"

Mom cleared the remaining breakfast plates, stirring rich scents of buttery pancakes and syrup into the air.

Her cream-and-olive wrap dress was modest, but elegant, emphasizing her youthful figure without drawing attention anywhere specific enough to rouse a blush. "Have you given any more thought to making Penelope the face of Furry Godmother?" She followed Penelope into the kitchen.

Furry Godmother was my dream come true, a pet boutique and organic treat bakery in the heart of New Orleans's Garden District. The slogan *Where every pet is royalty and every day is a celebration* was chosen for its all-inclusive nature. At my shop *every* pet got the royal treatment, from turtle to tabby to terrier. No discrimination allowed. I didn't want to give the wrong impression by choosing a mascot.

"No." I rolled my head against one shoulder and let my heavy eyelids drop. We'd had this discussion multiple times.

"Why not?" she pressed. "Every successful business has a spokesperson. You need a brand. Something people can connect visually to your business. Why not use Penny?"

I forced my eyes open and pulled my head upright. "Furry Godmother is more than kitty couture."

Mom returned with an enormous mug of coffee. Her third since I'd arrived. "Fine. We can talk about it more later."

"You're having another cup of coffee?" Not that I was judging, but Mom lived to preach the perils of over-indulgence. I should know. I was the poster child for her campaign.

She lowered gracefully onto the chair across from me, her bright-blue eyes avoiding mine. "I've been spring cleaning, and I'm exhausted."

I sensed there was a deeper meaning behind the words. With my mom, there usually was. "When you say 'spring cleaning,' do you mean you called a service?"

"No." She made a crazy face. "I mean purging. Out with the old and all that. For the record, I know how to do the day-to-day cleaning as well, Lacy Marie Crocker. I just prefer not to."

"Uh-huh."

"Besides, outsourcing boosts the economy and frees up my time so I can give back to the community."

"Yep." My mother was also known as Violet Conti-Crocker, sole living heir to the Conti fortune. To hear her tell it, Conti money had helped build the city, and she took her civic responsibilities very seriously.

I thought she tended to exaggerate.

She pursed her lips and held my stare for a long beat.

I looked like my mother, from her blonde hair and blue eyes to her narrow frame and ski-slope nose. What we lacked in classic beauty we made up for in spunk and chutzpah. Her chutzpah got on my nerves and vice versa, but we were learning to live with one another in the same city again.

I'd left for college nearly twelve years ago and rarely visited—outside the occasional holiday—until Pete the Cheat, my jerk of an ex-fiancé, broke my heart last spring and sent me running back to New Orleans. Specifically, to the Garden District, known for its stately historic mansions and megawealthy residents. As it turned out, I liked my new life here much more than I'd expected, and Mom was growing on me.

I smiled. "So hiring a cleaning service helps the economy, but you're doing the purging yourself?"

Her shoulders drooped away from her ears. Whatever she'd considered saying, she let it go. "This is different because it's personal. I'm going room to room boxing up anything I can bear to part with. A cleaner can't do that. So far, the work is endless, not to mention thankless, which is why I need the coffee."

"Room-by-room purging?" I did a long whistle and made a show of looking around the cavernous spread. The historic Victorian home had been in my mother's family for generations. It was a magnificent place to live—architecturally sound, immaculately kept, and in the most coveted section of the district, but it was stuffed to the frame with things no one needed. Five thousand square feet and nearly two dozen rooms with closets, cubbies, and built-ins. "Good luck with that." I worked through the information she'd given me. "Why are you doing this?"

She huffed, as if I'd somehow missed the obvious. "If I ever finish the insurmountable task, I'm going to redecorate." She curled both hands around her steaming mug and sipped. "I'm donating some things, and I have a pickup scheduled for this morning. I honestly thought she'd be here by now."

"Are all those boxes by the back door going out?" A sudden yawn split my face. I covered my gaping mouth with both hands.

"That's right."

"Wow." She had her work cut out for her. Mom was a certifiable packrat, exactly like her mother before her.

The attic alone was crammed with two lifetimes' worth of things she didn't need and couldn't part with.

She swept a thick swath of blonde and platinum hairs off her forehead and hooked them behind one ear. Mom had informed me long ago that our family didn't go gray. Those pesky white hairs that came along after thirty were called *platinum*. "There's a thrift shop on Jackson Avenue that guarantees anonymity and does pickups."

"A thrift shop?" I gawked. Who was this woman?

I'd recently caught her wearing jeans, and she'd changed her hair last week, adding waves and bangs to a shorter cut. The effect was drastic and glaringly opposite the sleek shoulder-length bob she'd worn for at least twenty years. Honestly, she looked nearly that much younger.

"What are you looking at?" She rolled her shoulders back and lifted her chin.

"I don't know," I marveled. "I guess I'm still getting used to your new look."

She raised a hand toward her forehead, but stopped short, opting instead to touch the new waves dancing against her cheeks. "I needed the bangs. You'll understand in twenty years. Sooner if you don't get some sleep."

"I sleep."

She hiked one perfectly manicured brow in challenge.

"I do." Not nearly enough, and normally after face-planting at my desk midstitch, but I slept. "And I love your new look."

A rare blush crept over her cheeks. "I think, perhaps, spending so much time with my daughter is changing my idea of beauty."

"What?" I made a show of looking over both shoulders. "Me?" I pressed a hand to my chest. "Well, clutch my pearls. You're getting soft." I rose to my feet and clamped my arms around her. "Now it's only a matter of time until my evil plan is complete." I rested my head on her shoulder.

"Get off me." She wiggled out of my grip with a peculiar grin. "Good grief. This is why I don't compliment you more often. You completely overreact." She grabbed her coffee and pressed it to her lips.

"I see you smiling."

"Do not."

I carried my cup across the threshold to the kitchen for a peek inside the boxes. "You didn't put any of my stuff in here, did you?"

"Not yet."

I didn't like that word, *yet*. I fingered the contents to be sure she wasn't lying, then lingered in the doorway between the two rooms. "Don't get rid of any of my stuff."

She rolled her eyes. "Do you mean the stuff you left here more than ten years ago? Why would I do that when you obviously use it so often?"

"They're memories. My memories."

"They're worn out books, of which you own multiple copies, and puzzles." She groaned. "Puzzles and games and brain teasers. I suppose you'd like to take those dusty things home and play with them again at your age."

I pulled my chin back. "Excuse me. I like puzzles." I shook off the bubbling frustration. "And I'm not old. I'm thirty and you're . . ."

She stabbed a finger in my direction. "Do not."

Penelope appeared at my feet, and I pulled her into my arms, carefully removing the little dress. "Grandma has had too much coffee, and it's making her grouchy." I set Penelope on her feet and folded the dress.

Mom ignored my jibe. "Who's the packrat now?"

"You."

She held a palm out. "Pot." And then the other. "Kettle."

I narrowed my eyes.

"New topic. Valentine's Day is next week," Mom said. "Have you made any plans?"

"Nope."

"Pity."

Yes. I was thirty and single, while every last one of Mom's friends was a grandmother. Heard it.

The back door opened and shut. Dad wandered into the kitchen and rolled his sleeves up to his elbows, then proceeded to scrub up as if he was preparing for surgery.

Mom moved to the doorway between rooms and cocked a hip. "Well, aren't you even going to say hello?"

He startled. "Oh. Hello, darling." He dried his hands on a dishtowel, then kissed Mom's cheek. "Sorry I'm late." He turned for the dining room and met me with a big hug.

"Everything okay?" I asked.

"Yes. Fine. Fine." His polite smile fell short, not quite reaching his normally bright eyes.

"He was out with Wallace Becker last night," Mom tattled. "He's probably hung over, but since he's finally chosen to bless us with his presence, we should talk about Friday night's award dinner and leave last night where it is."

Dad was the latest in a long line of Crocker men to fill the role of beloved Garden District veterinarian. He ran a private practice out of the renovated barn in their backyard, and he'd been nominated for a community service award. Mom was throwing a party to celebrate the fact. She'd celebrate the daily sunrise if she thought people would attend.

Dad forced the smile higher. "Great."

"Who's Wallace Becker?" I asked Dad.

Mom answered for him. "He's that man who runs the babysitting company for pets."

"The Cuddle Brigade?" The Cuddle Brigade was a fairly brilliant business concept—not a new one, but lucrative nonetheless. The pet nannies were vetted by a panel of local who's whos and rented out as in-home care to cover business trips and vacations. Some especially adoring pet owners hired the Brigade on a nine-to-five basis so their fur babies wouldn't be alone all day every day while they worked. Not every pet was as lucky as Penelope, who went everywhere I went. More or less.

"That's the one," she said.

"What a small world. The Normans are throwing their Saint Berdoodle a Bark-Mitzvah tonight, and I have twelve dozen dreidel-shaped doggy biscuits waiting in the car for delivery. I'm making a stop at the event hall next door to the Cuddle Brigade on my way to work."

She nodded. "That's Wallace's hall. The Normans are nice people. Their Berdoodle isn't bad either."

"How's Mr. Becker doing?" I asked Dad, enticing him to join into our conversation the way he normally did.

He set a kettle on the stove and cranked the gas. "Not good."

"I'm sorry to hear that. Is there anything I can do to help with your dinner Friday night?"

Mom made a crazy face. "Of course there is. I've already e-mailed a copy of your duties. I thought you said you got it."

"Right." I tapped my temple, pretending to have forgotten. I didn't always open Mom's e-mails. "Sorry."

She rolled her eyes. "Since you obviously haven't read it, dinner is at the Elms Mansion at eight. Be there at seven. Bring a date. Your cat doesn't count. And wear something pink. I'm playing off the valentine theme. Love for animals. Love the community. All we need is love. That mess. I don't want to clash."

"Got it." I packed my things and pulled Penelope's carrier onto the table. "I'd better get going so I can make that delivery." I caught Penelope as she tried to slink past and stuffed her into her travel pack. "Time to go." I kissed Mom's cheek and motioned Dad to walk me out.

He followed me silently into the warm Louisiana day, carrying Penelope in her pack.

I stopped to beep my car doors unlocked. "Are you sure you're okay?" I asked, squinting against the sun.

He kissed my head and loaded Penelope onto my passenger seat. "I'm fine." He buckled the seat belt around her carrier and forced a tight smile.

"Why don't I believe you?"

An older model SUV appeared at the end of the drive before he could answer. The vehicle crunched over loose gravel and stopped behind my Volkswagen. A woman in her forties fell out, stumbling for balance and mumbling under her breath. She straightened her blouse and elastic-waist pants over the lion's share of her curves. Her fuzzy brown hair fluttered in the wind. She gasped when she finally noticed me.

I did a finger wave and wondered if she was lost.

"Mrs. Crocker?" She fumbled in my direction, hand extended. A powerful cloud of essential oil scents wafted around her. "I'm Claudia Post. It's nice to meet you."

I held my breath against the olfactory assault of lavender and rose hips.

Mom bustled outside and down the driveway toward us. "There you are. I'm Mrs. Crocker. This is my daughter, Lacy Marie." She motioned for Claudia to follow her and turned back for the house. "I've got everything by the door for you."

Claudia returned a moment later with her hands full.

Dad jerked to life. "I'm so sorry. Let me help you." He hustled to her SUV and opened the hatch. "I'll carry the rest. Just a moment."

"No. It's no problem, Dr. Crocker." She slid the box inside and hurried after him.

Mom came to join me in the gravel and beamed. "Isn't this wonderful?"

Wonderful? Maybe Mom wasn't the hoarder I thought she was. "Yes?"

"I'm told Claudia's the best," she whispered. "She guarantees complete anonymity for donors. Finally, I can get rid of anything I want and trust it won't be gossiped about at the next big event."

"What do you have that people would gossip about?" *Dare I ask?*

"Please." She clasped her hands over her belt. "No one needs to know my dress size or what I keep in my closet. Can you imagine?"

"Not really, no." I wore a size eight, and I'd never considered it a secret. Also, I didn't want to know what was in Mom's closet.

Dad and Claudia loaded the final boxes into her SUV. She shut the hatch and approached me with an apologetic expression. "Sorry about the mix-up earlier."

"It's okay. People mix us up all the time," Mom lied.

"Well, if you ever have anything you'd like taken off your hands, just give me a call." She handed me a shiny white business card with curly pink letters in the center. "Resplendent," I read. "New Orleans's premiere thrift shop."

"Thank you, Mrs. Crocker. Dr. Crocker." Claudia wrenched open her squeaky driver's side door and climbed onto the seat with a little effort.

I kissed my parents' cheeks before following Claudia's SUV down the driveway and around the block where we parted ways. I zipped along the picturesque residential roads of our district, eager to make my delivery and get to work. More than that, I was dying to know what had my normally jubilant dad so melancholy. I would have blamed Mom, but she seemed sincerely clueless.

Penelope rode quietly beside me, ears rotating like tiny satellite dishes as the sounds of our district wafted in on the breeze.

A crowd came into view outside the reception hall.

"Uh-oh," I told Penelope. "Something's wrong."

Police cruisers blocked the parking lot entrance, forcing me to pass my destination in search of an empty space along the curb. A firetruck sat beside an ambulance outside the hall where my delivery was expected.

I parked two blocks away and powered the windows up halfway. "Wait here," I told Penelope. "I'll be back in a minute. I need to find out what happened so I know what to do with these dreidel biscuits." If there was a fire, I'd have to deliver them somewhere else, which meant throwing my day off schedule more than it already was.

I jogged back to the lot entrance. Lookie lous lined the sidewalks, snapping photos and buzzing with anticipation. I sidled up to a man standing outside the hoopla. "What's going on?"

"I'm guessing fire." He crossed his arms and rocked on his heels. "Could be a robbery or vandalism, I suppose. I'm not sure what they keep in there."

The hall was the big empty kind that folks rented out for special occasions. Unless the family holding the Bark-Mitzvah had stored something of value for the party tonight, I couldn't imagine any reason to break in. I snapped a few pictures with my phone. Photos had helped me sort things out in the past, and this felt like a moment to remember or at least document.

I lifted onto my tiptoes for a better view of the firetruck. Several men in New Orleans Fire Department T-shirts leaned against the giant vehicle, scanning the crowd and posturing. No gear or hose in sight. I ducked under the crime scene tape and went for a closer look.

"Hey," the man called from behind me. "You can't go in there."

I waved him off. "It's okay. I have a delivery."

I hustled through clusters of men and women in uniform, passing cops, firemen, and crime scene investigators with my chin up and shoulders back. A gust of wind whipped through the scene, sending goose bumps down both arms. New Orleans in February could be forty-five or seventy. Sometimes on the same day.

A knot of workers in matching uniforms huddled near the side entrance. "Hi," I said. "Sorry to interrupt, but I have a delivery for the party tonight. Is it okay if I leave the boxes with one of you?"

A puffy-eyed woman burst into tears.

The man beside her gave me a cold stare and pulled her into a hug. "Party's cancelled."

I cast a look at the not-burning building. "No party?" I had twelve dozen Jewish dog biscuits in my car. How the heck was I supposed to unload those if not for the Normans' Bark-Mitzvah? "I'm confused," I admitted. "What happened here?"

"I tried everything," the woman cried. "I was too late. He was so cold."

My gaze jumped back to the building. Fear prickled the skin along my collarbone. "Who was so cold?"

"Wallace Becker," the man said, pulling her closer. "She found him in there this morning."

I blinked long and slow at the woman sobbing against his chest. Behind her, a pair of EMTs drove a gurney into the back of a waiting ambulance. A closed body bag balanced on top.

"A real shame," one EMT told the other as they snapped the doors shut behind the body. "Wallace Becker was the nicest guy on earth."

It felt like ice slid down my spine and into my sandals. Dad was with Mr. Becker last night.

And now Mr. Becker is dead.